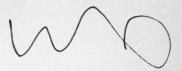

The Frog in the Bottom of the Well

By F. X. Mathews

The Concrete Judasbird
The Frog in the Bottom of the Well

F. X. Mathews

THE FROG IN THE
BOTTOM OF THE WELL

1971
HOUGHTON MIFFLIN COMPANY BOSTON

The summer insect cannot speak of ice; the frog in the bottom of the well should not talk of the heavens.

Thus saith the Lord God: Behold, I will send My angel, who shall go before thee unto the place that I have prepared. Take notice of him, and hear his voice, and do not think him one to be contemned, for he will not forgive when thou hast sinned, and My name is in him. But if thou wilt hear his voice, and do all that I speak, I will be an enemy to thy enemies, and will afflict them who afflict thee: and My angel shall go before thee.

The Frog in the Bottom of the Well

One

When my father, who is not a big man, crosses his knife and fork and then himself, rising from the rubble of breakfast, his balding head almost touches the soles of Grandma's feet. It wasn't always so. In the China Lake days he would push himself away from the table with his open palms, hike up his pants, inspect the buttons of his fly with his index finger, and say, "Well, so much for that." Now it's the sign of the cross. He still does not go to church, though. He says he gets dizzy spells, his kneecaps throb, the smells of mouths and armpits go to his head. He is still in the state of sin. So on Sunday mornings he lets us go off to Holy Angels while he sits in the cellar chain-smoking his roll-your-owns. He is forty-nine. Last year he had a full head of hair like a dark sea. Then all at once the tide went out. A tumbler appeared on top of the toilet tank and two rows of unnaturally even teeth grimaced under water.

Loss. Change. The biggest change is Grandma's feet every morning, clumping back and forth in the kitchen upstairs, while we three — my father and Paula and the boy — shovel down our Cream of Wheat in the cellar. My mother has already left for daily mass, early enough for a private novena to St. Anthony, patron of lost articles. One day the boy will look out the cellar window and see the lost house flying over the Kennebec like the Holy House of Loreto, angels bearing the four corners, wisteria trailing from the front porch, and behind, bushels of sun-swollen tomatoes tumbling through the winter air. For seven years the China Lake farmhouse with ten acres of land — the house first, set back from the road, then the vegetable patch, then the chicken wire fence to keep out the rabbits; behind that the crab apple orchard with the dried-up stone well; then the woods, and finally the point of land falling into the lake. All of it belonged to them (though of course they only rented), with certain parts belonging to certain people. The boy's father had the tomatoes and Paula had Paula's rock, a large rock flashing with mica sunfire in the middle of the wild cherry thicket. She spread her beach towel out there. The well belonged to the boy. In good weather he sat on the planks over the hole, reading under the shade of the little roof, because he did not tan like his cousin. Sometimes he removed the cover and lowered the bucket and waited for the splash that never happened. He had long thoughts about the depths.

My mother is working on her third novena, for we have been in the cellar for several weeks now. This morning she and my father kissed each other on the cheek at the foot of the cellar steps and she put on her coat and he got out of his, a black wool overcoat smelling of the Maine winter. He works the night shift at the paper company and gets in at seven-twenty-five in the morning. Paula and the boy are getting ready for school.

"Not today," his father says to the boy. "That snow doesn't look like it's going to let up till spring."

The boy gets up from the table, rubbing his sore eye with a fist. When they decided to live in the cellar his father came over one Sunday, rolled linoleum on the cement, whitewashed everything else — stone walls, rafters, pipes, the plank door leading into the furnace and bathroom, dead centipedes — and set a fluorescent light buzzing over the table. The boy reads under the noisy light and has grown a flaming sty.

Paula, who always finishes breakfast first, has taken the easy chair. She is curled up in her bathrobe with her bare feet on the doily, clipping her toenails with the kitchen shears. The father disappears behind the kerosene stove that cuts the room in half and the boy follows, and together they lean on the steel tubs Grandma once used for laundry and look out the cellar window. Half the window is already piled with snow. The Angel of the Snow broods over the gray world. They cannot see to the other side of the river. His father picks another brown leaf from the unblossoming geranium.

"No, you better stay home today. Paula can tell the nun you won't be in."

The boy gets nosebleeds. His mother makes him dump quantities of raw wheat germ over the Cream of Wheat to strengthen the blood vessels. He is twelve and a half and, like his cousin Paula, who is twelve, in the seventh grade at Blessed Sacrament. His father doesn't want them growing up speaking Deauville French. So even though Holy Angels, where they go to church on Sunday, is just a few blocks away, they walk almost a mile on weekdays to Blessed Sacrament School, where the nuns at least speak English. His father's name is Tom Dolan, but like everybody else he is married to a Vigue. Grandma is a Vigue. Grandpa was a Veilleux who streamlined the name to fit the signs on his grocery store and tavern. The boy does not understand why they are Dolans in the middle of French Canadians and Lebanese and Yankees, but it has something to do with the other Grandpa he never saw, a Vermont stonecutter who found his way to Gloucester and discovered the ocean. Grandpa Dolan and another man climbed into a rowboat and decided they were going to row right across the Atlantic. Several hundred people saw them off and a town councilman made a speech. But they were back the next day because the waves were choppy and the other man turned green. And the Dolans wound up in Deauville, Maine — because it was all over after that, and why not here as well as anywhere else.

"Hey, Dolan?"

Grandma, clumping halfway down the stairs.

"Hey, Dolan, you got any rum down there? I think I want to make some rum chiffon pie."

Grandma's rum chiffon pie again. At eight o'clock in the morning. With no confectioners' sugar because of the rationing.

"No, I don't."

"What you got then? Maybe something else is just as good."

"Not much. Bottle of Fairview wine. Half a bottle of Poland Spring gin."

"I'll take the gin."

The other Dolan was Uncle Andrew, who moved to Dorchester, Massachusetts and died when the boy was six. Uncle Andrew wrote songs, a whole trunkload of unpublished songs about going back to Ireland, where he'd never been. And he told jokes. The featured stand-up comic at every St. Patrick's minstrel show in Dorchester. But he was terrified of dying; he talked about it all the time. Finally he couldn't stand the fear any longer so he quit work early one day, went home and connected himself up to the gas stove. "Crazy Andy, had to have his last joke," my father said. That was because of the poem they found in his pocket, which began

4

Well, folks, I guess this is it,
The next time you see me I'll be an obit . . .

There were other lines which the boy cannot remember. One night his father recited the whole poem, his face flushed with unhappy laughter, then pushed his glass of whisky to one side, put his head down on the porcelain table and cried himself to sleep.

Though the boy doesn't go to school often, he is wise beyond his years. Already he has read more books than anyone else in the family. I am the boy. I am four-feet-eight, weigh eighty pounds, and wear a size four shoe. I will never be five feet tall. My knee joints swell up (growing pains, my mother promises), my shoulders slope and I have swamp-colored eyes (swamp fire, my father says). Paula is quite tall. She grows in front of everybody, she thinks about her underwear, and every morning over breakfast she practices a pout. She's going to turn out bad. "Small wonder," my father says, "what with the homelife she didn't have."

This is true. Two years ago Paula's mother threw the marriage into Uncle Fred's lap and moved down to Augusta with a man who sold sump pumps. Uncle Fred, a Vigue, had a breakdown and spent a month at Togus. Then the boy's mother invited him and Paula to live off them in the farmhouse on China Lake. The sick man sat in the rocking chair on the front porch, brooding into the wisterias for a whole summer, immobile except for the hands that kept doing something to his trouser knees. Once a week the boy's father drove him into Deauville to a doctor who shot electrical currents through him and told him to put on weight. Suddenly he snapped out of it and became Uncle Fred again and got a job in a mill up near Albion, drilling holes in doors on a trial basis to see how he'd make out. On summer evenings he would stop the now vigorous rocking chair and announce to the boy: "That's fast work, you know. Yessirree. They turn those doors out like hot cakes. Government contract, you know."

5

Then the war ended. No more stamping on tin cans and cutting off your cuffs. No more collecting kapok for life preservers. The loss of it all. In the war years they used to stand up in school assembly and sing, to the tune of "East Side, West Side":

> War bonds, war bonds, all around the town,
> The banker and Mrs. O'Grady, income up and spending
> down,
> And when the war is over, me and a few million more
> Will have more spending money than we've ever had
> before.

Which didn't happen. When the war was over the Poulins came back, and the Pellerins and the Ouellettes but nobody named O'Grady, and wanted to buy houses. None were being built. The roofless house that somebody had started down the road at the beginning of the war filled up with snow every winter, and the bare planks split in the summer sun. Even Deauville had a housing shortage, though of course it was nothing like what they were having other places, the boy's father said hopefully. He had been just over the cut-off age and stayed home from the war, but he had no more spending money than ever. A lot of it he'd given to the doctors — for the boy, of course, but also for Uncle Fred. An ex-Marine named Romeo Something bought the farmhouse. Uncle Fred had a fight with the boy's mother and said he was going down to Stratford, Connecticut, to build helicopters. He left Paula behind.

"But if it stops snowing later on and the sun comes out, can I go over to Holy Angels?"

"That's a big if, I'm afraid."

Because I love the angels. Angels are everywhere. There is an angel for every week and every month and every season. Every blade of grass has an angel over it saying "grow." A Bernardine sister once was shown in spirit the vast desolation

6

caused by the devil throughout the world, and at the same time she heard the Blessed Virgin telling her it was true, that hell had been let loose on the earth; and that the time had come to pray to her as Queen of Angels and to ask of her the assistance of the Heavenly Legions to fight against these deadly foes of God and men.

"But my good Mother," she replied, "you who are so kind, could you not send them without our asking?"

"No," Our Lady answered, "because prayer is one of the conditions required by God himself for obtaining favors."

For years the boy prayed to his brother Gabriel who died in childhood: "Angel Gabriel, pray for us." Then he discovered in a book called *Death Is the Beginning* that technically his brother was only a saint. But he still says the nightly prayer to the Angel of God, his guardian dear, to whom God's love commits him here.

Holy Angels is full of statues. When the boy was small he had a favorite statue of the Infant Jesus of Prague that he used to dress and undress according to the liturgical seasons. But in Holy Angels there is no Infant Jesus nor even any saint, only the angels. Outside it is just a brown-shingled little building with an oversized iron cowbell in the belfry. But inside angels peek out of every corner and niche, some in white marble, some painted gold all over, kneeling angels and announcing angels and angels with eyes upturned to the eaves, where more angels lurk. And my favorite, the Sorrowing Angel.

The Sorrowing Angel is a painted plaster figure, about three feet tall, in a niche on the gospel side. The boy has visited it every day for the past three weeks. It stretches on the toes of one foot, the other turned behind it, its eagle feathers about to flap, the folds of the gown billowing in the wind. In its right hand it holds a sword that, if you kneel in front of it, points almost directly at your head. It has long, softly curling hair like a girl, and an astonished mouth. But its eyes! They force their way out under the plaster lids, fiercely alert, a blue that is almost black in a wide-awake dream, tragic with knowledge. Michael the Archangel, his mother has told the boy. But I do not believe her. There is no serpent. I call it the Sorrowing Angel.

"It's not snowing as hard as all that," Paula says, mostly for her own benefit, because Paula is Paula. She uncoils from the armchair, twists her mouth at me as she passes, and climbs the steps to Grandma's kitchen. I hear her feet slapping across the kitchen floor, then the door slam on the back sun porch where Grandma lets her share a double bed with my mother. My father sleeps on a couch in the entryway to the cellar doors that open outside; I sleep on a couch in the furnace room where it is warm; my mother and Paula share the back porch, where Grandma shuts off the radiator at night and smothers it with a quilt to keep it from freezing. By now Paula has taken off her bathrobe. Now her pajamas. Now she is spreading those slippery panties out on the bed and selecting a color. Or just standing around being naked. I know all about Paula. One day last summer the boy went looking for her and found her on Paula's rock, belly down on the beach towel, trying to smoke a roll-your-own. A trail of tobacco dribbled across the towel from the Dill's Best box to half a dozen crumpled cigarette papers. Her bathing suit hung limp from a wild cherry tree. She was trying to get a tan all over.

Her eyes grew huge, but just for a moment. Then she smirked. The boy picked up a stick to defend himself because she might turn dangerous like an animal. But his eyes were hypnotized by the naked globes of her ass with the warm dark furrow between. His stare made them turn white. Then she said under her breath, "I dare you! I doubledare you!" He dropped the stick and went back into the woods. But he could hear her calling after him, "Go ahead and tell if you know what's good for you. If you feel like getting another bloody nose . . ."

8

He didn't tell. His mother and father had other things to think about. Every day, when his father finished breakfast, instead of going to bed he would sit down with the *Deauville Dispatch* and draw circles and X's on the classifieds. Then he would fetch his yardstick. He never looked at a house without immediately measuring all the rooms. Like the yardstick in London, England, the silver measure they keep locked up in a museum, exact to the billionth of an inch. If it were ever stolen, inches and feet would vanish from the earth.

But he always returned looking crumpled and went to bed with the green felt shade over his eyes. Twice, when they thought they had found a house, they asked Grandma for five hundred dollars for the down payment, but she shook her business head: "We don't invest in that chicken coop. You people, all you want to do is flush my money down the drain." A month before the eviction they found a house in Winslow, in smelling distance from the paper company. Five rooms with flush. Imitation yellow brick tarpaper. New picture window. View of the Esso station rest rooms. One tenant, old as the house. Took all her meals at the Rexall drugstore. Big back lot. The boy's father saw tomatoes groaning under their burden. He measured the rooms and they talked terms. The old lady cried and agreed to meet them in her lawyer's office the first of the week. His father closed out his insurance and collected six hundred dollars and they waited at the lawyer's for two hours until the telephone call came. She couldn't part with the house.

"I'm going to bed," his father announced then. He gave up reading the *Dispatch*, except for the live letters and the obituaries. The yardstick disappeared. He managed to be out of the house on the day the boy's mother accepted Grandma's offer that they pay her sixty a month to live in her cellar on Water Street.

He is getting ready for bed now. Paula comes downstairs in

9

her green Blessed Sacrament jumper and black stockings, takes her books off the top of the kerosene stove, kisses him on the cheek, puts on her mackintosh, shakes her hair loose over the collar, then goes up into the kitchen and out into the snow. My father has stripped down to his underwear and cellar-sleeping socks. He takes the kitchen clock off the stove where my mother keeps it warm and ticking, winds it, and sets it down on the cement floor in the entryway by his couch. He puts on his green eyeshade, sits on the edge of the couch, reaches blindly for the bedspread rigged up like a drape on a piece of clothesline, and begins to draw it shut. "Get the light, will you, there's a good fellow." But before his head disappears behind the bedspread he grins and says to the boy, "One peep out of you, young scalawag, and into a snowbank you go."

Now that he knows he is a defeated man, my father is sometimes more cheerful. Last Friday, instead of going to bed after breakfast, he poured a second cup of coffee and drummed on the table, smiling privately. Paula left for school but the boy, who could risk being late, waited, because all signs pointed toward a surprise. When the boy's mother returned from mass his father produced the surprise, out of the inside pocket of his black overcoat, an oblong package that he set in the boy's lap.

"What is that, Tom?" she asked, her forehead corrugated, as it always is when anything, good or bad, is about to happen.

"That," he said, "is an educational investment."

He respects education. Unlike my mother, who went to college at St. Joseph's in Portland and then was a nun for five years, he never finished high school. But his education never stops. He takes notes on everything he reads.

The boy tore open the wrapper and studied the perforated wooden tube.

"A recorder," his father explained. "Good thing for you to

learn your notes on. Then someday, when we get organized, Mama can teach you the piano."

The piano, a Baldwin upright, out in Grandma's garage with the rest of the furniture that wouldn't fit into the cellar. His mother played arpeggios: tip the piano on one end and all the keys fall down; then on the other and they tumble back again.

"What's a recorder, Papa?"

"Well, it's a musical instrument, of course. Like a flute. Only older. You see, back in medieval and Renaissance times there were these chaps called troubadours who'd go around in packs serenading the ladies. Princesses and milkmaids alike, it didn't matter. Poor as churchmice all of them, but that didn't matter either . . . Read the leaflet. Isn't there a leaflet that comes with it?"

The boy read, in his best classroom voice: " 'Most delicate is the headpiece. Particularly the cutting edge must not be damaged. It is advisable to play the instrument no longer than fifteen minutes in the beginning in order to injure it to . . .' "

"To what?"

" 'To inure it. To inure it to warmth and moisture . . .' What's the cutting edge, Papa?"

"Look at the diagram, you ignoramus. Isn't it on the diagram? . . . Well, let that pass. We don't have to worry about that for a while yet."

"All right . . . 'One tries from the very beginning to play as dry as possible, because otherwise the wood swells and one can no more take to pieces the instrument. When once it has swollen, one shall not use violence; one leaves it behind for some time open for being made dry by the air . . .' "

An explosion of laughter. My father's laugh is thunder. "German," he said. "That's the way a German explains a thing. That's how they won the war. German know-how."

" 'After the blowing — and this each time — the caused

moisture shall be removed by a sponge. In order to make insensible the instrument against moisture it shall be wiped out from time to time with oil free from acid; with it shall not soak any oil into the pith chip . . .' "

"Piss who?"

"Tom!"

"Piss who?"

"Pith chip, Papa."

Laughing then, the two of them laughing together, the father doubled up on his couch hugging a wound in his side, the boy hunched over in his easychair, shaking the floor out from under Grandma's feet. Suddenly the boy's mother began to cry. His father stopped short, drew himself together on the couch and said quietly to the boy, "Go to school."

He snores behind the bedspread now, in the ticking darkness of the cellar. I stand quietly by the table. Maybe I will go into the furnace room and work on my model boat, or sneak upstairs and see if Grandma is out. If Grandma is out I will take the *Dispatch*, read the funnies, then roll it up and put it back on the front porch so she won't know. Wash Tubbs. Boots and Her Buddies and Freckles and His Friends. Joe Palooka, my favorite.

What has happened? The window? The stairs. Nothing. Nothing has happened at all. Something has stopped happening.

"Papa, the clock has stopped." But of course he does not answer.

I tiptoe to my father's couch, pick up the clock, and shake it. Chut chut chut chut chut chut chut . . . But the moment it touches the cement it dies. Winding it, now, tighter, but the spring is already taut. I bear it through the plank door into the furnace room. Grandpa Vigue's old workbench. Mine now. The large drawers, with some of his tools and my clothes. The cubbyholes: coins, rocks, Vatican City stamps, balsa wood, my collection of holy medals, my camera, nursery catalogs — dozens of catalogs from nurseries all over the country. On the nights when he does not have nightmares the boy often dreams of trees — their secrecy, coolness, darkness, peace. Someday he will reforest an acre of land.

He sets the clock on the workbench and stares at it, and it stares blankly back. Then he takes Grandpa's ball peen hammer and gives it a deft whack on the side. Chut chut chut chut chut chut chut chut . . .

I have fixed Papa's clock.

But once again that terrible lack of sound. The white moonface staring back, saying nothing human, and hiding behind the face the sharp-toothed brass wheels and the tense mainspring. Caught in its own lie. I tip it on its side and it coughs out three minutes more and sputters to death.

And now the boy holds the clock in his outstretched hand and watches his fingers relax, then shuts his eyes, waiting the outcry of gnashing wheels, the ping of the springs, but hears instead a dull smash. The face is broken. Shattered glass speckling the cement floor. The black hands lying a foot from the clock, still attached to each other, but failing to twitch, not even that final twitch that is only nerves. The white moonface of a speechless idiot.

"What the hell are you doing in here?" My father stands in the doorway in his underwear and socks, his green eyeshade on top of his head, blinking into the light. He is a big man. He puts his hairy hands on my shoulders and shakes me. "What are you doing with that clock anyway?"

"It fell," the boy says. "I tried to fix it and it fell." Then he develops a nosebleed.

The color drains from my father's face; he too is losing

blood. "Here," he says. "Lie down. Let me take that pillow out of here." I lie on my couch while he goes through the door, rattles the insides of a drawer in the other room, returns with a dinner knife and holds it in back of my neck.

"How's it feel now?"

"Like ice."

"The nose, I mean."

"Better. It isn't going to be bad this time."

"I'm sorry," he says. "But you gave me a start, you know." He seems satisfied that the nose has stopped. "You just lie there for a while and rest. When your mama gets home tell her I want to get up a half hour earlier because it's haircut night." He goes out the door and the bedsprings sigh underneath him.

The boy lies on his back, checks the wet hankie from time to time for fresh stains. Is my father lying on his back now also, the two of us together, separated by the plank door but breathing the same dank quiet, even at the same moment, inhale exhale inhale exhale, in perfect unison? Drip. Another drip. But that is Humphrey, the water heater, dripping from the spigot into a galvanized pail. Humphrey blew a gasket Monday night, and the boy's father spent most of Tuesday without sleep, bailing them out with a makeshift bailer. "What you people trying to do monkeying with the water?" Grandma wanted to know. The next day one of the legs on the highboy came unglued from the flood and the big piece of furniture sank to the linoleum in defeat.

The boy leaves his couch and goes over to the furnace, pulling out an assortment of jars from a secret place behind it. His spider collection. He keeps them in peanut butter jars with holes punched in the top, the common house and garden spiders, luring them out of their hiding places by tickling their webs with a piece of straw from the broom, then swishing the jars over them and taking them captive. He feeds them the flies and wasps that hatch all winter long in the warm of the rotted window sills, or sometimes other spiders. Always the newcomer loses: the next morning only a few legs and the remains of a corpse sucked dry of its juice.

This morning there are five live spiders and one dead. He puts the jars back in their hiding place.

Beyond the furnace two wooden steps lead to another plank door; behind that the temporary bathroom Grandma had put in while she was having the upstairs one done over. A year ago now and the upstairs still isn't finished. That's so she can keep coming down here to the cellar, thumping down the stairs, pretending not to see anything but taking it all in. Grandma has a face like a zoo.

I close the plank door and drop the hook in the eye, but I do not turn on the light. Some gray winter light filtering through the little window by my head. *Life* and *National Geographic* mildewing on top of the toilet tank. In the soggy pages of *National Geographic* naked natives with their belongings on show.

On the back of the door there is a full-length panel of the mirror that used to hang in Grandpa's bar. The silver under the glass is speckled and crazed. The boy removes his shirt and undershirt (though the bathroom is unheated) and studies the five cloth scapulars on his chest: brown for Our Lady of Mount Carmel, green for the Immaculate Conception, red for the Passion, black for the Seven Dolors, and white for the Blessed Trinity. The rectangles of cloth are connected to two red shoulder straps, otherwise the scapular of the Passion would be invalid. And none of them sewed to another; that too invalidates. At night he prays to die on a Saturday, because the Blessed Virgin has promised that every Saturday she will descend into purgatory and bear off to heaven all the souls she finds wearing scapulars. This is known as the Sabbatine Privilege.

What have they done to the boy in front of the mirror? They have stripped him of his garments. He shivers in his underpants in the half darkness. And now they have rolled his underpants down to the hips, so that only a small pouch of cloth hides his shame. Tied him to a tree, his arms behind him, and the arrows pierce his side. He bears his martyrdom heroically. The sky is darkened. Ministering angels hover overhead. St. Sebastian.

And now they have stripped him altogether.

I am sweating. Icily I sweat all over.

"Yes, dear," his mother says. "I do think it's stopped after all. But wear your galoshes. And be careful because it's icy underfoot."

Up the stairs at last, out of the gloom, into the dazzling white of a snow change. Buckle down the pile-lined earflaps of the leather flying helmet, pull down the scratched isinglass goggles over the eyes. The march down Water Street. Past the theater that they turned into a laundry. Past the American Legion: BEANO EVERY WEDNESDAY NIGHT. Past a three-story house with laundry stiffened to the line on the top front porch. Past the First Church of Christ Coming with the neon letters over the door half-obliterated by snow — JESUS SAVES and AIR-COOLED FOR YOUR COMFORT — and the sign out front with the message for the week:

WELCOME

LIFE IS SHORT
DEATH IS SURE
SIN THE CURSE
CHRIST THE CURE

SUN 10 AM   REV ARCHIE LONGTREE
WHO IS THE EIGHTH BEAST OF REVELATIONS?

16

Past old Schatzie with his rubber-tipped cane, unhappy because he can't find any cigarette butts to whisk off the sidewalk into the storm trap.

Halfway to Holy Angels the sky opens up and it begins to snow again. I have stopped at a street corner. I am watching a very ancient lady in gray woolen stockings and a long mouse-colored coat. She has an orange wool hat pulled down over her ears. She stretches into a rubbish barrel on the corner, scavenging newspapers and folding them into a baby carriage. She is already half white from snow. And now, suddenly, she wheels about and extends an unfleshed forefinger and puts a hex on the boy. "Whoosh," she says. "Whoosh!"

The boy hurries across the street and shouts back at her from a safe distance. "Why don't you drop dead? You're old enough to drop dead, you know."

Alone with the Sorrowing Angel. For me alone the almost black, astonished eyes. I have said the prayer to St. Anthony, to my brother Gabriel the saint, to Sister Justine Bisqueyburu of the Green Scapular. I have said Jesus, Mary and Joseph one hundred times, moving my lips to gain the indulgence. But mostly I pray to the angel. After a while the prayer has no words: it is the dream I often have when I don't have the nightmares. The dream is a photograph, a dense forest of dogwoods teeming with May blossoms, and in a clearing in front of the forest, my mother, my father and Gabriel. Nobody moves and nobody speaks, but everybody is smiling. My mother from under the shadow of her wide-brimmed straw hat; my father (my father is almost laughing!) with his legs apart and his hands in his suit coat pockets so that the watch chain across his vest glitters in the sunlight; and Gabriel, shyly, hugging the cat. And they are all smiling at me, the picture taker.

But something strange is happening to the unbearable eyes of the angel. This is not part of the dream. The dream is gone and the boy is alone with the statue, staring into the angel's eyes, where something strange is happening. From the dark centers of the eyes, first one, then the other, then together, gathering momentum, trickling down the plaster cheeks, tears such as angels weep.

Two

Shall we take the young fellow first?"

"We shall," says my father, "and don't let him give you any nonsense about shearing it all off, Emile. I don't want him looking like every other Johnny in this town. He'll have a gentleman's haircut."

I do not want any of it off, that is just my father making talk. He hates crew cuts because of the Germans. Emile is cranking me skyward in the chair.

"Leave a little something on the sides to keep the ears company. And keep the razor off the neck. Just zip it with the clippers."

Because once you start shaving it, the hair sprouts like crabgrass. The boy does not like haircuts: they fill him with a sense of loss and failure. But he misses the ritual of the shaving: the warm lather, Emile's fingers around his earlobes and down the back of the neck, the thrill of the dangerous razor, the smell of barber sweat and Mennen talcum.

"I can't see why you stay open Thursday nights," my father says to the empty shop.

"Well, there's Tom Dolan and his kid. That's two good reasons."

"The exception proves the rule."

"Bad time of year," Emile says. "Here now, try to keep your head up a bit, sonny . . . A lot of people just don't have the money this time of year. Bills, income tax, doctors. So who needs a haircut?"

Tom Dolan and his kid. Every other Thursday. No matter what collapses around him, a gentleman keeps up appearances.

"Then there's this cold spell. Nobody wants to sit in a steamy barbershop and pop out into the cold again. Though I got to admit myself these last two weeks beat all. I'm crying into my towels . . . Ought to retire and go to Florida. Every body talks about the weather but nobody does anything about it. Except you, of course."

My father's eyes meeting the barber's in the mirror.

"What are you trying to do, Dolan, audition for a job on *Time* magazine? You're going to have the whole town down on you next thing you know."

"So they printed it?" my father says, and his face flushes slightly.

"That's not the half of it. They made an editorial out of you. I always thought that was for people who got elected to high office and died. Haven't you seen the paper yet? Over there — under Betty Grable."

That is my father sorting through the papers in the wicker basket under Betty Grable's ass and pulling out the *Dispatch*. He sits down and reads through his own letter in slow silence, because the words are all new to him again, and then the editorial on the opposite side of the page. Then he harrumphs.

"Still a job to be done on me, is there? What do they fancy, a dark alley someplace?"

"Well, if you're going to stick your neck out . . . I mean the weather's the weather, but why do you want to talk against your own job?"

"One million three hundred and seventy-five thousand men in America are talking against their jobs right now and putting their feet where their mouths are on the picket lines. And what am I doing? Just stating a fact about the air we all breathe every day."

"I been living in this town sixty-one years and I don't smell anything anymore. I'm surprised you do, after working there all this time. You're just setting yourself up for trouble, friend."

"Rubbish." He tosses the paper onto the floor.

"Let me see it, Papa," the boy says. He sticks his hands out from under the linen and takes the paper.

On the front page there is a picture of a man in a barbershop. That is a strange coincidence. I look into Emile's mirror and I am there and I look at the picture and I am there too. "Taking time out from his 275-mile snowshoe trek from Quebec to Lewiston was Cpl. Albert Dandurand, Canadian Snowshoe Champion, when photo above was taken yesterday. Still holding onto his snowshoes, Dandurand has a shave, massage and haircut at Adjutor Laverdiere's barbershop here, taking a snooze in the chair before continuing on his journey. He traveled from Jackman to Deauville yesterday and found the going perfect."

Senator Bilbo is heading down Filibuster Road and a Local Lad is entering Famed Boys Town. The boy finds his father's letter under an angry one about a streetlight by Ima Citizen. He reads while chips of his hair rain on his father's words.

Hey, who writes your stuff? his father wants to know. He refers to a recent piece of editorial piety called "Digging Out after Storm." He submits that the function of an editorial is something more meaningful than to tell us we're lucky to live in Maine since undoubtedly we dug out of the last blizzard faster than places that aren't used to them. Are Maine folks really so inadequate that they need to be constantly reminded how good they are? Good Lord, snow is snow — not a revelation of character.

(At this point there is a paragraph about something Disraeli said of the character of Gladstone and something John L. Lewis said of FDR.)

He goes on to suggest that the *Dispatch* might want to export its editorial writer as a cultural ambassador. Or tell him to clear his head by stepping out onto Silver Street for thirty seconds and whiffing the yellow fragrance that wafts across the Kennebec from the Progressive Paper Company.

(Here he begs the editor's indulgence while he makes mention of the Wobblies and Eugene V. Debs.)

Come on, fellows, his father concludes, let's knock it off, huh? Let's stop talking up Maine and start functioning as a newspaper. A first step might be to hire a journalist. Because whatever you call that stuff on your editorial page, it sure as hell ain't journalism.

And *they* say:

WE LIKE IT HERE

Reader T. Dolan, whose letter appears on this page this morning, evidently doesn't like Maine winters. But since it's the snow that seems to bother him, we suspect he'd have to go rather far west or far south to find a state with winters to his liking.

If he did he'd be confronted with a plethora of something else that bothers him — people who speak well of the area in which they live. Floridians, Texans and Californians are notorious boasters, he would find.

The writer of the editorial praising the efficiency of our snow removal people happens to live a half dozen miles in the country and is well aware of the problems in getting to work during a storm. He finds it less difficult, however, than getting into Washington, New York or Boston on a good day in the summer.

And he doesn't plan to ship out as a "cultural ambassador." There's still a job to be done with the likes of Reader Dolan.

My father would make a good journalist but they are all out to get him. Why is he always writing letters like that? Does he make them up while he lies on the couch behind the drape, staring into his green eyeshade, bug-eyed with excitement? He is waiting for me to say something. But I will suck on my tongue and read the newspaper.

They are out to get Joe Palooka too. The man in the rainstorm who tried to run him over one night last week. The gunman in the Washington Monument who swallowed poison capsules when he was apprehended. A man in evening dress, with a long cigarette holder and a sinister black beard, and his girlfriend Dolores in a slinky black gown. And Dolores says, "Palooka and his manager are in Drawing Room 1, in car 94. Are you going to try . . . ?" And the man, who calls himself Señor Juan Del Torres but that is not his real name, says: "No, my beautiful, this is not a cinema melodrama. It will be done properly and no chance of our being stupidly caught."

Death.

"I must sleep now." The last words of Lord Byron, preserved on the fine India paper of *Death Is the Beginning*. Rabelais rolled over on his bed, cried "Let down the curtain, the farce is over," and made a great leap into the dark. Saintly Charles VIII of France promised never again to commit a mortal sin, or even a venial if he could help it, and gave up the spirit. "This box was presented to me by the Emperor of Prussia," said the dying Czar Alexander III. Crazy Andy Dolan: "The next time you see me I'll be an obit."

So sad and sudden came the call
Your sudden death suprised us all.
The sudden change in a moment fell
Without a chance to say farewell.
I often sit and think of you
And then of how you died,
To think you could not say good-bye
Before you closed your eyes.
You never complained, you weren't that kind,
One of those brothers so hard to find.
But God made a special heaven for you
For you never deserved what you went through.
Sadly missed by Sister Filly and Brother-in-Law

A few months after they moved into the farmhouse on China Lake, Gabriel went to bed with rheumatic fever. Gabriel was seven, two years older than the boy. It was a beautiful summer and the boy spent long afternoons playing with his lead soldiers on the lid of the well. But when he came in for supper he always felt guilty about his happiness, because of Gabriel upstairs with the shades drawn, and suppers were silent, except that occasionally his father would attack the unsuspecting silence: "A man can bear it with one sick child. But why in the name of Almighty God must it be both of them?" Then the boy felt sorry for his father, who looked like he might cry, and for his brother behind the drawn shades, and for himself. One evening he leaned across the supper table and said to his father's sad eyes, "I hope Gabriel dies soon, Papa."

His father's mouth widened, and he half-rose from his chair, clutching a menacing pork chop.

"Because," he added in a hurry, "then he can go to heaven, because Mama says you have to die to go there."

His father sat down, dropped the defeated pork chop onto his plate, and began chasing the peas with his fork.

IN MEMORY OF MY DEAR HUSBAND TONY CLOUTIER
Tony, your death was so sudden
You made us all weep and cry,
But the saddest part of all,
You never even said good-bye.
If we had seen you to the last
And heard the last words you had to say
We would not feel so sad this day.
The time and years will be going swiftly by
But, Tony, the loving memory of you will never die.

Wife Alice

Nobody, not even his father, ever blamed him afterwards for what he did to Gabriel. It was a dark thing not to be mentioned. One Sunday morning they were looking at the funnies together, the boy in his maple rocking chair and Gabriel in bed reading him the words. When they got to the Katzenjammer Kids Gabriel said he was tired and wouldn't read anymore. The boy climbed up on the bed with his rocking chair, set the rockers on either side of Gabriel's body, and began rocking furiously. His mother rushed in and dragged him off the bed. A few days later the priest came and anointed Gabriel and he died.

TONY CLOUTIER, 1943–1946
Just when his life seemed brightest,
Just when his hopes were best,
God saw him getting tired
And a cure was not to be,
So he put His arms around him
And He whispered "Come to Me."
With tearful eyes we watched him
And saw him pass away.
Although we loved him dearly
We could not make him stay.
Dear God, please light a candle
For our Grandpa's third birthday with You.

And if there are any flowers
Could our Grandpa have a few?

        Frankie, Bobby, and Ann-Marie

And a few weeks later, when his father sent him upstairs to fetch him a fresh pair of socks, he found the pack of white balloons in the sock drawer. And then after that his father told him about the death of Grandpa Vigue. He knew about the automobile accident, of course, but there was more: the death was strange, his father said. Medically strange. The wounds were supposed to heal, but didn't. And after Gabriel his father stopped going to church. These are all facts. They go together like forced jigsaw pieces, somebody's head sprouting in a blue sky: Gabriel dying under the rocking chair, Grandpa Vigue dying with medical strangeness, white balloons blown up in memoriam and tied to the little headstone over my brother, my father staying home on Sunday mornings.

"Wet it a bit?" Emile asks the boy, but is looking at his father in the mirror.

"Hell no," his father says. "We've had colds enough for this winter."

The barber dusts him with his brush, whisks the cloth away, cranks him down and motions to his father. I watch my father ease into the leather chair and close his eyes and say nothing. I wish he would open his eyes again. I wish he would say something. But he has abandoned me now. To death. Loss. The voices whispering things about me in a dark place. Gabriel. Grandpa Vigue. Crazy Andy Dolan. Tony Cloutier. What has he to do with me? I do not even know you. I am sorry for what happened to you. What more do you want?

*

Jerome's is my father's bar. Even when we lived on China Lake, because it's just a hop across the bridge to the paper company for the midnight shift. And on haircut nights mine too.

Until recently his father used to take the boy to a drugstore for an ice cream soda after the haircut, while he had a piece of pie and a glass of milk. That was when, as he said, he was getting the old creature by the tail. Then one night he took a swig from his glass, scowled, rose from his booth with glass in hand, a faint milk mustache trembling on his upper lip, and marched up to the counter.

"What's the big idea watering down the milk?" he said to the girl.

"Pardon me?"

"You heard me. WHAT'S THE BIG IDEA WATERING DOWN THE MILK?"

After that they went to the bar instead.

The bar is quiet tonight. A few students from the college by the tracks, playing cards. The old-timers at the bar, in lumber jackets and overalls and felt hats — always wearing those felt hats. We sit down in a booth. Jerome coming down the aisle, carrying a circular tray with a wet bar rag in the center. His hand is tattooed with an eagle and the wrist is strapped in leather.

"Evening, Tom." Swish with the rag. "Usual?"

"The usual, Jerome. And a triple Manhattan on the rocks for the young lad."

We are sitting opposite each other, our hands off the sticky table till it dries. Just the two of us, face to face, but he is staring at the bar. He is Reader Dolan. I will wait.

Then, at the right moment, the boy will reveal the secret that is singing hosannas in his head.

"Here we are, you young reprobate. Set them down, Jerome."

A large Coke brimming with crushed ice and garnished with two maraschino cherries. A double shot of whisky.

"Bottoms up!"

But there must be a place to start. My father has never been inside the church. I could tell him about the statues, slowly, one by one, and then, when I have his interest, lead him at last to the Sorrowing Angel. Who will throw him on his knees at his feet, pierce with his bright sword the sin-hardened heart, and contrition will flow like balm. Then I will tell him the simple but astonishing fact: that my angel sheds tears. That at first the boy was so moved that he too shed tears. But then he dried his eyes on his sleeve and put his finger to the left eye of the statue, and the drops rolled over his finger. And put his finger to his tongue and tasted salt. All this is true. The boy does not lie.

But my father is far away. Maybe he is disappointed because Jerome hasn't mentioned the letter. His mouth is not disappointed, though. It is his car-driving mouth, stuck half open, gulping the carbon monoxide fumes and taking energy from them as he eases down on the accelerator. Last Sunday he took me for a ride down the Augusta road past Sidney because gas is back again, and there is a huge sign in front of Silver Street Service: WE HAVE 600 X 16 TIRES! Halfway there he leaned on the horn and did not remove his hand. The boy searched his face for some explanation, but the eyes bore straight ahead and the car-driving mouth did not close. For five minutes he kept his hand to the horn. Then he burst out laughing, and a cop swung past and motioned him over to the right.

"What's the trouble, mister?"

"Horn. Just blasts on and off again. Must be a short in the wiring, officer. You don't suppose there's a gas station open around here on Sundays?"

"Try the Gulf Station at the second intersection. About a hundred yards down on the right."

"Good enough, officer. Thanks for stopping."

He has never explained. He is still tearing down the Augusta road in the old Dodge, with the horn hooting.

A girl stands by the back door of the bar, alone, pulling bangs out of her eyes. She is wearing an oversize Army-Navy sweater and a wool hat with a long tassel and a pompom. She has a little-girl face and a skirt almost up to the knees, like Paula's, but everything else about her is full grown. She smiles. Her name is Jean.

"Bon soir, Tom."

"Bon soir to you," he says, and his face brightens, and the old Dodge careens over a cliff with nobody at the wheel. She sits down beside the boy, pulls off her wool hat, sets a pile of books on the table and combs her tangled hair with long white fingers.

Jean is from the college. She studies French. My father found her alone in the bar one night, crying, and drove her back to school. He does not tell us why she was crying. But always at breakfast he tells my mother all about her. "Jean was in last night, you know. She's a bright little kid. Smart as a whip. Pity she's never had any real homelife." She is on scholarship, and always picking up odd jobs because her parents are separated and each is waiting for the other to pay her bills. My father wants to have her over for a meal sometime to meet my mother. Dinner on the porcelain table under the fluorescent light under Grandma's feet. "Tom Dolan, everybody's gentleman," my mother said to that, "with special consideration for waifs of all ages."

"In many ways she reminds me of you," he said, circling my mother's waist with his arm and pecking at her cheek. She pushed him away. She was having those hot flashes again that she treats with turnips, raw carrots and lots of oatmeal. On the inside of her coat my mother wears a gold medal of St. Dymphna, the patron saint of nervous conditions.

But the boy is sitting next to Jean now, so close that he can

29

feel her heated hips even through his corduroy pants and her own wool skirt. Her soft white hands are talking to my father's resting hands, his hairy knuckles, the black moon crescents under the nails. The tips of my mother's fingers are knobby with arthritis and the hands are sandpapery. But Jean's hands are soft and white and they play a harp when she talks. The nails are luminous like the inside of an oyster shell. Her hands come to rest on the table and the boy is embarrassed seeing them exposed like that, almost like Paula in the woods. Why doesn't she cover them up with the furry mittens?

"Hey, here's one," she says. "Apportez-moi encore un oreiller, s'il vous plaît. Vous pouvez enlever le traversin." She is reading out of a yellow book.

"Apportez-moi . . ." my father says.

"No, no," she laughs. "You're making it sound Canuck. Mwah. Ap-pawr-tay-mwah . . ."

My father tries again. "What am I saying, anyway?"

"Please give me another pillow. You can take away the bolster."

She snickers and he laughs. "Very valuable indeed. I can see myself saying that on all sorts of occasions."

She is teaching him French. And he tells her stories about the mill. About the union standing up to the big bosses. About the sulfite process and the breakers and the half-stuff machine and the sixteen-foot-high bleaching towers. About the old modified Hollander that should have been scrapped half a century ago. Those were my stories once, but now they are hers too.

"Your father makes me feel very humble. He's a natural man. Capital A, Capital N, Capital M."

My father grinning like a boy at the compliment. Jerome's leather-strapped hand setting a glass of beer in front of Jean. "Combien vous dois-je, Jerome?"

30

"No no no," my father insists. "On me. Plenty more where this came from."

We are all silent now, but Jean's silence is not like mine or my father's, it fills up the spaces between the words. My father throws a handful of nickels at the silence.

"Go ahead," he says to the boy, "make some music."

Down the aisle, past the backs of the hatted men, past the Hav-a-Hank display on the corner of the bar, past the cigarette machine saying YES, THEY'RE BACK. Sergeant Johnny Desmond, the Creamer, on the front of the jukebox in two-tone. The boy touches the sticky knob with two fingers which he will have to wash now. Many people fail to wash their hands after the toilet. When he was five his mother took him on a train ride down to Portland and he had to use the toilet. She led him into the ladies' room but would not let him sit on the seat. She held him in the air above it, his pants around his ankles, encouraging him — "Go, now! Go!" — her legs braced wide on the lurching floor as they roared through the night to Portland, his mother holding aloft the terrified boy who could not go.

A lady gets up from a booth and comes toward him, manipulating her hips and smiling, a thin sweater rolled up above the elbows, and under the sweater two inverted ice cream cones. She says, "Lissen to the jukebox that broke down, Dentyne chewngum, Dentyne chewngum, Dentyne chewngum . . . You like what you see, huh? Believe me, cousin, I could show you more than you ever saw in your life. But you're just a kid. You don't even belong here. What are you playing?"

"I haven't decided yet."

"Play Bing Crosby. Play 'Saddy, Sundy, and Mondy.' J6."

He plays J6 to make her go away. He looks for "Mairzy Doats" but it's been taken off, so he puts on "Chickery Chick" and the "Hut-Sut Song." Back to the booth as the last notes of "Sunday, Monday, or Always" fade into eternity. Jean is leaning over the table, laughing a secret into his father's ear. She looks up at the boy and says, with sudden interest, "I bet that's your favorite."

"No."

> Chickery-chick cha-la cha-la
> Check-a-la-romey in a bananika . . .

"Then *that's* your favorite."

"That's my second favorite."

"Second bests aren't first enough," Jean says. "And third bests are too third. Come on now, tell us."

"It's not there anymore." The boy is almost shouting. Why is she tormenting him? She is trying to make him cry because they have taken "Mairzy Doats" off the jukebox. But the lady with the tits has come over to the table.

"Those are two nice-looking kids you've got," she says.

"They're not my kids," my father says. "Only him."

"Well, they're two nice-looking kids. I'm a mother, I ought to know. I been married seven years already. Married to a real jewel."

Nobody says anything.

"The boy's got real nice hands," she says, leaning over and patting one, her left tit jabbing at his face. "Sensitive. He's going to be a doctor. But don't drink so much, sonny, or you won't be able to operate." She winks fiercely. Suddenly she draws back and looks at them all darkly, especially the boy, and says to him out of the side of her mouth, "You soft kid, you don't even know what trouble is like."

"What's *your* trouble, lady?" his father says.

"You think I don't know what trouble is? I ought to know, I married a Jew like you."

He corrects her: "Jewel."

"No, a Jew, just like you. You make all the money but what good can you do? Can you make my baby better? You can't even make my baby better."

32

"Everybody has his cross."

"My baby's a year old and he's got a fissure. You know what a fissure is?" she asks the boy. "That's right, it's a cut. He's got an eight-inch fissure in his bowels. And they don't do a thing for him. Well, no kid of mine is going to lay in pain every time he has to have a BM. He shouldn't have to scream in pain every time he has a BM."

The boy is going to be sick. He hates the lady with the tits and her baby; she will make his own bowels bleed. For two weeks last winter his father brought home rolls of extra-soft toilet paper from the mill and his mother fed him liquids.

"Would you please go away," Jean says.

"And he's got a ball that's three times as big as the other." Her hands creating an enormous globe in the air. "And an eight-inch fissure." Her voice is climbing up treacherous stairs.

"Please!" Jean says.

"Sure. That's right. You're from the college, aren't you? You go to the finest schools in the land and you study all the minor things, but you can't make my kid not scream in pain every time he has a BM."

"THAT WILL DO!" My father rises from his seat. But then, because the woman has started to cry, he puts his hairy hands on her shoulders and says softly, "Why don't you go home and get some sleep? You look as if you could use a little sleep. Come on, now. We all have our cross to bear."

The boy does not see what happens after that because he has hurried from the booth and gone into the bathroom to be sick.

"Feeling better now?"

"Yes, Papa."

He has followed me into the bathroom and is wiping my

33

face with his bandanna hankie soaked in cold water. The boy closes his eyes under the wet hankie, and they open to his father's face in the mirror under a sign:

DIRTY HANDS SPREAD DISEASE
WASH THEM!
Deauville Dept. of Health
Environmental Sanitation

The sign bears a black hand print to dramatize the terror of toilet diseases.

"Well now, it's getting past your bedtime. Nine-thirty already. I'd better drop you off at the house."

He wrings the hankie out over the sink, pats it flat, and puts it back wet into his pants pocket.

"Papa?"

"What's the matter? Are you feeling sick again?"

"No. No, it's not that. Papa, I want to tell you something."

"Well, of course. Go right ahead." His hands reach for the cigarette papers and the Dill's Best, as they always do when somebody is about to tell him something. The boy does not turn to face his face, is still looking at him in the mirror back in the barbershop.

"Well — at Holy Angels? There's an angel at Holy Angels and it sheds real tears."

He has spoken — not to his father's eyes, which he dares not meet, but to the black hand on the DIRTY HANDS sign. And immediately he is angry with himself and with his father. The wrong words in the wrong place. Spewed out like sickness. A green stain in the center of the sink, the Lava soap streaked with black fingers, the odor of unflushed urinals with piny soap cakes in the bottom, "Lick My Lollipop, TR 2-3748." The taste of my sickness still in my mouth. O my defiled angel!

34

A wisp of smoke drifts into the mirror. My father has lit a cigarette and is drawing on it silently. "A statue?" he asks finally. "A statue of an angel?"

"Yes. It's a statue. And it sheds real tears. I tasted them."

"You tasted them." He is telling it to himself, twisting his mouth strangely because of the smoke or the statement.

"Yes."

Then he smiles, puts an arm around the boy's shoulder, and draws him from the sink.

"Well now, I've got a story for you, too. You know that crazy dog down the next block — the one with the face like Chiang Kai-shek? You'll never believe what he was up to this morning. Digging a great hole down through the snow to bury two bones. But they weren't bones at all. Do you know what they were?"

"No."

"Icicles! Yes! Setting away two icicles in the deep freeze till the spring thaw. Can you imagine Chiang Kai-shek's face when he comes back looking for his bones in March?"

He guffaws. His face is flushed. He pats the boy on the back and says, "Be with you in a minute."

He is over at one of the urinals, unbuttoning his fly, fighting with his underwear. "Damn these things! Somebody's got a pretty curious idea of human anatomy. Well, the company's going to hear about it, by God. I'll blister somebody's ears with a letter first thing in the morning."

Three

Spring came fiercely over the weekend, as if it had never happened before or would again. Everybody in Maine knows that spring at the end of March is a lie. But in the middle of the night the ice floes exploded on the Kennebec and the boy woke in the dark frightened, thinking for a moment the Germans had broken the treaty, that after all the years of practice blackouts the invasion was finally on them. And every day now the water rises, the deep brown rush of river flecked with yellow foam along the banks. The boy's father stuffs old socks in the cracks between the stones of the cellar where the cement has sprung loose. The geranium has put out a tentative bud. Heavy rains and heavy sun. Strange birds are baring their bellies to the edges of the wind. Laundered slipcovers flap in captivity on the back line.

For the boy has returned from school to find his mother

helping Grandma with the spring cleaning upstairs. Grandma follows her around on afflicted legs made out of mahogany, muttering orders as the boy's mother takes down the curtains, rubs the furniture with lemon oil, reverses the mattresses, rolls up the rugs to scrub the floor underneath. "All right, Mama . . . I'm sorry, I didn't notice that, Mama . . . Yes, Mama" (Mama says). The boy helps on the lighter jobs, like squirting the windows with Windex for his mother to rub clean. "You leave streaks," Grandma says.

Then his mother starts on the pictures while Grandma makes spastic sounds. She takes down the picture over the lowboy of Grandpa Vigue in front of his tavern with three other men, each wearing a fedora and a rumpled tarpaper suit, Grandpa Vigue squinting defiantly into the winter sun, a cigar in his fist. Under his mother's hand time skips seasons and suddenly a full summer sun blazes in the plate glass windows of the tavern. Encouraged, she moves on to the oil painting over the fireplace.

"What you doing with that, Anna? You don't put the Windex on that. There's no glass."

" 'Course not, Mama. All it needs is a little mild soap and water. Can't you see that dingy film all over it? "

The boy's mother is an artist. Though he has never seen her at work, she still keeps a box of oil paints and saves picture postcards to turn into oil paintings someday. She has sensitive blue veins on her temples. Almost every room in the China Lake farmhouse had pictures she did before the boy was born, seascapes mostly, to remind her of happy days in Portland.

Out in the garage now with the furniture, growing fungus.

Grandma's painting has a massive gilt frame. In the left foreground an olive-skinned boy beside a hay wain gazes into the eyes of an olive-skinned girl, whose skirts are knotted up around her hips and who offers him coppery grapes from a basket. A purplebrown stream starting in the right corner twists into the center of the picture through yellowbrown fields in some place like Rumania, catches a mill wheel on the side of a redbrown cottage, and disappears in the brown gloom of a murky horizon. The sky is dull cinnamon. You are looking at it all through a pair of old sunglasses. The picture is like Grandma.

His mother's sponge skims the surface. "That's a two-hundred-dollar picture," Grandma says. "Do you know that? A man was here once to talk about the property on Front Street. Before we lost all the property." She always speaks of the property Grandpa sold on Front Street as lost. "He wanted to buy that picture for two hundred dollars. But of course I don't sell . . ."

As his mother's thumb slices through the girl's bare legs.

"O my God, Anna!"

Grandma covers her left cheek with her hand. Only I know why she does that. My mother sets the painting on the table, wipes her soapy hands on her hips, picks it up again and strokes the back side with her fingers to help the wound to mend.

"I'm sorry, Mama. It couldn't be helped. It's because the canvas is all dried out."

"So that makes everything all right? All you people can do is be sorry. Why don't you just throw all my pictures into the garbage can?"

"I'll fix it, Mama."

"Go ahead. Throw them all into the garbage can."

"Mama, I can fix it."

"Sure. You can fix it for two hundred dollars, maybe?"

"Please, Mama. I said I'm sorry. All it needs is a bit of tape on the back and I'll match the paint on the front side so the rip won't even show."

All this time Grandma has kept her left cheek covered with her hand. The boy knows what she is hiding.

Under that hand there is a fresh gash in her canvas-colored skin.

Now she clumps out of the room, and the boy and his mother descend into the darkness of the cellar bearing the brown harvest with them.

A letter has been lying on the porcelain table since the noon delivery. Now it is suppertime and my father comes out from behind the hanging bedspread, sees the letter, tears open the envelope and reads to himself, standing in the center of the room in his underwear. Then he turns to us, fills his chest with air, and announces, "Behold the man! Tom Dolan in his performing briefs." He does a pirouette on the linoleum. Then he passes the letter around.

"Oh for heaven's sake, Tom, put your pants on." My mother is worried about Paula, but Paula is busy gnawing on a licorice rope to spoil her appetite.

> Sartor Resartus Underwear Corporation
> P.O. Box 4110
> Winston-Salem, North Carolina
> March 20, 1946

Mr. T. Dolan
54 Water Street
Deauville, Maine

Dear Mr. Dolan:

Somebody once said, "Anything clearly expressed is well wrote!" This gramatically incorrect — but semantically precise — statement describes the contents of your letter of March 3 perfectly.

Mr. Dolan, I am real concerned over the fact that you have been dissatisfied with the performance of our briefs.

Would you be so kind as to send all eight pair of briefs to me as I want to turn them over to our Quality Control Department for examination. I will then replace the eight pair of briefs promptly.

We have always been proud of the quality of our products, and when we receive a letter from a long time customer such as you have been, it really disturbs all of us.

Thanks again for your letter, and rest assured that we have no intention of having you desert SARTOR RESARTUS for another "name brand" of underwear.

Cordially yours,
R. "Bob" Bembow
Men's and Boys' Division

Supper is done. The boy's mother whisks the dishes off the table, mops it with a rag, sets the painting down, and out of storage from the garage she brings a shoe box of oil paints. This means that the boy will have to go to St. Francis Xavier devotions without her. Every Wednesday night Monsignor Fallon, an old displaced Irishman who is pastor of Holy Angels, runs these devotions, because he owns a splinter of the saint's bone. But how did he get hold of it? Because St. Francis Xavier's body is incorruptible. Four hundred years after he expired on the island of Sancian off China, dreaming of the harvest of souls there — and even after a band of atheist pirates stole the body and threw it into a vat of lye — the tongue which received the sacred host is still intact, the body as fresh as the day he died, entombed in a glass vault in the cathedral in Goa. Except for the right arm, which baptized thousands of pagans in a single day and which his Holiness the Pope has honored by having it shipped to him personally in Rome. After devotions and benediction the congregation files up to the altar rail to kiss the gold and glass case that holds the relic — the cold, thrilling kiss of sanctity — and Monsignor Fallon wipes it with an embroidered linen cloth between each kiss. Then he and Father Tetrault hear confessions.

"Paula dear," the boy's mother says (Paula is in the easychair again, watching her bare toes), "why don't you go along?"

"I've got homework."

"Isn't it about time you went to confession again?"

"No. I don't have anything to tell. I just went."

"I'm sure you can find something," the boy's father says.

"How long ago was that?" his mother asks.

She is pretending to remember. But I know: "Three weeks."

Paula uncoils and shoots out of the chair. "O for Christ sake why don't you mind your own business?"

My father laughs. "Well, there's a little item for the good father's ears, anyway."

"That's enough, Tom. You go upstairs and change into a dress, Paula."

"They're as clean as anything *he's* got on," she says, rolling the cheeks of her ass as she leaves the room so that we can appreciate the two worn spots in her blue jeans.

Father Tetrault is the boy's friend, the intense young priest to whom he confesses twice a week, on Saturday afternoons and on Wednesday nights. To Father Tetrault he revealed his shame, the conscience that rises up in the night.

"If it happens at night that's nothing to worry about."

"And sometimes in the day."

"Well. That just means you should think about something else. When you get bothered start thinking about — Oh, imagine that you're Johnny Mize and you've just socked a home run for the New York Giants."

The boy does not play baseball. And it does not seem right to think about Johnny Mize when you are receiving holy communion.

"At holy communion?" The priest sounded surprised.

41

"Yes, Father. Whenever I receive holy communion."

The priest became nervous then, the shadowy figure shifting his weight on his haunches, drifting away in denial of what he had heard. But when he spoke again his voice was confident.

"Do you know what I think? I think you're altogether too sensitive about things." Father Tetrault went on to distinguish three kinds of conscience — normal, lax, and scrupulous. Scrupulous people should not listen to their consciences. It was all in their head. "So for the time being," Father Tetrault said, "I'm your conscience. Whatever I say goes. You just fly blind."

Then, to prove to the boy that he was still his friend, despite the things he had heard, he asked him if he would like to be an altar boy.

Shortly after that, when the angel began to weep, the boy was afraid to tell Father Tetrault, who might say it was all in his head. And when, after three days, the tears dried up, there was nothing to tell. He flew blind through the dark snowstorms of the late Maine winter, all the lights on his instrument panel out, not a star in the sky. Then he heard a voice. And Father Tetrault did not laugh at him or say he was imagining things.

"You say it speaks to you?"

"Yes, Father."

"And the lips move?"

"No."

"Then how do you know it's the angel?"

"Because that's where the voice comes from."

"I see. And what language does he speak?"

"I don't know."

"You mean you don't understand what he's saying?"

"No, not that. I mean the words sound like they're a foreign language. But I understand all of them."

"What does he tell you?"

"He tells me not to fear those who persecute me. To forgive my enemies."

"Well, that's sensible, I suppose. Though at your age you shouldn't really have enemies. Now let me tell you something. God speaks to us in different ways. To some he speaks through the beauty of a sunset or a symphony or — or the splendor of the liturgy. Or the light in a child's eyes. To you, possibly, through the angel. Do you see what I mean?"

"And he says I should pray to him."

"I see. Tell me, does he have a name to pray to, this angel of yours?"

"He's the Sorrowing Angel. His eyes are very sad."

"But has he ever told you his name?"

"No."

"Well, maybe the next time he talks to you, you should ask him his name."

The boy thought there was a smile on the gray face behind the grille. But he must have been wrong because the voice was solemn.

But tonight there is nothing new to tell him. That is why the boy says nothing to Paula on the walk to Holy Angels and does not mind that she is punishing him with her own silence. But Paula has spotted old Schatzie under a street light, working his rubber-tipped cane up and down in the wet refuse clogging a rain sewer. When he finishes with that he will go back to flicking all the cigarette butts off the sidewalk into the gutter. Paula is determined to speak to him.

"Hi, Schatzie. Pretty messy, huh?"

He does not look up.

"Pretty messy, huh Schatzie? You ought to get the city to pay you for all that work."

This time she gets an answer. "They'd owe me so goddam

much by now they'd be broke. All those old butts. Most of
them got lipstick on them. Women are the dirtiest damn
smokers. Dirty whores."

His cane jabs angrily at a butt and skids to one side. "See?"
he cries. "See?"

Paula laughs and says to the boy, "Do you know what happened to old Schatzie?"

"No."

"I do." She hisses the loud secret into his ear. "They
caught him doing something not very nice and THEY CUT OFF
HIS PINOCHLES." Then she giggles.

But that is not funny. Human suffering is not funny. The
baby with the eight-inch fissure. Gabriel dying under the
rocking chair. Schatzie without his pinochles.

The terrible revelation of the angel.

> O Father Saint Francis, thy words were once strong
> Against Satan's wiles and an infidel throng,
> Not less is thy might where in heaven thou art,
> O come to our aid, in our battle take part!
> Saint Francis Xavier, O pray for us!
> Saint Francis Xavier, O pray for us!

Monsignor Fallon climbs the pulpit and tells an involved story
about the saint going outside the city limits of Goa, removing
his sandals and shaking the dust of the city out of them. Then
down from the pulpit, lace skirts swishing around his ankles,
into a huddle with Walter Caron and Philip Proulx and a new
altar boy. A cloud of smoke spiraling from their midst. Up
the three marble steps. Puts the bone in the huge monstrance
reserved for the Blessed Sacrament. Arms extended, a flash of
gold and rubies, the saint's bone aloft, genuflection, all heads
bowed, a clatter of bells, incense. "O most lovable and loving
Saint Francis Xavier . . ." The final singing of "Holy God
We Praise Thy Name." The cold kiss of the relic. Finished.
Candles snuffed, all lights out except for the red vigil lamp

and the dim lanterns over the confessionals on the side aisles.

They wait on Father Tetrault's side. From where he sits the boy can see an old woman hunched in front of his angel, but nothing is happening for her. Father Tetrault comes down the aisle, smiles at his penitents and enters the box. Two old women part the curtains, one on either side.

Paula is next. She blesses herself the way girls do, her fingers suggesting her tits but not touching them. Now she folds her hands tightly and sucks on her whitening knuckles in an examination of conscience. She looks unhappy. She is in the state of sin.

But now she raises her head and the gloom disappears. She even smiles slightly as if her sins are already erased. Inside the box a slat bangs shut and a woman emerges, blinking sorrowfully into the light. Paula rises, takes several confident steps down the aisle, but then, to the boy's astonishment, passes the box and keeps going till she walks right out of the church. He gets up, confused, momentarily thinks of running after her and making her go to confession, but enters the box himself.

Thud. The open slat. The acid male smell. The breathing of the priest's averted head in the gloom.

"Bless me, Father, for I have sinned. It is four days and six hours since my last confession. I accuse myself of the following sins . . ."

Pause. Because the boy has none. Not since the angel. Flying blind over the contamination of earth. When he was seven and about to make his first confession, he worried that he might have to commit a sin before they would let him go to confession. And until he made his first confession they wouldn't let him receive communion. On First Communion Day the rest of the class would file happily up to the altar rail and he would be left behind, and nobody would know why. Maybe they would think he was a great sinner who had committed the Unpardonable Sin.

Tonight, sinless, he repeats the sin from his past life that he is particularly sorry for. That time in the third grade Miss Lipchick praised the new boy from Elyria, Ohio, for his skill in arithmetic: "Why this is as simple as apple pie for you, isn't it, Leonard! If we keep this up we may just have to skip the fourth grade." By the time the boy got home from school he was convinced the teacher really meant to say it to him. For several weeks his mother made hopeful trips in the evening — to Miss Lipchick, Mr. Violette the principal, Mr. Boutelle the superintendent of schools — because of what the boy now knows was a lie.

My poor mother! Why have I made her suffer?

Father Tetrault listens patiently to the old story. Then he turns full face to the boy. "Now then. About this angel of yours. I spent the better part of an hour there the other day saying my office. I think I should tell you it strikes me as a rather unexceptional piece of plaster. In fact . . ."

"He spoke to me again. He told me his name. He said . . ."

"Yes?"

"I am the Angel of the Bottomless Pit."

The priest shaves his chin with the flat of his hand. "I don't think I like the sound of that. What do you suppose he meant?"

"I don't know."

But I think I do. It is because of the dark unfathomable truths the angel knows.

"He said that unless the world venerates him there will be another terrible war and a third of the human race will perish. He told me I will suffer greatly in my lifetime."

"I think," Father Tetrault says, and for the first time his voice is not completely calm, "I think maybe you've carried this business far enough. I don't like it. I don't pretend to know what it's all about, but I don't like it. It sounds too much like a form of spiritual blackmail."

"I don't know what you mean, Father."

"Listen, I'm going to give you some advice now. And I

46

want you to follow it to the letter. I want you to forget about this angel. Don't go anywhere near it. Say your prayers elsewhere. I tell you these things for the good of your soul."

"But if the angel wants me to . . ."

"If the angel wants you he'll find you. If it really is an angel he'll understand that you're following my advice, that I speak as the voice of your conscience. Do you understand?"

"Yes, Father."

"Good. And remember, I'm always available. Any time you need me — any time anything's bothering you. The rectory is always open. OK?"

"Yes, Father."

"Good. And now for your penance say three Our Fathers and three Hail Marys and make a good Act of Contrition."

The boy recites the Act of Contrition while Father Tetrault makes the sign of the cross over him. Then, before he shuts the slat, the priest says to the boy, "Pray for me."

The night is windless but cold. It feels like snow again, like winter coming back. The boy buckles his aviator's helmet and looks for stars, but the sky is black except for the unnatural rose glow over Winslow from the paper company. The Angel of the North Star has covered his golden eye with his dark wings.

I am alone. Though it could have been worse. Father Tetrault might have talked about Johnny Mize. And it's important that he called it advice. He said he wanted me to forget about the angel, but he didn't say I *have* to forget about the angel. Technically the boy is still free. Otherwise how can the angel be known and venerated?

But it would be terrible to lose his friend Father Tetrault and be all alone with the truth.

When the boy is halfway home the night suddenly explodes. A dog, invisible but close at hand, barking. A dead privet hedge turning into three kids. One of them, a big teenager, squeals like a girl. Then they come at him. He lashes out with his knee, hurting somebody where it is soft, and the kid bounces away and goddamns him. Then arms pin his arms and he cannot move. They drag him to the front of a very narrow but high three-family house, riding the night like a monstrous ark. One of them clambers up the front porch steps and drums the door of the old house.

An old lady opens the door, her face sour in the porch light. In summer there will be moths over her head, a whole flock of them, beating their wings crazily against the lamp and her colorless hair. She strains at the boy through half-moon glasses and says, "That's him . . . that's the one."

Another light goes on upstairs and a moment later a second and younger woman appears, descends the porch stairs and looks into his face. She smells like weeds that flower in the night.

"Why, I know him, Mother. He lives just down the street."

I know her, too. She is Miss Duplessie, who teaches fifth grade at Blessed Sacrament, is in charge of buying pagan babies at five dollars each, and runs the school library. Whenever I ask her for a good book on angels or astronomy, she gives me *The Life of St. John Bosco for Boys*. Joseph Maroon says she hands out pellets of ant poison on Halloween.

"Well, he's the same one . . . same color jacket and everything . . . that's the one." The old lady has come down the steps now too and breathes the insides of her mouth on me.

"Nobody wants to hurt you," Miss Duplessie says, trying to be kind, dropping pellets into my paper bag. "Why did you break the window?"

"What window?"

"He's the one all right."

"Nobody wants to hurt you. Tell us why you broke the window."

"He'll pay for it . . . brat."

The kids have loosened their grip on his arms, and the boy breaks from them and runs down the street. Half a block later he looks back but nobody is following. But he runs on until he is home. Paula steps out of the shadows by the side of the house where she has been waiting for him.

"What's the matter?"

They have made the boy cry.

"Here," she says, "give me your hankie." She feels in his pocket but can't find one. She gives him her own and he wipes his eyes and blows his nose. No blood this time.

"What happened?"

"Miss Duplessie says I broke her window."

"Did you?"

"No," he says, and begins to cry again. Paula puts her arm around him because he is shaking. Then she kisses him on the cheek. "Please don't cry," she says, and he is so surprised that he stops crying to wonder what her motive is. Paula has motives for the things she does.

My mother bending over Grandma's canvas, her face only a few inches from the picture, daubing nervously.

"It's all changed," Paula says.

She looks up irritably.

"This is only the beginning. Not what it's going to look like after I tone it down. You have to get something down on the canvas before you can get the right shade."

But she doesn't sound convinced. The girl's bare legs are Disney pink. My mother aims at the hay wain with a brush tipped in crimson. "Get out of my way, both of you, and let me finish this." The table is littered with the wrinkled old tubes of paint, split in the middle because the tops are caked shut, the colored intestines leaking out onto the porcelain top.

My father comes out of the furnace room on his way back from the toilet and smiles when he sees us. He pulls a scrap of paper from his pocket. "It's only a rough draft," he says.

Mr. R. "Bob" Bembow
Sales Manager
Men's and Boys' Division
Sartor Resartus Underwear Corporation
Winston-Salem, North Carolina

My dear Mr. Bembow:

It was indeed kind of you to take a sympathetic interest in my plight as described in my letter of March 3. I deeply regret, however, that since I do not make a practice of keeping old shreds of ill-fitting underwear as trophies, seven of the eight pair of Sartor Resartus briefs were consigned to the rubbish bin before your letter arrived. The last pair — in a slightly less deplorable state of disintegration than the others — I am sending you under separate cover. The briefs have, of course, been thoroughly laundered.

Yours ever truly,
T. Dolan

He sticks the letter back into his pocket, pins his foreman's badge onto his jacket, and leaves for a few drinks at Jerome's before work.

Joe Palooka is in Florida training for a fight with Phantom Dill, a big dark man with five o'clock shadow. Joe's friends are disappearing and dying off mysteriously. The assassin lurking in the palms has killed his sparring partner Tiny and dumped his body into the sea. Mrs. Sampson, the cook, tasted a turkey intended for Joe and died of cyanide poisoning, then she burned up over the hot stove, leaving no evidence. The hired killers have got his friend Marty and left him dead in the road, pouring liquor into his mouth to make it look like he was in a drunken brawl. And masterminding it all is the sinister Juan del Torres. "Corazon," Dolores says, "why do you not tell your beloved who you really are? I follow you blindly . . . I act even as an accomplice in murder."

"One day you shall know . . . the world to its sudden shock will know . . . and you shall share the glory . . ."

Every evening for a week my mother has worked on the painting. The flesh has not lost its pink glow; instead, the rest of the picture has been made to harmonize with it, my mother working outward from the two figures in ever widening blocks of color, every brush stroke demanding another, brightness spreading out to the very edges of the painting like an uncontrollable stain. The stream winds, blue and untroubled, through a sunny gold field; sun floods the sky and blazes in the tiny windows of the cottage; the girl's mouth, like the grapes in her basket, is a gash of scarlet.

And now she is done. It is a Thursday afternoon and Grandma is out for a walk. We sneak upstairs to hang the painting. But before we can escape from the room the front door slams and Grandma stands in the living room, fish-eyed. The wound in her cheek has healed.

"I fixed it, Mama."

Grandma says nothing.

"And I brightened it up a bit. It was so drab . . ."

Still Grandma refuses to speak.

"And you see, you can't notice the rip at all. Even up close. I put some tape back there . . ."

"Shut up," Grandma says. "You take that thing off my walls. All you people can do is ruin things."

Tonight, Grandma in the front room listening to Gabriel Heatter, the boy enters her bedroom. He unscrews the perforated top from the jar in his hand and turns it upside down. The spider springs up to the bottom of the jar. He slaps the jar with his palm — and again — and finally the spider drops, in infinite slow motion, trailing a filament of silk, hits the floor, freezes, then scurries off in back of her massive mahogany wardrobe. And waits.

Four

About. Above. Across. After. Against. Along; amid; among; around, at, before, below, beneath beside between-beyondby . . ."

"Slowly!"

"Uh . . . between. Betwixt."

"Betwixt is between. Same thing."

"Beyond. By. Beneath."

"We already had those."

"Down?"

"Yes."

"Down. Except. For. From. In. Into. Of. Off. On. Over. Through. Throughout. Till. To. Toward? . . . Toward. Under. Until. Up. Upon . . . Up. Upon. Uh . . ."

"*Uh?* Is that a word? Are you finished already?"

"No, Sister."

"What about the w's?"

"With! Withwithinwithout."

The boy gasps out the last three and sits down.

"Only thirty-nine," Sister Polycarp says. "There are forty."

Why are there forty? Who made up the numbers for things? There are seven gifts and twelve fruits of the Holy Ghost, four signs of the one true Church, ten commandments of God but only six commandments of the Church, nine First Fridays and five First Saturdays and four Last Things, fifteen mysteries of the rosary and fourteen Stations of the Cross. And three things necessary for a mortal sin.

"What's in back of you?" Sister Polycarp asks.

He turns. Joseph Maroon is in back of him, engraving something on his desk, and hurriedly puts down his pencil. The boy cannot understand the question.

"What do you call what's in back of you? What's the word for it?"

A word for Joseph Maroon?

"Class?"

Rita's right arm flagging the air, her left hand bracing the elbow against exhaustion.

"Rita?"

"Behind."

"Yes. *Behind*," Sister Polycarp says meaningfully. "You left out *behind*. Now let's try to get all forty in proper sequence without all the fumbling and hesitation."

The mystic forty. Forty days of Noah and the flood. The forty-year reign of Solomon, David and Saul. Christ in the desert fasting. Forty days, therefore Lent. Christ rose from the dead and walked the earth for forty days before ascending into heaven. And left behind him forty prepositions. The boy begins the litany again.

"About. Above. Across. After. Against . . ."

But Sister Polycarp has never really explained what prepositions mean. The whole idea of preposition. Instead you carry forty words around in your head like a Junior G-Man with a portable file of fingerprints. When one of them matches a word somebody said or wrote somewhere, you have caught up with a preposition.

The boy does not like school. In China it was better; no one broke into his mind to ask him about prepositions. Several grades studied together in the one room, and the teacher never seemed to know who was in what grade. On bad days in China he stayed home and played, and on good days he went to school and played, waging the war on yellow sheets of arithmetic paper, two Corsairs and a Spitfire swooping out of the corner of the page, a Messerschmitt splitting open in midair, an unlucky Nazi paratrooping into the line of fire of an antiaircraft gun, ack-ack crisscrossing the paper in relentless dashes drawn in along his steel-edged ruler. But at Blessed Sacrament paper is rationed. And Sister Polycarp's voice is a little rattail file rasping away at the iron bars around him. He summons up all his powers in the fight for peace, sealing off his kingdom from the hostile world that keeps sniping at its borders. He is happiest when he turns the classroom into a dull gray weather and the other children into pieces of furniture.

"Eddie Gagne! Is that your own pencil you're sucking on?"

"No, Sister."

"To whom does it belong?"

"The school."

"That's right, it's school property. So stop sucking on it. No child wants to handle a pencil you've been sucking on."

She does not like the Gagne twins, Eddie and Edie, anymore, because they lost on the Amateur Hour. In February Major Bowes gave them an audition: Eddie played the spoons and Edie tap-danced. A few days before the big night the nun let them do their routine for the class, Eddie in a plaid vest and bow tie and Edie in purple spangled tights with a leg band of her blue panties peeking through when she went into her split. Sister Polycarp played the piano chords from some sheet music of "Hey-Bob-a-Re-Bob" while Edie stamped across the floor and Eddie's spoons made vulgar noises on his cheek. Then the twins went to the lavatories to change and Sister Polycarp told the class, "The winner is up to you, children. If you want Eddie and Edie to win you'll have to vote for them." She had them all make rough drafts of the post cards they would send to Major Bowes at Box 191, Radio City, New York. Several nights later the boy tuned in the old Majestic radio in the entryway of the cellar, a few feet from the head of his father's couch and next to the kerosene tank. The grille cloth over the speaker had been stripped away long ago, exposing a cardboard cone with a large gash that turned voices into death rattles, and an electric nut that was good for magnetizing screwdrivers. Here, between death rattles for Serutan and Geritol, and Major Bowes coughing out the post office number from a ruined T-Zone, he listened to the familiar chords of "Hey-Bob-a-Re-Bob" and the curious plonkity-clickety noises that were the twins. He tried to feel excited for them.

But they didn't win. The post cards from the class were mailed too early and were disqualified. And the twins became part of the furniture again like everyone else.

Across the aisle from me Rita is flagging the air again, but this time the nun will pretend not to see her. Rita is my enemy. She betrayed my love.

Three weeks ago a white hand stretched across the chasm between them and flicked a note on the boy's desk. "Polycarp's a pill," the note said. "Write!" He did not write. But he could not clear her out of his head, and that night at dinner Paula said slyly, "Who're you dreaming about now?"

"Nobody."

"Says you. Rita Coté is who."

"I am not. Why should I dream about Rita Coté?"

"Because she writes notes to you. She likes you."

"How would you know?"

"It's scratched into the back of her mirror. I saw it in the girls' room."

The next day she sent him another note and he responded with one of his own. The notes got longer and more elaborate. His desk was full of her secret words. He thought of his father and spent hours composing letters in his mind. Rita began signing her notes with a row of X's, and one with a lipstick kiss too ripe to touch. That same afternoon the nun noticed her lips and took her down to the girls' room to scrub them off, Rita protesting that it was from a Popsicle she had for lunch, but the boy knew it was lipstick. For him.

Sister Polycarp does not like Rita because she is impertinent: she knows all the answers and breaks all the rules. Like wearing shiny patent leather shoes that the nun has forbidden because boys will see what is reflected in them. Or short-sleeved blouses with loose sleeves that show things if you look up her armpit when she raises her hand. She is the most developed girl in the class. Sister Polycarp gave them a lecture on breast-feeding once. It is the only natural way, she said; she herself was breast-fed and the Blessed Virgin breast-fed the Infant Jesus. It is nothing to snicker about, Joseph Maroon. But everybody was embarrassed, especially the girls who had nothing under their jumpers yet. And the boy cannot look at Rita anymore, even though she is the enemy now, without the danger of impure thoughts. Streams of sweet white milk squirt out of her two little tits.

But not her own, said Joseph Maroon, who is the natural leader of the boys because he is fourteen and has stayed back two years in a row. She stuffs cotton in her brassiere, he said. If anybody should know he should know. He calls her the

Cotton Queen because he has names for everybody. The boy is Holy Dolan and also, because of the notes, the Coté Killer. The boy hates Joseph Maroon because his mouth is a cesspool.

I loved her and she has betrayed me. For two weeks the boy loved her so deeply that he could not even say hello to her on the playground. Then it all fell apart, abruptly, as he rounded the corner of the brick school building at recess and came upon Rita and Paula crouching on the cinders and poring over what were unmistakably his own words. Rita covered her mouth with her hands but she was giggling underneath them. "Excuse me," she said, "I think I hear my old lady calling me," snatched the notes from Paula and hurried into the building.

"Rita wants them back," Paula said.

"What?"

"Her notes of course."

"Why?"

"Just because, that's why."

"Then why did she write them in the first place?"

"Because. I bet her a quarter," Paula said indifferently. "I bet her a quarter she couldn't get Holy Dolan to notice her . . . The little snip. She thinks she's so great."

I still do not understand. I understand only that Rita has returned to the general grayness, and I am alone again in the kingdom of the mind. Threatened for a time but impregnable. But I am not like the others. The boy has known this ever since he knew anything, he drank this knowledge in with his mother's milk. And outside, like the rumble of distant wars, Sister Polycarp and the class squabbling over the possession of forty prepositions.

The recess bell gongs overhead, slowly, sadly, the funereal bell up in the tower that Joe Bisson, who has been in the special dunce class for five years straight, is privileged to ring on the appointed hours, hauling on the long hemp rope, sadly and penitentially. The boy dreams while the leaden circles of sound radiate outward from him in the gray weather. But the others, who must have heard the sound differently, are throwing books, slamming desk lids, punching their way into the cloakroom. When the room is empty he too starts to leave, but Sister Polycarp stands at the door, shrouded in shadows of her own making, and says quietly, "Miss Duplessie would like to see you."

Her classroom is empty. The boy walks over to the windows where, stacked in triple rows on the ledges and on several low tables, Miss Duplessie keeps the school library. The last of these tables is piled with booklets on South America, made by her fifth graders out of construction paper and pictures cut out of magazines like the *National Geographic*, the words "Our South American Neighbors" stenciled on each of the covers, and a series of paint blobs repeated with uniform irregularity. A toilet flushes in the teachers' room across the hall and Miss Duplessie enters, redolent of soap.

"Aren't they nice?" she says. "The children are studying about South America and learning about bookbinding at the same time. We make those patterns with linoleum blocks. Did you ever try that?"

"No."

"It's really quite simple. You draw your design on a piece of linoleum, then you take a linoleum knife and cut out the spaces you don't want to show . . . here's one over here that one of the pupils is working on. You see? How she's cut out the spaces? Then you paint the surface and press it on the construction paper. Afterwards we shellac them all to make them permanent. I bet you'd like to try that sometime."

"Yes," he lies.

"It's really quite simple."

He looks out the window beyond the books. Joseph Maroon and Bobby Durrell are choosing up sides for baseball, towering over all the smaller kids who are rubbing their hands

59

vigorously and breathing frosty puffballs in the April cold.
Joseph Maroon gets first choice because he has the top hand
on the bat; Bobby pretends that he can get a hand over it, but
can manage only a few squashed fingers, and Joseph is insist-
ing on the no-fingers rule.

"How is your mother?" Miss Duplessie asks.

"She's OK."

"I bet you didn't know I knew your mother?"

"No."

"I see her practically every morning passing the house on
her way to mass. She's a very good woman, your mother.
You're a lucky boy to have a mother like that."

For five years the boy's mother was a nun. When she
left they asked her not to upset the other sisters or her third
graders by saying goodbye. They simply explained that she
had been transferred to a new assignment. "I remember how
utterly lost I felt," she said once, "facing the world for the
first time at twenty-five with bus money in my pocket — not
even *my* pocket, it was a little wool suit belonging to a novice
who'd just entered a few days before . . . But God has been
good."

"She's an exceptional woman."

Baseball always means the same thing. Joseph Maroon
pitches and everybody strikes out except Bobby Durrell, who
belts home runs into the bike rack, all the outfielders knotted
at the other side of the field, trying not to get hit with the ball.
Then Bobby Durrell pitches and everybody strikes out except Joseph Maroon, who belts home runs into the bike rack.
Some of the kids are playing boy-catch-girl.

"You're a very quiet boy," she says.

He says nothing.

"You shouldn't spend so much time by yourself. You
ought to get out and play with the other children more."

She glances out the window, realizes something and brings

her eyes back to him in a hurry. He resents his captivity. The fact that he is being kept from playing with the children he would not have played with anyway makes it doubly painful. The spot under the fire escape where he usually stations himself is deserted now. Sooner or later the game of boy-catch-girl will head toward the fire escape, and a girl will run squealing up the steps with somebody in pursuit. And I, underneath, could have looked up through the grating and got a glimpse. "Suppose," the boy asked Father Tetrault, "we had a fire drill at school and I was down already, I was down in the playground already, and I just happened to look up when some of the girls were coming down and I . . . saw something." That would not be a sin, Father Tetrault said.

"You're not very well, are you?" Miss Duplessie says. "I mean you have something of a history of illness?"

"Yes."

"I'm very sorry," she says. "But you shouldn't let it make you bitter."

I am not bitter. How can you be bitter about something that is a fact of your existence for as long as you can remember? If they took that away the boy would not know who he was.

"Now then," she says. "I'd like you to tell me about the other night. In your own words."

"What do you mean?"

"You know. I want you to tell me about the window." I have nothing to tell.

"Maybe you don't fully understand yourself why you did it. Or maybe it was just an accident. But I'd like you to tell me in your own words," she says helpfully.

"There's nothing to tell. I didn't do it."

"Please. There's nothing to be afraid of. I'm not going to hurt you. I just want the truth."

"That's the truth," he says.

Leda Michaud goes tearing up the fire escape and my heart aches.

"I don't intend to encourage lying. Do you want to tell me the truth?"

"No," the boy says, meaning something else, but she pounces.

"So you admit it? You admit you've been lying?"

Her eyes are hungry for the kill, two glitter-green poison pellets. In a moment she will sink her teeth into the nape of my neck. I try to blink her away but she is there, too, in back of my eyelids. And suddenly, from somewhere in the boy's vocal chords that he has no control over, a voice says calmly, "You are the devil."

"WHAT?"

He does not repeat it. Her right hand swoops over him like a bird of prey, but her mind must have told the hand that he is a sick boy who cannot be hit, because the hand flutters down to her hip and she says through her teeth, "Then obviously I cannot help you. Good morning." And leaves the room.

The boy reaches the playground just as Joe Bisson, in his lonely tower, gongs the mournful end of recess.

My mother is eating coffee grounds again. She doesn't know that I am watching her, sitting here in the stuffed chair, reading about ratio and proportion. If one locomotive travels east on a six-hundred-mile section of track at a rate of sixty miles an hour and a second locomotive travels west at a rate of fifty miles an hour, how many miles east of the point of departure . . . And my mother opens the lid on the coffee can, dips a spoon in, and puts the raw grounds into her mouth. Then a second time. It makes no sense. Don't we have enough food? I am afraid to ask her what it means.

Mr. T. Dolan
54 Water Street
Deauville, Maine

Dear Mr. Dolan:

We received the one SARTOR RESARTUS brief, which you returned, about which you have corresponded with our Sales Manager, Mr. Bembow.

Our Quality Control Department thoroughly tested the garment, and it is an old one, as we changed the bind leg operation a few seasons ago.

The garment returned showed the edge of the bind legs completely worn off; and, frankly, this is the first return of this nature that we can recall.

Also, the garment showed that it had been bleached heavily. The defect conceivably was caused by abrasion in the washing machine. Nevertheless, we are sending you six new garments, size 34, feeling confident that you will discover them to be entirely to your liking.

Sincerely,
Arthur Renfro
Quality Control Department

Looking up from her Jello, Paula laughs. I do not laugh because I am suddenly very sorry for my father, who is writing letters about his underwear so he won't have to think about other things. My mother is somewhere else.

"What's the matter, Anna?"

"Is something the matter?"

"Something's always the matter when you pull a long face like that. You look just like your mother. Now what's happened?"

"Well . . . it *is* Mama, Tom. She had a little spell this afternoon."

"Too much to drink again."

"No, Tom, she fainted. I heard her take a fall and I ran

63

upstairs to see what happened. There was an ugly spider on her bed. I squashed it with a broom."

"Did she hurt herself?"

"I don't know. I don't think so. Mama's pretty strong. But then she blamed it all on us, Tom. She said there weren't any spiders in the house until we came, and that they were obviously coming around because we were careless about the food."

"Careless nothing," my father says. "Fact is we're very choosy about what we feed our spiders, aren't we?" he says to me, winking. "Nothing but prime Grade A black market hamburger. Next time you see her tell her we're running a spider farm down here, going to export them to Latin America and start a revolution."

The boy feels the blood desert his brain. Paula scoops out the last spoonful of her raspberry Jello, licks the edges of her mouth with an unnaturally red tongue and says to him, "One of your pets must of busted loose."

"What are you talking about?" my father says.

"He keeps them in jars. Back of the furnace. Go and see for yourself."

"Do you mean to tell me you're saving spiders again?" There is a paper-thin edge between my mother's words and hysteria. "Didn't I tell you not to bring spiders into the house?"

"I didn't. I found them here."

"Well you don't have to *keep* them here! Throw them out!"

"It's cold out there . . ."

"O my God!" she cries, and this time the words leap over the edge. "We're living in a cellar and Mama's having fainting spells upstairs and I've got a son who's worrying about his spiders catching cold and a husband who keeps writing letters about his underwear." She puts her hands over her face and begins to sob into them.

64

"All right," the boy's father says darkly, "I'll give you five minutes to get those spiders out of the house. Every goddam last one of them."

Waking now into a darker darkness. I wake into fear but I cannot locate the thing I fear. This prison has invisible bars. My legs ache as if they have been walking again. The boy is known to be a sleepwalker. In China he shut the window of his bedroom every night, even in summer, to keep out the nightmares, but they came anyway and drove him from his bed — down to the kitchen once where his mother found him making a peanut butter sandwich in his sleep, once even out of the house and as far as the well, where he woke and found he had taken off his pajamas.

Maybe it has happened again. But I should remember something; a corner of my mind always remembers something the next morning. My underwear is warming on the furnace pipes, but I will not get up yet. I will wait. It will come, slowly, like the sweat that forms, drop by drop, on those other pipes overhead, the rusted water pipes.

But it does not come. Grandma, hugging herself inside her quilted housecoat, comes through the plank door into the furnace room and goes up the steps to the bathroom. Grunt. Flllpp. Flush. Down again, with the toilet gasping behind her. My turn now.

And here, sitting on the warmed seat in the cold bathroom, the boy remembers. A long walk in the middle of the night to the other side of town. A darkened bedroom, smelling of musty age. An old woman sleeping on the bed and he could hear her labored breathing. And then?

No.

Say it. It is true.

No.

Say it! And then?

And then the boy killed her.

He lurches from the seat, his pajama bottoms still around his ankles, hurries to the sink and gets sick. His head is a balloon swollen with gas. You must be reasonable. The boy has lots of dreams. This was a dream. How could you possibly kill an old woman without waking her?

A knife.

Prove it! Where would you get a knife? Go and look in the drawer. You won't find anything missing.

One of her knives. Out of her own kitchen.

Can't prove a thing.

It takes a knife to make a sandwich. A boy who makes peanut butter sandwiches in his sleep . . .

You can't prove any of it!

But that makes it worse. To go on living day after day with the guilt of a crime that can't be proved.

The boy's mother, who has just returned from morning mass, takes one look at him and tells him to lie down on his father's couch until his father finishes breakfast. "You don't look at all well." She turns on the Majestic for the morning news. Lying on his father's couch, eyes shut in a double darkness, he waits for the broken voice of the newscaster to announce the horrible fact. But the newscaster says nothing about it. The Senate has passed an Emergency Housing Bill, but the boy's father says that's only for veterans, not for them. Killer McFarland has been picked up by the FBI in Knoxville eight days after he broke out of death row. Six lightly clad girls, age ten to fourteen, have been lost in Five Mile Swamp near Bath in subfreezing temperatures. The boy tries to think of himself saving the lightly clad girls. It is the first anniversary of Roosevelt's death. "My husband's spirit lives in this house," Eleanor said, "in the library and in the quiet garden where he wished his body lie."

They have not found the body yet.

The weather has held warm since the weekend. It is Tuesday and all the children in the school stand in a long queue in the playground, waiting to file into the convent. Nuns are posted at various points along the line, encouraging them through the decades of the rosary. Tuesday is the Sorrowful Mysteries, and when they finish the last of them, the Crucifixion, they begin all over again with the Agony in the Garden, the line inching along toward the convent, bead by sorrowful bead.

Last Friday, the day of the fear, the boy stayed home from school. He played with his coin collection most of the afternoon, making paper envelopes for the coins and sorting them into Dill's Best boxes. Every so often, in the midst of this work, the panic returned and he clenched his fists and pressed them into his eyeballs.

When he sneaked upstairs to read Grandma's *Dispatch*, even the funnies were no relief. Joe Palooka, too, was being tormented by terrible dreams. By voices calling to him in his sleep — Marty, Tiny, Mrs. Sampson — all murdered. Marty summoning Joe to the world of the dead: "Say, Joe, why don't you join us? . . . No more trainin' . . ." Tiny looking in fear at something Joe cannot see: "Here they come . . . We gotta go . . . So long, Joe . . ." Vanished in smoke, beyond his power to call them back.

Then the man with the beard. I almost know who the man is. "No . . . WHY, YOU'RE THE ONE!" But which one? The cruel eyes have grown enormous, filling the whole frame of vision: "Of course . . . you know you know me." Then a huge mouth, white teeth, sensual lips, framed by the hateful beard: "Think hard . . . think hard . . . think of hatred, cruelty . . . greed . . . think of death, torture . . ."

"Y—you are . . . who are you . . ."

"THINK."

"Think, Joe, think," says Marty, reappearing. "Think, Pally," Tiny says. "Try harder, Joe," says Mrs. Sampson.

I spin in a dark vortex, holding my tormented head, while the man in the beard points at me and laughs maniacally. I swing at him, but my champion's fist passes through the vision. And the mad laughter fills the page as I awaken: "HA HA HO HO HEE HEE HEE HAW HAW HEE HAW HA HA . . ."

By dinnertime the Majestic still had no news.

The next two days were Palm Sunday weekend, dazzling with sun, and the sun scattered the shadows of the fear. On the way back from Sunday mass the boy found a brown woolly caterpillar on the sidewalk and brought it home in his pocket. He cleaned a dead spider out of one of the jars and made a home for the caterpillar.

On Monday he went back to school. But he knew that something was wrong when, five minutes after Joe Bisson had tolled the mournful beginning of the day, the nun still had not appeared. A few minutes later Sister John Nepomucene, the mother superior, came in and told them to file quietly down to the assembly for an announcement. There, in front of all the classes, she broke the news.

That early Palm Sunday morning God had called Sister Polycarp home to rest.

Bead by sorrowful bead, the line inches into the convent chapel to view the last remains. The room is heavy with a sweet heat. Large candles in massive gold candlesticks, as tall as the boy himself, stand at the head and foot of the casket. The smells of chrysanthemum, gladioli, incense, formaldehyde: he tries to keep from gagging. Sister John Nepomucene has warned them not to stare — simply to look, say a little prayer and then move on. But when he reaches the casket he forgets all about the prayer, comes to a dead halt and gapes. He has never seen a nun lying down. It is like finding her out in her own bedroom, her head pillowed on a satin cushion, beads in her fingers, sleeping in her habit as nuns do. But in life her face was always sallow; now it has a pink lacquered glow like a china doll's. Her mouth is set, uncertainly, as if at any moment it will open and all that stuff they pumped into her will suddenly leak out and dribble onto the satin cushion. And she will utter some horrible wisdom from beyond life. He hurries on.

Afterwards (for the rest of the day has been declared a holiday) he consoles himself by going into the Five and Ten and buying a package of morning glory seeds. These he plants deep in the yet cold earth by the foundation at the back of the house.

Spy Wednesday, the day Judas sneaked off to the high priests: overnight the weather turned around and snowed on top of the morning glory seeds. It is the morning of the funeral. Along with five others in the class the boy was chosen to be an honorary pallbearer, but the thought of walking alongside that box with the dead woman inside it, his hand actually touching one of the bronze rails, is too much and he stays home.

It is the middle of the morning. The boy's mother is up to her elbows in suds, washing the shirts and bed linen by hand in the steel tubs. It was no washing machine that ruined his father's underwear. He passes behind her without her noticing, goes outside and lets himself into the garage, not through the front doors but through the little side door in the alley. The door opens grudgingly because that corner is littered with afterthoughts of Grandpa Vigue. A scythe handle. A cast-iron cash register. Three opened cans of Bondex Quik-Plug for Damp Basements. A rubber plunger. Two left-hand work gloves. A bottomless watering can. An assortment of disappointing cigar boxes, each containing maybe a single elbow joint, or a tube of graphite, or a mismatched nut and bolt. A truss hanging on a nail. A 4-Way Easy Setting Choker made by the Lovell Mfg. Co. of Erie, Pa. Two 1934 license plates. The rusted ball from a toilet tank. A deuce of clubs on the oil-stained floor. All that's left of the man who stood in front of Vigue's Bar in the tarpaper suit and fedora, brandishing his cigar at the sun.

Then the boy picks his way past their own stuff — trunks and cartons, a rolled mattress, his mother's paintings in yellowing newspaper, an open box full of girdles — squeezes through the space at the edge of the upright piano and sits down on the unsteady springs of the easy chair.

This time there is nobody to tell it to, not even Father Tetrault. For almost a month the boy has followed the priest's advice, fearing to lose his only friend. He has shunned the statue of the angel, averting his eyes when he passes it, suppressing the pangs in his heart.

But then the dream. He knows now that it was a dream, yet that is no true comfort. He cannot simply reason away the death of the nun shortly after the dream. For a new, subtler fear is growing in the place of the old terror. That the dream was not a memory (as he first thought) but a prophecy — a power that can shape history to its own imaginings. It will neither be controlled nor denied.

He draws his heels up onto the cushion, tucks his hands into the warm between his thighs, and rocks gently back and forth the way he did when he was little, emptying his mind. For a long time he rocks, and objects begin to recede, cartons and trunks lose their solidity, the piano itself becoming a mere dark shadow. Suddenly the garage is almost totally black. Then a faint glow where the piano was, a yellowish light, then a thousand brilliant points of bluish flame, and all of them are eyes, and then the figure itself, with the sword pointing directly at him and a drop of something terrible glistening on the tip, and the dark sorrowing eyes boring into him, wise with the burden of bottomless depths.

"I have been waiting. Why haven't you come?"

"The priest told me not to."

"And for whom does the priest speak? What does he offer you? I offer you love. And I ask only love in return. And suffering. For suffering is a proof of love. The souls that I choose must be victims of love."

The priest was right: if the angel wants me he will find me out.

"Believe in my love and mercy. You have sinned against me; I forgive you. You have denied me; I love you. You have wounded me; still I wish to do you good and let you share all my treasures. Do not imagine that I am ignorant of your state of soul."

"What do you want?"

"I thirst!" the angel cries, and his cry is torn from the depths of suffering. "I thirst for souls. Live with me and I will live with you. Hide in me and I will sink deep into your heart. We shall comfort each other, for my pain will be yours, and your suffering mine. Those whom I choose I call to a life of intimate union with me. It is their privilege to know my longings. Theirs, above all, to become more and more closely united with me and never abandon me, never to leave me alone! Do you understand what it is to be alone?"

"Yes."

"That is your cross in this life. Not to be one of them. But you are a divine instrument of my love. Put aside the things of this world. Come to me in utter nakedness and I will be manifest to you."

The boy takes off all his clothes and kneels, trembling in the cold bluish light, and trembling more when the voice cries out again, "I thirst for souls! The time has come to make me known."

It is too much. How can I make them believe? Father Tetrault, my mother and father, Paula, the nuns, the children. The angel asks too much.

"Do you know of the Temple of God?"

"Yes." That is where Grandma goes on Sunday afternoons. On Silver Street. Crackpots, my father says. Founded by a man who was sent to prison for tampering with young girls and stealing money from husbands by promising to heal their wives.

"Do not despise them. They are misled but do not despise them. Go to the Temple on Easter Sunday afternoon and they will listen to you. They will be the first. Tell them to come to my statue and I will prove my power."

"But Grandma won't like that."

"She does not matter."

"And my father told me . . ."

"One day he too will understand. I promise you the joy of his conversion. Do you love me?"

"Yes."

"One single act of love in the loneliness in which I leave you repairs for many acts of ingratitude. I leave you now. Put on your clothes."

Five

In 1933 Romeo St. Cyr was just a cornet player. But one day when he was in a butcher shop on Richmond Hill a man walked in, picked up a meat cleaver, and cut off his head. It fluttered to the floor like a handkerchief. But then the Spirit entered his body and he arose, reunited, and knew that the Spirit of God had entered him. And that day — it was Lincoln's Birthday — that the cornet player rose from the dead in a Richmond Hill butcher shop marked the beginning of the Spiritual Humanistic Alliance of the World, Inc.

That, at least, is how the boy's father tells it.

Then he gathered a flock, mostly women, who came to him in sickness of body and soul and were healed. Then they came to him with money. He bought a piece of property on the better part of Silver Street, where the fat cats of Deauville had built homes at the turn of the century — a large white house with a guest cottage in back and another small building that was once a carriage house. He walked about his estate in diamond stickpins and the women followed in white angel robes. He drew up articles of incorporation for the cult, "to promote the equitable happiness and the spiritual and material welfare of mankind by stimulating love, obeisance, piety, gratitude, thanks, and public worship of God."

Then fate struck like a second meat cleaver. An angry man, who claimed that the mortgage on his farm was foreclosed while he paid for his wife and daughter to be treated in St. Cyr's house, went to the police. The police raided the house on Silver Street and flushed out an assortment of women and a fourteen-year-old girl who was in the family way. He was arraigned in 1937 on two counts of conspiring to steal money from husbands by promising to heal their wives and one morals charge, and sent to Thomaston for three years.

Those were dark days for the Spiritual Humanistic Alliance of the World, Inc. But the women did not abandon him. They paid the taxes on the property, they baked cakes and cookies and brought them to him in Thomaston, and on Sunday afternoons they gathered to read and reread his letters from prison. He signed them all simply "The Transubstantial Christ." And once he wrote: "I shall move with my manifested body when I see the stones shed tears." Not long after that, a spring began to flow on the property of its own accord, and one of the faithful bathed her eyes in it and was cured of glaucoma, and another drank and was healed of pernicious anemia.

In his third year in prison he died of an unexplained illness. The faithful refused to believe that he was really dead and did not come to claim the body till a week later. They were told that he had been buried in the common prison graveyard, but when they demanded that the authorities show them the exact spot, nobody seemed to know. The faithful went away indignant, but of course secretly rejoicing, because the meaning was quite clear: the Transubstantial Christ had not really died, he was still among them. The cult grew. Mostly Catholics, who sent their children to Holy Angels School, went to mass on Sunday mornings and gathered at the Temple of God on Sunday afternoons to drink the miracle water and read the letters from prison.

Uncle Fred joined in 1942, the first time that his wife left him. Several months later, when she came back, he became disillusioned with the cult and quit. But Grandma picked up where he left off. On Sunday afternoons she too drinks the water for the pains in her legs.

My father is handsome in his new pinstripe suit. Every so often he catches himself standing in front of the mirror over the steel tubs, frowns as though he isn't very fond of mirrors, but stays there long enough to pat the wide lapels flat again. My mother surprised him with the money for the suit a few days ago, dumping quarters and dimes onto the table out of a change jar nobody knew she had. Though it is now afternoon of Easter Sunday, nobody has changed into old clothes. The boy's mother has a lavender suit with a violet corsage, Paula a canary-colored dress, and the boy a large houndstooth jacket that he is supposed to grow into, with extra shoulder pads because of his slope. Jean is coming for dinner.

"I'm going out for a walk," the boy says.

"Ask Paula if she'd like to go along."

"Paula doesn't want to," he says, and is relieved when she agrees.

He is relieved, too, that Grandma is sick this afternoon. At least half a dozen times since Wednesday he has tried to ask her to let him go to the Temple with her, but fear and the enormity of his mission have choked the words off. Then last night she came downstairs carrying an empty mayonnaise jar.

"Dolan, you got any wine? I got to marinate some meat."
She stuck the jar about a foot away from his face.

"Say when," my father said. He filled the jar about half-way, paused, but she didn't say when. So he filled it to the top.

An hour later she was down again. "That is some tough meat! I should buy on the black market instead of being honest. Give me some more wine."

It is a long walk down Silver Street to the Temple of God — time enough for the doubts to form again like hard little pellets in his stomach. On Good Friday the boy visited the statue for the first time in over a month to give the angel a chance to perform a miracle. For over an hour he prayed but nothing happened. And now the angel is sending him to these strange people, with no idea of what he should say or do when he gets there. Maybe it is to test his faith. Because that was the sort of people Christ chose too — the suffering and the outcast, fishermen and publicans, and women taken in adultery. He will not be proud. They are misled but he will not disdain them.

On the front lawn a little man stoops over to examine the first crocuses of the season. When he sees the boy coming up the sidewalk he stands up to watch him. He wears a black suit and a red necktie and gold-rimmed glasses. His hair is silver. He looks like an insurance man, except that his left eye is leaking copiously. He narrows his one good eye shrewdly but says pleasantly enough, "Hello there. Nice day, isn't it?"

"Yes."

"What can I do for you?"

"Isn't this the Temple of God?"

"What brings you here?"

"I want to talk to the people."

"I see." He turns from the boy and bends to the lawn again.

"Crocuses," he says. "This one's going to be yellow, I'm sure it is." Then, straightening up: "I'm Mr. Fortier. I'm what you might call the caretaker. Keep up the property. But I'm also a member. I used to live in the cottage back there but nobody lives there now because of the vibrations."

"Oh."

"Divine vibrations. So we turned it into the shrine . . . Who sent you here?"

"I came by myself."

"But somebody sent you, didn't they? I bet some of your friends put you up to it."

"I don't have any friends."

"I see. . . . He was a friend to everybody, Professor St. Cyr. Rich and poor alike. And especially the weak ones, women and children, the lame and the sick. Are you sick?"

"Yes."

"What is it?"

"I have nosebleeds. And swellings in the joints."

"I see," he says, and pulling out a hankie he daubs at the leakage from his left eye. "What about your parents? Do they know you're here?"

"No." Though he didn't intend it, the word is heavy with mourning.

"We usually like to have the parents," the man says, about to close an invisible door. "Oh please. You're not going to start crying, are you?"

"No."

"For a minute you looked as if you were going to cry."

"You know my grandmother," the boy says. "Mrs. Vigue. She comes here."

"Oh. Mrs. Vigue . . . Well, I just don't know. Would you like to see the spring?"

He leads the way to a small hillock in back of the house

77

where a lead pipe is planted. Water trickles from the open pipe, down a gravel-lined causeway, and into a pool the size of a small goldfish pond. The overflow from the pool empties into a passing brook. In the brook a small waterwheel turns lazily.

"That's to generate electric power," the man says. He kneels down beside the pool, plunges his hand in over the cuff of his sleeve, and pulls out a drinking cup full of water. He tilts his head at an angle and raises the cup to his bad eye. The water dribbles down his shirt front and stains the red necktie. Then he swishes the cup around in the water a few times and brings up a second cupful.

"Do you want to drink?"

"No."

"Then you'd better not. If you fully believe in the water it will cure you. But if you don't it will hurt you."

On a second hillock, ringed with Christmas tree lights, there is a white headstone, but the man explains that this is not a gravestone, simply a commemorative marker. In the center, under glass, a photograph of the Transubstantial Christ, a fat man with long hair, a floral tie, a triangle of hair sprouting from his nostrils, a circular pin in his lapel like the union pin my father wears. "Look at the eyes," the man says. "Look at the eyes. They move. See? No matter where you are the eyes look right at you. I have a copy of that picture in my car. It saved me from an automobile accident once."

"Where are the other people?" the boy asks.

"In the house. There's an executive meeting, I can't take you in there. But they'll be out in a minute or two."

A few minutes later about two dozen people emerge from the house, crossing the lawn toward the cottage, mostly women and all in white robes. One of them is very old and one is young, no more than fifteen or sixteen.

"Mrs. Goodman," Mr. Fortier says to the old woman, "this young man has come to see us."

"By himself? Well, I don't know about that. We don't usually take young boys. Why have you come?"

"You know my grandmother," the boy says. "Mrs. Vigue."

"He's not well," Mr. Fortier says. "He has nosebleeds and swollen joints. He needs our help."

That is not true. "No," the boy says, "I've come to help you."

Mrs. Goodman smiles. "That's what we're all here for, to help and be helped."

"I've come to tell you about an angel."

The moment he says it the fears return. Why must he make the angel public to these strange people? Will the angel still be his own when he has done so? He thinks of fleeing down the sidewalk with the vision undefiled while there is still time.

This time Mrs. Goodman is not smiling. She studies his face thoughtfully, then turns to the young girl, a solemn girl with a wet lower lip, and says, "Take his hand, Evelyn." Evelyn takes my hand and the procession continues to the cottage. At the door Mrs. Goodman stops and says to the boy, "This is a special privilege. We don't often let people come here. This is where the Professor lived most of the time, not in the big house. He was a humble man . . . I'm eighty-eight but he keeps me young. I come down here every Sunday all the way from Farmington Falls."

We enter the cottage through what was once the kitchen. Several of the women begin to snuffle, though it looks like any other kitchen, except that there are pictures of the Transubstantial Christ all over the walls and even on the plates of the cast-iron stove.

The eyes follow you.

In the bedroom we look at the bed the professor slept in. Some of the people approach the dresser and kiss locks of his hair preserved in glassine envelopes. On top of the dresser are two crosses that he glued together from unraveled socks

79

while he was in jail. A huge pair of shoes, in bronze. His eighth grade diploma. The cornet he played before his resurrection. And the usual picture. "If you keep looking at it you can see halos," Evelyn explains, and the boy takes advantage of the explanation to slip his hand from hers and pretend to study the picture.

The ceremony begins in the parlor, in front of a flower-banked altar and another photograph. Evelyn lights two candles and opens an old loose-leaf notebook and begins to read from the prison letters:

"Peace be with you. Peace in this home and may peace also reign in every home where I am not denied. No doubt the people in general shall soon admit that it does not pay to deny the Truth, the Light of the World, as they cruelly did . . ."

Afterwards everybody meditates for several minutes on a glass of water, sitting in a large circle around a wooden table. The glass goes from hand to hand and each member takes three sips, saying with each sip, "Professor Romeo St. Cyr, help me," and finishing with the sign of the cross. When the glass reaches him the boy simply stares at it.

"Don't you want to drink yet?" the man with the bad eye asks again.

"No."

"Then why have you come?" he says, not kindly this time, even with something like menace in his voice.

"To tell you about the angel."

"Hush," Mrs. Goodman interrupts. "That comes later. The testimonials don't come till the end . . . I'm eighty-eight years old. I guess I ought to know how it's done."

After the drinking of the miracle water a number of the faithful file up to the altar, genuflect and place envelopes on it. Everybody recites something like the Lord's Prayer, but with different words to it. And finally it is time for the testimonials.

But nobody has any testimonials. All eyes fall, then, on the boy, who becomes suddenly terrified, his thighs pressing tight together in instinctive panic, who remembers his father in the bathroom at Jerome's bar and the hostile smell of the urinals, who fears again that his time has not yet come. But he begins to speak: "There is a statue in the Church of the Holy Angels . . ."

"No no no," Mrs. Goodman says irritably. "Not there. Out here. Out into the center of the room."

In the center of the room then, circled by these strange people in the Temple, the boy tells his story. He is scrupulous about the details, describing the statue so accurately that Mrs. Goodman breaks in and says, "That's true. I come down here every Sunday all the way from Farmington Falls but I've seen that statue and that's exactly what it looks like." He speaks of the tears, the vision in the garage, the prophecies. By the time he has finished his voice is no longer a twelve-year-old's, is not his own voice at all, and when he dredges up the angel's cry "I thirst! I thirst for souls!" several of the women begin to weep.

"And what does your angel want of us?" Mr. Fortier asks.

"To go and see for yourselves. He will show you his power."

"We will have to pray first. We will have to ask the Professor what is to be done."

They thank him for coming and file out toward the house. The boy is about to follow but Evelyn detains him.

"You can't go in there."

"Are they going to ask the Professor now?"

"No. Not now. They're going to have some cake and beer. They always do that after a service. But only members can go in."

Now I am alone in the kitchen with the young girl and the eyes are everywhere. She is watching me curiously and then, it seems without moving her wet underlip, she says, "You'd better not be lying."

"I'm not lying! It's all true."

"Because if you're lying I wouldn't want to be you, that's all."

She is an enemy. She wants to frighten me. "I don't believe any of this stuff," he shouts, waving his hand toward the other rooms. "You're misled. The angel said so. There aren't any vibrations here."

"You won't feel them unless you believe. Or unless somebody helps you feel them."

"I don't believe you."

"Hold my hand," she commands. He backs away.

"Hold my hand, I said."

The boy takes her hand timidly. "Now shut your eyes." He does as he is told.

"So?" she says.

"I don't feel anything," he says.

But then he feels something. The light fingers of her other hand searching confidently between his legs.

"So I said to them," he says, "I said 'I do not make a practice of keeping old shreds of underwear as trophies . . .' "

"Oh for heaven's sake, Tom. Jean doesn't want to hear about your old underwear. You might as well open some wine. It's going to be a while yet."

"Whatever it is, it smells delicious," Jean says.

"I don't smell anything at all," my father says. "Are you sure it's still lit?"

"Of course it's still lit. Just be patient a few minutes."

A few minutes ago the stove gave out just as she was about to put the final glaze on the ham. She gave the boy an angry shove outside to fill the kerosene tank from Grandma's barrel. "What you people do with all my kerosene?" Grandma wanted to know. "That's the third time this week you fill up the can." Grandma, now recovering in her housecoat, is sitting at the head of the porcelain table because she owns it. Jean is at her right hand, wearing a pale blue blouse that is almost transparent. The boy can see her brassiere.

"That's pretty," Grandma says, pinching a piece of the sleeve between two raw fingers.

"Yes," my mother agrees. "It's lovely. What a lovely blouse, Jean."

"Thanks. I think it's pretty snazzy myself. It's nylon."

"*Nylon?* How did you ever manage?"

"Oh, I have friends who have friends . . . who have friends. You know. In Boston."

Last week the boy's mother stood in line for several hours in the cold morning because there was a rumor that Boutelle's was going to sell nylon stockings. Several times the manager came out and pleaded with the ladies to go on home, said it was all a mistake, but the crowd just got larger and angrier. At noon they shut up the store.

"I'd love to get you one, Mrs. Dolan. You've got just the figure for it."

My mother's face is dark with denial. "Oh, I'm too old for that now. Those styles are all well and good for you young girls — you and Paula."

Paula smiles hard at Jean, to see what she will say to that. But Jean doesn't say anything. She turns to my father beside her and gives him a young girl smile.

My father does not notice: he is rising from the table with a bottle of dark wine in his upraised hands, like Father Tetrault at the elevation of the Blessed Sacrament. A rusted metal corkscrew is embedded in the top. "Nineteen thirty-nine," he says, as the bottle reaches his eye level and keeps on going upward, "that was the last good year. They haven't made a decent wine since nineteen thirty-nine." By now his hands are fully extended and the loop on the corkscrew grazes the two-by-tens overhead, flirts a little to the left and right of a spike in one of them, then hooks over it. "Got it," he says, relaxing momentarily before the final tug. Now the veins bulge as the wrists tighten, and, half-chinning himself, turning as the bottle turns, my father descends to the table, the cork swinging free in the rafters on the end of the corkscrew. Jean claps. "He refuses to buy a decent corkscrew," my mother says, "has to do it his own way."

He pours himself a half inch of wine, sniffs, sips, rolls it around from cheek to cheek, swallows and is happy. Then everyone gets a glass, "even that young rapscallion at the foot of the table," because it is Easter Sunday.

"Scrumptious," Jean says.

"No, it should have been left in longer," my mother says. "The glaze isn't right."

"Oh, that's not true at all. I think it's absolutely scrumptious."

The boy knows the sacrifices his mother has made for this meal, how she paid extra to persuade Mr. Bolduc to give her the ham and used up coupon thirty-nine on the sugar though it's supposed to last them till the end of the month. But she flutters around the table apologizing for the food and giving people nervous stomachs.

"Why don't you sit down and eat something, Anna?" my father says. "Have you heard about the robins in San Francisco?" he asks Jean, pouring her another glass of wine. "Seems they're getting drunk by the thousands on some kind of red berries. Pyracantha bushes, they're called."

"How can you get drunk on berries?"

"They ferment somehow. They develop a formidable alcoholic charge. And it happens every year, apparently. The robins come barreling in right on schedule and get drunk as lords gobbling up all the berries in the area, falling off the rooftops and staggering down the streets causing traffic jams."

"That's another of Tom's little jokes," my mother says. "Pay no attention, Jean. Won't you have some more peas?"

"It isn't. It's the absolute truth."

"No robins yet. Not for a long time," Grandma says through a mouthful of food.

"Please have some more peas, Jean."

"No, *San Francisco*, I said," my father says. "It's what the good Lord must have had in mind when he told us to consider the birds of the air," he tells Jean.

"That glaze isn't done. You should leave it to bake longer," Grandma says, reaching down the table and hacking off another hunk of ham.

"I *know* that, Mama. I already said that." But Grandma, who is selectively deaf, is eating again and doesn't hear what she didn't hear the first time.

"I disagree," Jean says. "I think it's marvelous. I'd love to have the recipe."

"Oh please! I don't do anything with recipes anyway. It's just a little wine, some brown sugar, a few spices . . ."

"I just wouldn't have the patience, Mrs. Dolan."

"Ohh," my mother says unhappily.

My father sees what I see but he cannot speak: my mother has sliced the chocolate cake into six triangles and placed the first on Jean's plate, but something is moving down the side of the cake. One — another — three, now — three tiny ants are coming down the side of Jean's cake. She digs her fork in and raises it to her mouth. My father's mouth opens at the same moment, as if he is going to save her by eating it for her, but his mouth says, "Speaking of birds, there's the poor old woman in England who was sent to jail on her fifty-fourth conviction for drunkenness, and when the judge asks her if she can offer any reason not to be locked up, she ups and says, 'I will die — I am like a wild bird and must be free.' "

Now Jean sees it too, blanches, and lays her fork to rest on the plate, the chunk of cake still on it.

"Is something the matter?" my mother asks.

Jean too cannot speak.

"There are ants on the cake," Paula says.

"ANTS?" Grandma says. "Where are the ants?"

"On the cake."

And now my mother sees. "Oh my God. I bought this cake fresh just yesterday at Bolduc's."

"Bolduc is no good. Bolduc is a bad businessman. You should buy at the A & P."

My father is angry now. "Couldn't you see it wasn't fresh when you bought it? By God, Bolduc's going to hear about this. It's not wartime anymore. He could be sued for things like that. There was a fellow in Bangor who found a cockroach in his root beer and sued the company for a thousand dollars' discomfort."

"It's only a few ants," my mother says desperately, putting all the triangles back onto the big plate and hustling it from the table.

"One thousand smackers," my father says to Jean.

"That's why you get spiders," Grandma says.

The cake crashes into the garbage, plate and all.

"Don't throw it away," Grandma says. "Bring it back and get your money back. If you go to the A & P they always give you the money back if you got ants in the cake."

The lights have gone out again. Fumbling at the table, Grandma wants to know who's been monkeying with the electricity. Somebody giggles once. Then somebody else is sobbing in the darkness. Then the sobbing stops and my mother has put a hurricane lamp on the table and strikes a wooden match. My father rises from the table, slams the plank door behind him and tries to locate the fusebox in the furnace room, cursing the darkness.

The clumping of the Grandma feet overhead now. The boy's father has taken Jean back to the college and his mother is washing the dishes.

"Did you see what Uncle Tom did when the lights went out?" Paula whispers.

"No."

"He touched her."

"Who?"

"Jean. He touched her like this." She cups her hand a few inches from one of her little tits and squeezes the air. The boy winces, remembering the girl with the wet underlip who touched him impurely and —

"That's not true!"

"Suit yourself."

— and how last winter on the playground Joseph Maroon threw a snowball at him by the fire escape, and he ducked and it hit Leda Michaud right there. It was not the boy's fault. But he was an instrument and the damage was done. She would never give milk.

"How could you see? It was dark."

"I can see in the dark," she says. "I have radar. That's radar spelled backwards."

Six

May. The second spring this year, though still there are no leaves, only hard little shells on the tips of trees, waiting. Yesterday the boy received a circular from the Fernwood Forest Nursery Co. in Fryeburg who for only $9.50 postpaid will mail him 65 evergreen trees — 23 dense Scotch pine, 13 majestic blue spruce, 8 elegant Black Hills spruce, 5 shapely American arborvitae, 5 towering Norway spruce, 5 handsome white spruce, 3 enduring Fraser fir, and 3 rapid-growing red pine. And last night he dreamed again of the dogwood forest, but it was changed. Gabriel was no longer in the photograph, and Paula and Jean had somehow managed to get into it, crowding in front of the boy's father so that he could no longer see the gold watch chain glittering in the sunlight. The boy awoke crying and did not understand why.

Any day now the gray cocoon will burst open in the old spider jar, and the brown woolly caterpillar will step out

transformed, stretching his great multicolored wings. This is
the second one; the first died because it was born out of season
and the boy could find no leaves to feed it. When he found
the second he was afraid that too would die of hunger, but it
did not want to eat, not even the geranium leaves he put in
with it. It ran up and down the stems of the leaves crazily, and
even before his eyes its head changed color, as if all the juice
were draining out of it. Then it clung to the underside of the
lid, against the jagged little puncture holes, and began secre-
ting that strange gray film around itself. Now it is quiet, waiting. He prays it will not emerge at night.

My father is writing letters again, but he does not enjoy
them. No package has arrived and he has not heard about his
underwear in over a month. So he sits down and writes his
angry letters — to the President of the Sartor Resartus Corporation, to the Better Business Bureau of Winston-Salem, to the
Interstate Commerce Commission and the Attorney General
of North Carolina.

He is bitter about other things, too. They have taken him
off the night shift at the Progressive Paper Company. My
mother is glad, because she says she will see more of him now,
but he is bitter. The day shift means a twelve and a half per-
cent cut in salary. He stood up to the big bosses with his gold
union pin staring them down and told them about his senior-
ity. But they told him about people who had high school di-
plomas. There are dark conspiracies against my father. He
finds it hard to learn how to sleep at night, spends his nights
taking long walks, or at Jerome's. His green eyeshade lies un-
used in the bureau drawer.

One day when no one was home the boy opened that
drawer, put on the eyeshade, and lay down on his father's
couch. The green felt darkness pressing gently against his
eyelids. The secret darkness of the father. It was very sad.

*

"My dear people. And particularly, my dear mothers, for this is your special day. I hope you will not think me an old sourpuss if I choose this Mother's Day to lay a finger on some grave and widespread dangers besetting this beloved nation of ours. But I must speak frankly. To those of you who haven't been in this parish long enough to get accustomed to my frankness I apologize sincerely, but sometimes all of us — and especially our young women and their mothers — need to be shocked into a sense of reality.

"I should like to begin by setting a scene vividly in your mind's eye, a true incident that took place not in some remote period of dry-as-dust history, but at the turn of our very own century, among the people on the island of St. Pierre, Martinique — a people jaded, bored, surfeited with sinful pleasures. In this modern Sodom of the Western Hemisphere, moral restraints had long since been cast aside in the frenzied quest for greater excitements and newer thrills. But this time there was no Noah, no Abraham, to warn them. Nothing but silence from heaven as (I am almost afraid to speak it) they carried a pig to a hillside and nailed it to a cross, in blasphemous mockery of the crucifixion of Our Lord and Savior Jesus Christ.

"Five stories down, in solitary confinement, lay a man condemned to die. He knew nothing of the sacrilegious outrage being perpetrated on the hillside. He was aware only of a series of ominous rumblings, louder and louder, like the roar of a gigantic express train overhead. He knew nothing till many days later, when rescue parties from nearby islands revived him. It was everybody else who had been condemned to die. Mount Pelée had suddenly erupted, and of the 28,000 inhabitants of St. Pierre, he was the only man alive.

"A sign? A warning? Or just an idle tale? Oh but Father, I hear you say, this has nothing to do with a Christian nation like America. Perhaps, my dear people, perhaps. But I ask you: where were the mothers on that impious day to restrain the hands of their sons and daughters from this sacrilegious mockery? And I ask again: where are the mothers who will stem the rising tide of paganism in our own land today? There is an ancient proverb, 'As the women go, so goes the nation.' And sad to tell, the women of America are going very far indeed!

"In 1815 Our Blessed Lord appeared to Mother Mary Rafols, a Spanish nun, and told her: 'The offenses that I have received, and those that I shall yet receive, are many; especially the offenses of woman, with her immodest dress, her nakedness, her frivolity and her evil intentions. Because of all this, she shall accomplish the demoralization of the family and of mankind. Such shall be the corruption of morality in every social class and so great unchastity that My Eternal Father shall be forced to destroy entire cities, should they not reform after these merciful calls.' And who heeded those calls? In 1917 Our Blessed Mother appeared to the three children at Fatima and warned, 'Certain fashions will be introduced that will offend Our Lord very much. More souls go to hell because of sins of the flesh than for any other reason.' How have the women of America responded to these warnings? Look around you.

"With each passing summer (and I remind you that summer is almost upon us again) our streets become more and more like open-air burlesque houses, with many of our women and young girls parading around publicly in the shortest of shorts, and other indecent attire. Our bands are led in parades and in athletic events by drum majorettes, who prance to and fro in next to nothing — even in the coldest weather. Sad to say, even many Catholic schools, supposedly dedicated to the all pure Blessed Virgin Mary, join in this lockstep behind the Pied Piper of pagan fashions. Though they may not realize it, or may refuse to acknowledge it, all of this brazen display of the flesh leads to countless thousands of sins of impurity in thoughts, desires and actions. The F.B.I. in its official bulletin declares that there is always a great increase in crimes in the summer months, when women wear scanty clothing. Only last year in Aroostook County a psychiatrist, examining a man charged with molesting a ten-year-old girl, reported that the man habitually bought books and magazines which were illustrated by pictures of women wearing varying amounts of clothing assuming suggestive positions.

"Need I say more? Today young girls everywhere eagerly seek out the opportunity of entering various and sundry 'beauty' contests, even though it means parading around half-naked like a bunch of cattle before the eyes of lustful men. We present Miss America, Miss Rose Bowl Queen, Miss Cucumber, Miss Dill Pickle, Miss Potato Blossom right here in Houlton in the State of Maine, Miss this and that, ad nauseam — in their half-naked display of the flesh — as models for our young girls to imitate and emulate. The ideal of nakedness has replaced the ideal of purity and modesty. In many young girls' lives the goddess or queen of the flesh reigns in the place of the Blessed Virgin Mary. No wonder the morals of our nation have fallen so low. It's actually gotten so bad they even have beauty contests for little girls of three, four, five and slightly older, seeking the title of Miss Wading Pool. At tender ages they are being taught to seek after the pagan and empty honors of the world, to become vain and self-seeking — and their parents think it's cute. O tempora, O mores! How stupid can we get? What will these empty titles mean when these same young girls come before the Judgment Throne of Almighty God?

"But there is one title, my dear people, there is one title which is not empty, one which was instituted not by man but by God himself — the simple and beautiful title of Mother. And as a proof of his esteem for that most beautiful of titles,

God gave it to Mary herself. Our young girls today would be wise indeed if they would consecrate themselves completely to the Mother Most Pure, imploring her help in protecting them and preserving in them the priceless virtue of purity. I am most happy to report at this juncture that since the organization of the TWIFs little more than a month ago membership has risen at a spectacular rate and now numbers almost forty. The TWIFs, for those of you who may have missed the earlier announcement, are a group of our own teenage girls dedicated to doing everything Through and With and In and For Mary. Any girl between the ages of twelve and eighteen who is interested in this worthwhile organization should see me in the rectory after Mass.

"Unfortunately, however, some of the new breed of priests and religious and laity today seek to soft-pedal and play down the importance of the role of the Blessed Virgin in our daily lives and in the course of human affairs and world events, to minimize the rosary and the wearing of the brown scapular, and to become lax about novenas and other time-honored Marian devotions. I here serve them notice that I have no intention of forgetting the pious practices that I learned at my own mother's knee, and that she learned at her mother's knee in the mystic climate of Catholic Ireland.

"The mission of Mary, my dear people, is essentially maternal. She was constituted in the mind of the Trinity before all time as a mother — not merely of those in the fold, or of those who love her, but of all men, those who do not know her, even those who hate her, in the souls of whom, however much they mistakenly deny it nourishment, there is the germ of love for their Mother. If we are going to enter with any sort of proportion or reality into Mary's mothering of souls, it is essential that we in turn gain from her some part of her mother instinct for these souls. No human creature, it is easy to believe, had so great a love for Christ as had his Mother, not only because of the ever incomparable love-relation that a mother has with the fruit of her womb, but also because of the Charity of the Holy Spirit which was in her a vivifying and loving principle of her divine maternity, which associated her with the Passion of her Son and with every mystery of Christ's salvific mission, and which, at Pentecost, overflowed in her heart and so dilated it as to make her the spiritual mother of the newborn Church, and indeed of the Church throughout the centuries; and we who belong to this Church rejoice in being able to address her with that title which she prophesied would be hers: 'All generations shall call me blessed.'

"And therefore, my dear people, I say to you: let your souls experience the unspeakable happiness of this sweet and strengthening vision. It will not take away from you that other sad and oppressive one of present world conditions, but it will give you light to see, along with the dangers, the defense again, to witness anew the crushing of the serpent's head. May my blessing obtain for all of you the sweet and powerful blessing of the Queen of Angels, our universal Mother."

Monsignor Fallon crosses the air hugely with his fingertips, plicks off the reading light on the lectern and climbs down from the pulpit. I rise from the wooden bench on the epistle side and hand him his vestments. Beads of satisfied sweat are trickling down his face. He kisses the stole, slips the gold chasuble over his head, fastens the maniple to his left sleeve with a straight pin and ascends the marble steps to finish the mass. I kneel at the foot of the altar, palms pressed together over my breast.

But underneath the cassock and surplice the boy's flesh is on fire. He invokes the fierce purity of his angel to defend him from the summer girls in their short shorts and scanty clothing.

*

94

The door yawns overhead and Grandma's legs, in surgical stockings, come down the steps as far as her ankles. "Somebody for Dolan," she says, and goes away. The boy's father and mother quiz each other with silent stares. Except for Jean nobody who really counts has visited them since they moved. Then she says, "For us, Tom?" and he says, "That's what she said." "That's strange," she says. "Who the devil could it be?" he says. Then, answering his own question, "Probably another damn encyclopedia salesman," he goes up the stairs to see who it is.

The boy winces at the memory. Several weeks ago Sister Eusebius, the replacement nun, handed out post cards and told the students to check one of six boxes for a free booklet on Abelard, Algae, Ants, Aqueducts, Artillery or Atom. The boy picked Algae. No booklet arrived, but a salesman did, after supper on haircut night. He spread out sample pages on the rug in Grandma's parlor upstairs while she hovered darkly in the drapes between the parlor and dining room. He was a tall young man with an electric blue suit, an enormous college ring, a gold key on his tie clip, and brilliant shoes. The boy's father sat on the edge of Grandma's sofa in his work clothes, running his hand through the scruff at the back of his neck, looking diminished. "Tonight's my haircut night," he explained once, angrily. The young man called him "Mr. Dolan, sir," and told him he was not actually selling the set but placing it in a selected model home as a goodwill gesture. He urged the boy to read the folders spread in front of him, but the print swam, and when the boy looked up his eyes met the outraged eyes of the father he had betrayed by bringing this visitation on the family.

"Who is it, Tom?"

"Some priest. A young chap."

"Father Tetrault."

"Yes, I think that's what he said."

"Where is he?"

"Out on the front porch."

"Well, for heaven's sake, don't leave him standing on the front porch. Invite him in."

He goes back up the stairs and my mother bolts for the bathroom. She emerges smelling of too many lilacs, the toilet hissing and the plank door slamming behind her, as Father Tetrault comes down the steps.

"Beautiful afternoon, isn't it?" he says, tipping his straw boater to my mother. His intense eyes seem to photograph the cellar in a split second. His blue cheeks glisten as if he just finished shaving.

"Just passing by," he says. "It's such a beautiful afternoon, and I thought to myself, what could be nicer on Mother's Day than to stop in and pay a visit to a few of those mothers who keep the parish running."

My mother's hands fidget with the front of her dress. Then, to keep the hands busy, she fills the kettle with water, lifts one of the iron plates off the stove, and lights a fire. "You'll have some tea, won't you, Father? I've got a special tea that's very nice . . . Now where did I put my special tea?"

"Oh please. Nothing special. I'm just passing by . . . I don't believe we've met, Mr. Dolan?"

"I'm Mr. Dolan," my father says. "We just moved in last winter."

"Yes. Happy to know you. It's such a large parish I never get to know some of the most interesting people. That's one of my big regrets. Your wife is one of our stalwarts, rain or shine. And of course I've met your son."

For the first time he looks at the boy, who is playing Monopoly with Paula, and smiles his company smile. I know that something is wrong then. And he knows that I know, because he tries to make it right by smiling again, and says to my father, "My prize altar boy. Really has the form down. Some of these kids genuflect like old men. And they rattle through the Latin as if you're hovering over them with a stopwatch. If you're lucky you catch a few words at the beginning and the end. Suscipiat Dominus sacrificium buzz buzz buzz buzz suae sanctam. That kind of thing. But not him. Every vowel comes through like a bell."

Suscipiat Dominus sacrificium de manibus tuis ad laudem et gloriam nominis sui ad utilitatem quoque nostram totiusque Ecclesiae suae sanctam.

And the priest says "Amen" and bends to the secret prayers of the mass. From this point on the mass is tense. By the time Father Tetrault reaches the consecration his face is white and the words come out in a gasp like Christ himself crying from the cross: "Hoc est enim corpus meum." When he breaks the host in his hands he breaks it reluctantly, knowing it is Christ's body. The boy has seen him after communion spend as much as five minutes wiping his fingers across the paten held over the chalice, to make absolutely sure no minute particles of the sacred host are lost. And once, when he mounted the altar to begin mass, the boy was surprised to see him lift up the altar cloth and peer under it.

"Why did you lift up the altar cloth, Father?" he asked later.

"Well, of course, there has to be a consecrated stone in the altar if mass is to be valid . . ." Then he stopped and looked at the boy curiously, as if he had been interrupted in a private thought.

*

"Now what's all this, Mrs. Dolan? Please, I must insist. You're treating me like one of the crowned heads of Europe." My mother is furiously polishing the silver tea service that hasn't been used since V-J Day. "Paula," she says, "straighten up that bed, will you," pointing to the mass of twisted bedclothes on my father's couch. Then, to the priest: "God's priest is higher than all the crowned heads of Europe. Now you just sit down in the comfortable chair and talk with Tom for a few minutes while I get things ready."

Paula finishes making the bed and sweeps all the Monopoly pieces off the table with ruthless hands because she was already six hundred and seventy dollars in debt. My father sits down on one of the bentwood dining chairs with a plywood seat where the cane used to be, pulls out the Dill's Best, sprinkles some on a cigarette paper and his lap, licks the gum, twists the ends and lights a soggy cigarette. Then he tilts back on the back legs and blows smoke rings at the fluorescent light. The priest opens a neat pack of Camels, taps one against his thumbnail and also lights up. He holds his cigarette strangely, between the thumb and the anointed fingers, the way he holds the host. Unlike my father he does not inhale.

"Well," my father says finally, "I see you've got a full house again."

"Pardon me?"

"I mean all those new cardinals the Pope made. Seventy-two is it? How many Italians this time?"

"Oh, a handful, I guess."

"More than that, I'll wager. But at least there are a few Americans this time."

"We're all very happy about Archbishop Spellman."

"Are we?" my father says, lofting a white zero into the air. "He always struck me as something of a boy scout. All those postage stamps. What's a grown man doing collecting postage stamps? And I wonder where he got the money? But any-

98

way he's not an Italian. Sometimes your Pope sounds just a bit like FDR with the Supreme Court."

"Well, after all, it is the Roman Catholic Church," Father Tetrault says stiffly.

"Except in America where it's the Irish Catholic Church."

"I'm afraid I can't agree with you there."

Tea and Lorna Doones. The priest takes no sugar; he splits a Lorna Doone smartly in the middle and eats half. Paula has three spoonfuls of sugar and four cookies. She is going to get acne. My mother is too busy to touch anything.

When tea is over my mother suggests that we take our Monopoly upstairs and play on Grandma's sun porch.

"No, let the children stay, Mrs. Dolan. Actually there's something I'd like to discuss with all of you."

My father looks alarmed and his hand dives for the tobacco.

"It's a rather curious story. Now of course I don't think we should set much store by it — certainly nothing to be alarmed about — but it is rather curious. I had a visit last night from one of my parishioners. At least I think he is, though I couldn't place him — although as I've said in a parish this size that doesn't mean very much. A fellow named Fortier."

"Fortier?" my father says. "That's the Fortier whose wife went cuckoo and burned down the house."

"No, I don't think so. Well, I couldn't get very much out of him at first because he was crying. But he kept pointing to his eye and saying, 'Father, it's a miracle. My eye! My eye is cured!' "

He has kept his word! The angel kept his word! The boy feels the blood pulse into his temples. He swallows hard to keep from fainting.

"Too much to drink," my father says.

"No, not that. And he told me about how his eye . . . it seems he's had a weeping eye for seventeen years. Then after a while I realized he wasn't talking about his own eye anymore but the eye of one of the statues in the church and apparently *that* was weeping. Then it turned out that his eye stopped weeping when the statue started. He said that he wet his handkerchief with the tears of the angel — it's a statue of an angel, we have them all over the place — and put it to his eye and was cured. He pulled out a soaking handkerchief to show me, although God knows with all the crying he was doing that didn't mean anything. I went back to the church and looked at this statue, and naturally nothing was happening, so . . ."

"Wait a minute," my father says. "WAIT JUST A MIN-UTE! I've heard this story before, haven't I?" He is looking at me now, his dark eyes brighter than a spider's.

"I'm glad," Father Tetrault says. "I'm glad your son's taken you into his confidence. That makes it a lot easier for me."

"What does?" my mother says shrilly. "What are you all talking about? Will somebody please tell me what's going on here?"

"That's what we're trying to get to the bottom of, Mrs. Dolan. Your son — you see, your son had this same notion about the very same statue. That it was shedding tears and — well, even talking to him."

"O my God!" my mother cries. "What are you talking about? What's this all about? What kind of nonsense has he been telling you?"

"Now now, Mrs. Dolan. I wouldn't say it's nonsense. It's just something that he thought was happening and it does him credit that he told me about it."

I told him about it in the secret darkness of the confessional. He is violating the sacred seal. Sister Polycarp said that once the priest leaves the box the Holy Ghost grants him a special gift of forgetfulness, so that even if he were tempted to tell what he heard he wouldn't be able to remember it.

"It's not uncommon for children to have notions of this sort, Mrs. Dolan. No, my concern is simply that we put an end to this business before it gets out of hand. That's why I come to you."

"Well, of course we'll put an end to it," my father says. "As far as I'm concerned we've already put an end to it. As of this very moment. Who started this yarn?"

"Nobody started it," the boy says. "It's what happened."

"Rubbish! What about this Fortier character? How did he latch onto it? Do you know him? . . . Listen, I'm talking to you. I'm asking you a question. Will you please look at your father when he's talking to you?"

If I look at him he will devour me.

"Please, let me try," Father Tetrault says. "This isn't the time for anger. Now then. Would you like to tell me about Mr. Fortier? You can trust me, you know. I'm your friend, remember?"

Not any more. He has never believed me. And now he wants to destroy the angel.

"Maybe you met this Fortier person somewhere and told him the story? Is that it?"

"Yes."

"I see. That makes it all come clear."

"Where the hell would you meet a character like that?" my father wants to know.

"That's not important now," Father Tetrault says mildly. "The important thing is that we just put an end to it all, quietly and simply. There's nothing to get alarmed about here. But you see, don't you" (he is talking to the boy now), "you see what happens when a story gets out of hand. We're going to need your help. I want you to promise us — your parents, myself — to forget about the whole affair. What do you say to that now?"

"No."

"What the hell do you mean no?" my father says. "Where's the manners your mother taught you? Is that any way to answer the priest?"

"I mean I can't."

"There's no such word as can't."

"No, he's right," Father Tetrault says. "That's asking too much of him. Tell you what, let me put it this way. Will you just promise not to go around telling that story to other people? That's fair enough, isn't it?"

Yes, that is fair. The angel has no need of stories now, now that he is making himself manifest.

"Promise?"

"Yes."

"Good lad. You see, Mrs. Dolan, there's nothing to be alarmed about here. It's just something that got a bit out of hand and nobody's to blame. And now we've cleared up the little mystery. As for you, young man" (he is smiling a real smile this time), "are you scheduled to serve St. Francis devotions this week?"

"Yes."

"Well, why don't you drop over to the rectory for a few minutes? I've got a little surprise for you. I hear you're a great reader, aren't you?"

"Yes."

"Well, I've got a few nice books that are just taking up space in my study and I've been looking for a bright young boy to give them to. What do you say to that?"

"Say thank you to Father," my mother says.

"Thank you, Father."

"And thank you, Mrs. Dolan, for the delicious tea. I don't think anybody's brewed me a finer cup of tea since my own mother was alive."

"Oh, not at all," my mother says.

*

On the other side of the plank door they are talking about the boy. Their words, like the fluorescent light, seep into the furnace room through the spaces between the planks, thin and sad, and over the half-inch crack at the top of the door and under the one-inch crack at the bottom. Once the door opens about a foot, but he is lying down now with his eyes shut tight. "No, he's sleeping, Tom," she says, and the door darkens. The boy sits up on the couch again and watches, intently, the words coming through the planks.

He says: "Always a loser. Everything. The whole show. And now this. To be made a laughingstock by my own son."

She says: "Tom, nobody's making you a laughingstock."

He says: "And what's-his-name coming down here — Father Wet Behind the Ears — to humiliate me with his sanctimonious airs. As if I couldn't manage my own household. Who the hell does he think he is?"

She says: "He's only trying to help."

He says: "And those lily-white hands. Did you notice the way he holds his cigarette? Like this. He does, like this. Like some prancing queen at a fairies' convention. Thank you, Mrs. Dolan, for the excellent tea. Oh no, just half a cooky, thank you — must watch the little tum tum. Please come and see me in my silk and satin at the high mass."

She says: "Stop it, Tom."

He says: "Do you know what I think? I think there's something a little funny going on behind my back. Sure, every kid's a bit screwy, and when I was a kid I had all sorts of crazy ideas. For a while I thought all the doorknobs were poisoned. But the point is I didn't go sneaking around outside the family making up stories for lunatics with leaking eyeballs or the holy priest."

She says: "Maybe he's lonely, Tom. He doesn't really have any friends, you know."

He says: "And it's a fine lot of friends he'd make in this

town. What could he learn from all these juvenile delinquents except maybe a few new words?"

She says: "I don't think he's a happy child. You never see him laughing like the other children."

He says: "Maybe he's already found out that life isn't just a bunch of laughs . . . poor kid, he hasn't got much to laugh about, has he? Anna, what's wrong with us? Just what the hell is wrong with us? First Gabriel. Now him. Do you know, sometimes I lie on that couch and I can't get to sleep and I feel my fists tighten up like rocks as if they want to pound themselves into the stone wall. And I can't figure out what we did to deserve everything. There's no way out. God damn it, there isn't any way out."

She says: "Tom? . . . please don't get angry but maybe . . . maybe Christ is the answer."

He says: "Christ be damned, what's the question? That's what I'd like to know."

She says: "I guess we'll just have to try a little harder to make him happy."

He says: "You read about kids who turn out funny because nobody gave them love. But he's had love, hasn't he?"

She says: "I know. Maybe love just isn't enough."

They are silent.

Then he says, almost inaudibly: "Well, it's about all we've got. Honey, do you know something? You're still a very pretty woman."

(Not like the other Deauville women, fat and toothless, waddling down the aisles of the A& P in their Bass Weejuns and cotton anklets, old before their time.)

She says: "I love you, Tom."

Now they are silent for good.

*

104

He is coming at last. He is almost here. The mouth of the tomb has opened and he is stepping forth into the light. Thank God by daylight. Now the head and half the body are visible. And now, painfully, he pulls the rest of his body out of the gray tomb and steps, carefully, upside down, onto the underside of the lid. He trembles violently and a reddish brown flow gushes from his entrails. His wings are still matted flat against his body.

And now he is opening them with infinite care, fold by fold, like a rare piece of parchment with a message inside, and with the agonizing opening of each fold he shivers. The wings glisten wet.

And now they are opened and ugly. It is a moth. Eater of trees and wool. Betrayed inside the cocoon. He went to sleep a brown woolly caterpillar, soft as a kitten, and when he awoke he was transformed by his nightmares into a flying monster with scaly black-brown wings.

The boy takes the lid off the jar and dislodges a moth onto the floor. It wobbles on uncertain legs and falls to one side, rights itself, slowly opening and closing its wet wings against the air.

Fly, moth. Fly out of here. In the darkness behind the furnace and hide.

But of course it cannot fly yet. It is pumping more of the reddish brown fluid out of its horrible insect bowels.

And the boy brings his heel down on the cement floor and listens to the soft crunch. Then he goes outside into the warm spring weather and grieves. The lemon-yellow willow trees are beginning to leaf on the other side of the Kennebec.

On the front of the old upright piano in the darkness of the garage the boy has set up his shrine: a fifteen-cent red vigil light from the Five and Ten; a bottle of holy water; a blue glass vase with a single flame of jonquil; an ashtray with several cones of Fuji Mystic Orient Incense; the New Testament. He strikes a wooden match and lights the vigil, then touches the match to a stick of incense. It does not catch. The match burns down to his fingertips and he drops it in pain and puts his fingers into his mouth. Lights several more matches. Now the tip of the incense cone glows orange under gentle breathing. The smoke rises, purple and pungent, lazy swirls caught in the thin light coming through the side door window.

A face appears in the smoke. But it is not the angel. Paula, screwing up her face against the grimy window, squinting into darkness out of daylight. He cannot stop her. The door opens and she comes toward him, picking her way among the debris.

"So this is where you sneak off to," she says.

"Go away."

"Why? What're you doing? What's all the junk for?" She wrinkles her nose. "Something stinks."

"That's the incense."

"That may be what you call it. They got other names for that stuff, I bet. What's it here for?"

"Never mind."

"No, come on. Tell me. I'm your friend."

"You'll tell everybody."

"I will not. Why should I want to tell anybody anything?"

"Do you promise?"

"Scout's honor."

"No, on this. Swear it on this." He hands her the New Testament. "Put your left hand here, raise your right hand, and swear to God you won't tell."

"Oh come on, for pete sake."

"Then I won't tell you."

"Oh all right. I swear."

"Say: I Paula Vigue swear to Almighty God not to reveal any of the secrets of this place."

"I Paula Vigue swear to Almighty God not to reveal any of the secrets of this place."

"Under pain of eternal damnation."

"Oh for Christ sake, I already promised."

Paula's hand is trembling slightly. She knows what this means.

"No, say it. Under pain of eternal damnation."

"OK, underpainofeternaldamnation . . . now what gives?"

"This is where the angel appears."

She laughs. "Pretty funny place for an angel. Does he play the piano?" But now she is not laughing but looking at the boy with a knotted forehead. "Hey, come on, cut it out, huh? You're just trying to give people the creeps. All that stuff the priest was talking about. You made all that up, right?"

"No."

"Honest to God, you shouldn't go around making up stories like that. Grandma just found out about this Fortier guy and she's boiling mad. I guess he's some kind of friend of hers."

"Everything I say is true."

"OK, so where's the angel, then? I don't see any angel." But she looks hastily over her shoulder as if she expects he might really be there.

"You won't see him. Now go away."

"Why not?"

"You have to be prepared. You have to pray hard. And you have to come to him in — in utter nakedness and he will be manifest."

"You mean take off your clothes? Is that what you do in here?"

The boy does not answer. That is a mistake. He should have made up a lie.

"Well, no thanks anyway," she says, smirking. "So that's what you do in here. Wait till you-know-who finds out about that!"

"You promised," he cries. "You swore an oath. It's not like you think."

"Oh, who cares anyway? I won't tell."

"Please go away."

But she doesn't go away. She picks up a dead match and teases the wick of the vigil lamp. Then she turns from the piano and looks at the boy curiously. Then she looks at herself — at her yellow T-shirt, her white shorts, her saddle shoes. Then she stares at the boy again with those crazy Paula eyes, a painful bright green under blond eyebrows that almost meet, and the phlegm in his throat thickens with fear.

Once, when they were seven and visiting Grandma Vigue for Thanksgiving dinner, Grandma handed them each an orange and sent them back to the sun porch to play while the adults had drinks. That was when Paula told him about orange seeds: how if you swallowed ten in your lifetime you would get appendicitis. She had already swallowed four, she said, so she had only six to go. So had he, the boy said, though he could not remember how many. "But I don't believe that. You made that up."

"OK, then, let's see you swallow six more."

"Why should I? I'm not afraid. You're the one who's afraid," the boy said.

"I'm rubber, you're glue," Paula said.

So together they swallowed the seeds, and both got sick afterward, but it was not appendicitis.

And Paula says, "Hey, listen, if I do it . . . does that mean you will too?"

"No."

It is a sin to take off your clothes with a girl. Unless you have a good reason.

"You're scared."

"I am not either."

Though it's not the same as it would be with Rita Coté or Leda Michaud because Paula is his cousin, after all, and part of the family now. People in the same family are allowed to undress together.

"I knew it," Paula says. "There isn't any angel."

"There is too!"

That time in the woods he looked at her and did not sin. He will pray to the angel, who is wise and has his own reasons. The angel will shield him from sin.

"You first," the boy says.

"No. Together."

"Turn your back then."

And he won't really look at her. Back turned, he fumbles with the buttons on his shirt. He takes off his shoes and socks, carefully rolling up the socks and stuffing them into the shoes. Pulls off his pants. But now, still with his back to her and only the underpants left, he suspects what is happening: she is tricking him. She hasn't made a sound. Is watching him and doing nothing herself. He turns to confront her.

She is naked.

"You cheated," she says. "Take them off." He peels off the underpants.

Though this is not the first time he has seen Paula, it is the first time from the front. She is half sitting on the altar — the lid over the keyboard — her legs pressed tightly together. Her tits are like two little doorbells. She has a pouting belly button and puckerlines around her waist and thighs from the elastic bands on her panties. Her underbelly blushes with the vigil light and curves gently downward to a little nest of hair. He had not expected that. Hair soft as incense.

I will stop looking now.

"First you have to close your eyes and pray," the boy explains. "The prayer to the angel."

But he cannot stop looking because even when his eyes have seen all of Paula it is too much for them to take in. Her eyes, too, remain open, looking down at him.

"Kneel down. Say the words of the prayer after me . . ."

"It's funny," she says. "Course I've seen plenty of those. But it's funny."

"You have not! Close your eyes and say the prayer."

"On little boys who their mothers bring into the ladies' bathhouse with them. But theirs were bigger." And she snickers.

O my God, what is she doing now? Still half sitting on the lid. But opening her legs. Parting the hair with her fingers. The rosy glow there. To show him something incredible.

"Fair's fair," she says. "I bet you've never seen one before, have you."

"You're evil," he whispers.

But his conscience is awakening out of the dark moss like a toadstool with a life of its own. Reddening. Purple veins tensing along the stem, the membrane stretching tight over the fleshy cap. The slit eye dilates, stares up at Paula, and a single poisonous tear forms in the eye.

Giggle.

"You are evil!" he cries, and slaps her.

The slap on her cheek is white. Then slow crimson. She does not retaliate. She yanks on her pair of sky blue panties, the shorts, the T-shirt, jams her toes into the saddle shoes without lacing up, and hurries to the door. Now, at a safe distance, says through her teeth, "I'm going to tell."

"You can't! If you do you'll go to hell."

"See if I care. You're there already."

Gone.

Not a sin. No consent of the will. Her sin, not mine. The goddesses of the flesh. Especially in the summer months. Nakedness and frivolity and evil intentions.

It has shrunk back into the moss. The temptation is over. The boy is still sinless.

But a sinister new voice is whispering to him, torturing him: *more beautiful than the angel.*

The boy has a nosebleed.

Seven

Slap!

"Ha ha ha ha ha ha ha ha ha ha ha ha," Grandma says. "You don't make it again, Dolan. That's only two hundred forty meld. You shouldn't take the bid when you don't have the big fellows."

My father says nothing. He will probably take the bid again on the next hand, and lose, and he and my mother will be out of the game, and he can excuse himself and go down to Jerome's. This happens every Tuesday night. Grandma has her friend, Viola Violette, over for pinochle. Grandma and Viola are always "We" on the score pad; my mother and father are "They," and lose; I keep score. During the game Grandma and Viola keep up a steady undercurrent of mumbling in French — "ma meilleure carte" and "reine des carreaux" and "coupez" and "merde." My father knows they are cheating but doesn't say anything. Even my mother doesn't say anything tonight; she bites her underlip and looks past her hand to the darkness outside the curtains. She is not well.

"So," Viola says, in English, as a sign that everyone should listen, "every year we go down to Hartford in the summer to see my daughter and her family. And it's such a shame to leave all those flowers in the garden with nobody to appreciate them. So Roland, he says to me, 'Viola, why don't we give the flowers to somebody to appreciate them?' Only what we do, we don't tell them where they came from. Roland sneaks out at night and puts the flowers on the doorstep. He's so clever, my Roland. Last year he put some roses on the door of this nice young man who was getting married. I can hardly wait till this summer when we're going to surprise a sick old lady down the street. Isn't that nice?"

"Sometimes people die and nobody even gives them any flowers. That's nice to give people flowers before they die," Grandma says. "You deal, Dolan."

My father riffles the cards down onto the table, then presses the edge of the deck and makes them all rise, magically, off the table into his left hand. One-handing the deck, he cuts it in midair and deals.

He takes the bid again. "Spades," he says.

Grandma snorts happily. "Why do you bid spades when you don't have any?"

"I like spades, that's why. How do you know what I don't have?"

Slap. Slap slap slap.

"What is that, Anna? Why don't you play spades?"

"I'm sorry, Mama. Isn't that a spade? What's trumps?"

"Spades is trumps. That's a club. Pay attention."

"I'm sorry. I guess I don't have any more."

And she bites her lower lip again and looks at the window. My mother is in pain. She is not well. Slap slap slap slap.

Grandma has forbidden toilet flushing except for serious

things because she says the water pressure is down. And last night, after his mother left the bathroom, the boy saw the blood. Two months ago Paula was bleeding somewhere secret, but he overheard his mother telling her that was normal. But not his own. Or hers. When is blood normal and when isn't it? Maybe the whole family is going to die of bad blood.

Slap.

Everybody is looking at my mother. She has just put down a king of spades.

"Where did that come from?"

"What, Mama?"

"That big spade. Three times ago you don't have any spades."

"I'm sorry, I must have forgot."

"That's not fair," Viola says.

"Well, she must have forgot," my father says.

SLAP!

Grandma has flung all her cards down onto the table. "Shit!" she cries, rising in triumphant anger, "we're not going to play baby's game."

My mother hurries from the room in tears.

A terrible word like hysteria. Hysterectomy. They are going to operate and remove the strange growth inside her that is making her bleed. They came and took her away after dinner last night while Paula and the boy were at the movies. The boy hadn't wanted to go but his father insisted. The movie was a Jane Withers rerun at the Opera House. Paula stuck her feet up on the chair in front of her and settled down with her Holloway's Milk Duds while the voice in the previews of "Getting Gerty's Garter" said naughty things: "Yes,

it's a very *snappy* story! . . . She's got it . . . and they *want*
it." Then the feature came on, with Jane Withers growing up
and making smart remarks to her brother like "Hi, Mushface"
and "Oh, hold your lava, Vesuvius." And her brother spent
all his time upside down on the sofa making crazy talk into the
telephone: "Anytime so-and-so gives a tumble to a drooly
meatball like that she takes her feathers right out of my tee-
pee." Everybody, including Paula, was laughing, but the boy
felt very sad. He wanted his mother more than at any time
since he was a small child. "Oh don't be a sadapple," Jane
Withers said. And when they got home from the movies his
mother had been carted away to the hospital.

Evenings now Jean comes over to make supper. Jean is
teaching Paula how to cook because in another week, with
school over, Jean has to go away to Vermont to camp-
counsel. Paula pretends to resent her help. "Sauce could use
some wine," Jean says, "don't we have any wine?" "Who's
we?" Paula says. "I wouldn't know. See for yourself," and
makes her search through all the shelves and drawers. But
every time Jean puts a pan in the wrong place Paula knows
where it really belongs. Sometimes they have long pouting
silences or temper tantrums together. They are as thick as sisters. When they aren't being enemies they have solemn discus-
sions about their hair. The boy is cut out of it all; it is somebody else's family. But his father is pleased. "By God," he
says, "it's not every old codger gets two pretty young girls to
fuss over his supper," and gives Paula an affectionate pat on
her ass, and smiles at Jean.

After supper last night we visited my mother in the hospital. Jean brought along six tea roses and my father a box of

Whitman's Sampler. My mother's hair was spread out loose on the pillow like a fan, showing all the gray hairs that are invisible when it's up in a bun. She wore no makeup. She was feeling much better but they would just have to wait and see.

"Wait and see what, Mama?"

"If everything's going to be all right."

"But didn't they remove the growth?"

"Yes, dear. At least we hope so. But the doctors can never be completely sure of a thing like that. Whether it's malignant or not. We'll just have to wait. And pray."

Malignant. He looked it up in the dictionary when he got home: "being disposed to evil." It went on to explain about tumors, malignant and benign. The boy was terrified. Why couldn't the doctors really be sure? Because the sickness was not physical at all. The holy body of his mother, that took in the sacred host every morning, inexplicably possessed by a being disposed to evil.

When he was very small his mother would take him to mass with her. She would return from the communion rail, eyes lowered and hands folded on her breast, and kneel happily beside him in thanksgiving. He would put his hands up and draw her face down close to his. And she would kiss his lips with lips tasting of Jesus.

Possessed now by a being disposed to evil. No doctor can touch evil. Only God. Or a priest, perhaps, with special powers of exorcism.

The boy began to cry. But the angel said to him, "Do not weep, little one. This is your mother's cross. But the evil cannot touch her soul. She is without sin."

"But the malignant being," the boy whispered. "Where does it come from then?"

"That is a great mystery. God allows evil to exist in the midst of good. In the holiest places there also will you find evil. It is a mystery."

"But whose fault is it?" he pleaded. "Am I responsible?" The angel did not answer.

The boy has never seen so many books in a single room. Two sides of the tiny study are lined with bookshelves. A large metal bookcase, in the center of the room, tilts at a dangerous angle, only the back of a little secretary-desk keeping it from toppling to the floor. Books run two deep on many of the shelves, and then crosswise on top of those. An irregular pile about two feet high balances on the corner of the desk, and on top of that a cherry-colored pipe with half a bowl of caked ashes.

Della, the housekeeper, is still standing in the doorway making vulture eyes. She runs the rectory like a female bishop. She does not like boys, who are obscene. "Don't touch any of Father's things," she warns, hesitates, then withdraws.

Father Tetrault is still over in the church hearing confessions. The boy sits in the leather chair by the desk and studies the spines on the irregular pile. Foreign titles — the Latin, of course, that he recognizes — but others in strange hieroglyphics, maybe Greek or Hebrew. One black book in the middle of the stack has no title. He lifts the others, balancing the pipe on top, and slides it out.

In French: he recognizes some of Grandma Vigue's words. With weird illustrations that must be from the Middle Ages. A man lies strapped to a wooden plank, and somebody is feeding him, head first, into a beehive furnace like a bread oven, and out of a vent on top a blast of air full of tiny figures — horses, lizards, goats, houses, mandolins, naked ladies. The naked ladies have clumps of hair in their forks. But maybe priests have special dispensations . . .

Footsteps. The boy closes the book and tries to slide it back

116

in place. The pile topples onto the desk and the pipe sails off, hits the rug, kicks into the air, alive, falls again, dead ashes on the rug. Father Tetrault comes in, notices the boy and then the mess, and says, "I ought to be a bit more organized, I suppose." He picks up the pipe, sniffs it, but pulls a pack of Camels out of his cassock instead, the cigarette balanced in his fingers in that funny way. He returns to the door and closes it.

"Well, where've you been hiding yourself?" he says. "I expected you might be over a couple of weeks ago."

"My mother is sick."

"Oh, I'm sorry to hear that. I noticed she hadn't been at mass lately. Nothing serious, I hope?"

"She had a hysterectomy. Her eucharist had a growth in it."

"Uterus. Oh, dear. You should have told me so I could offer an intention."

I *said* uterus. He is trying to humiliate me.

"Well now, where were we? I haven't seen you at confession lately, have I? Anything been bothering you?"

I have nothing to confess. I am in the state of grace.

"No. Sometimes I go to Monsignor Fallon."

Not true, but only a venial sin.

"I see. And I hope there haven't been any more difficulties about this angel of yours — this what's-his-name . . ."

"Samuel."

"What did you say?"

"Samuel."

"That's a new one, isn't it? I think it was something else last time."

"He has other titles. He says he has many titles because he has many manifestations."

"I take it this means you've been visiting the statue again." His face clouds over.

117

"No. I don't have to anymore. He comes to me."

"Where's that?"

"In the garage, mostly."

"Uh huh. And you actually see him? He looks the same as the statue here?"

"Yes. No, not the same. I mean he's the same one but he's different too. He is full of eyes."

"Samuel. The Angel Samuel." Father Tetrault is obviously not happy. He starts several sentences — about the workings of the mind, a grain of salt, religious scruples — but he is not talking to the boy anymore; he is talking to the books on the overcrowded shelves. And the books tell him something else. They remind him that he is going to give the boy a present, and he brightens and says, "Suppose we turn to other matters. I think I promised you a few books, didn't I?"

"Yes."

"OK. Now you see the third shelf from the top over there? Pick out anything you can use."

The boy is still standing by the desk, looking at the spilled pile there. Father Tetrault notices and laughs.

"No, I'm afraid not. I can't let you have any of these. But anything you see over there."

Timidly his finger reads the titles of the books on the third shelf from the top. He takes down a collection of views of Brussels. A book called *Astronomy for the Layman*, which is not about Catholic astronomy. Liddell and Scott's *Shorter Greek-English Lexicon*. The priest laughs and the boy, confused, starts to put the book back.

"No, take it if you want it. I've got the unabridged. You'll be the only kid in Holy Angels with a copy of Liddell and Scott, you can be sure of that."

The Imitation of Christ, in green limp leather, and on the flyleaf, in pencil, Eugene R. Tetrault, May 1939.

"Say, what's that you've got there? Let me see that one

. . . I wondered where this had gone to. It's an old friend. My mother gave it to me shortly before she passed on. Now how did it get mixed in with the stuff on that shelf?"

Reluctantly the boy surrenders it on the desk; the soft leather was beautiful to the touch. And the priest, noticing the reluctance, says, "Hey, listen, would you like that too?"

"No, thank you." His mother is present and he is refusing a second helping of dessert.

"Please," Father Tetrault says. "I'd like you to have it. I wouldn't give that book away to just anyone. But I promised you anything on that shelf and I'm no Indian giver. Go ahead. It's yours. Just let me erase the writing." He rummages underneath some papers for a gum eraser.

"You don't have to erase it," the boys says. "I like it the way it is."

The priest smiles and puts a hand in the boy's hair and musses it. The boy tries, unsuccessfully, to duck out from under the friendly mussing fingers.

"Nineteen thirty-nine," the priest thinks aloud, keeping the boy from leaving by that simple announcement. "That was my first year out. Though I wasn't out long because they sent me back to the seminary to teach theology. One of those spooky stone mansions that used to belong to the Carnegies, I think. Dear God, nineteen thirty-nine. Some strange doings then."

He has settled into his green Morris chair. He pauses to see if the boy will ask him about the strange doings. The boy stands patiently.

"There was a thief, you see. Things started disappearing from some of the seminarians' rooms. We were in a particularly tough section of South Portland so naturally we figured somebody was sneaking into the house. The rector gave an order that all doors were to be locked at all times. But the thefts continued. So then, of course, we all knew."

"Knew what, Father?"

Father Tetrault has a blister on his right thumb, and there is fluid under the blister. He presses the nail of his forefinger against the tender flesh, forcing the white liquid bubble into one corner of the blister. Then releases the pressure.

"Why, that it was an inside job, of course. You can imagine the chill that put on everything. Nobody knowing whom to trust. And then several of the seminarians started getting threatening letters. 'I've got your number!' 'You are in danger!' That kind of thing."

Why is he telling me this story? The liquid bubbles again under the skin.

"And then *I* started getting the letters. Let me tell you, that was unsettling. I went so far as to string up wires around my door and let the word get out that I had burglar-proofed my room. And whenever I entered the room I'd go through an intricate business of defusing the system in case anyone was watching. Something like this."

He has risen from the Morris chair and set his left hand gently on the doorknob. He opens the door carefully about four inches. His right hand slides up the edge of the door and disappears over the lintel on the other side. Then, suddenly, the door has opened and closed again and the priest is gone. The boy stares in wonder at the closed door. A moment later the door opens again and Father Tetrault reappears, chuckling softly. He sits down in the chair, stops laughing and begins to tease at the blister once more.

"I felt I owed it to the boys. It helped them, I figured, to have somebody in the house who seemed in control, who wasn't going to let this strange business overwhelm him."

"Why didn't somebody call the police?"

"Yes. Well, I guess we all thought it would be better if we worked it out ourselves. Religious societies are a kind of world of their own. And we did seem to be making headway, too, at this game of amateur detective. I got a number of the seminarians together in my room from time to time and we started comparing clues. What were the likeliest times? Which floors? Who got the letters? Who didn't? In a month's time I'd built up a fairly complete case on the culprit."

"Then did you go to the police?"

"No. Then it occurred to me. Here I am with all this information on the thief. I've pored over it for heaven knows how long trying to establish a pattern, an identity. Now obviously this man isn't a common criminal. He's a sick man — the mind, I mean. Now if I were to bring all this material to a specialist in such matters — a psychiatrist — maybe he'd be able to figure out a pattern behind it all and help us discover the identity of the man. I talked this over with the rector and he gave me the green light. There was a friend of the rector's, a Boston psychiatrist, who came down to a vacation place in Camden on weekends, and the rector arranged for me to see him there — because of course there aren't any psychiatrists north of Boston normally. I drove out to Camden one Saturday afternoon and told him what I knew of the case."

"And he found out who it was?"

"Yes. He found out." The priest's voice becomes almost dreamy. "He sorted through the papers and listened to what I had to say. Then he smiled and told me who it was."

"Who?"

"Can't you guess? Go ahead, try."

"I can't guess." The boy is suddenly frightened. He doesn't want to hear any more. But there is no stopping it. The fingernail is bearing down savagely on the blister and the bubble is going to explode. The priest's voice is almost a whisper: "He told me I was the one."

Silent now. Studying the broken flesh as if it were someone else's. Putting the thumb to his lips and sucking it for a moment. Then wiping it briskly on the sleeve of his cassock and managing a thin smile.

"Of course I didn't know any of that at the time. I was as surprised as anybody. Imagine, I was even writing those letters to myself. But you see, I'd been working awfully hard that summer — at the spiritual side of things as much as anything else. Striving for instant perfection. As if I expected they should have canonized me along with the ordination and finished off the job right there. So the whole strange business was just a kind of warning signal, you might say. The mind's way of telling me that I was wound up too tight. Do you see what I'm driving at?"

The boy sees nothing. He wonders if the bookcase is going to topple finally to the floor.

"Please, don't be frightened. There's a reason why I let you in on these confidences. I've never told that story to any young boy but yourself. Because, of course, I can trust you and I want you to trust me. You understand, I think, that this isn't the sort of story that's meant for the ears of your friends."

"I don't have any friends," the boy says.

"But you understand what I'm saying — that this is a confidence between the two of us."

"Yes, Father." Like the sacred seal of the confessional.

"The mind, you see, is still a largely unexplored continent. It has sides we're only beginning to understand. It's a rather shattering experience to find out, as dramatically as I did, that the mind can lie to itself. Yes, that's just it — that the mind is a liar."

That is not just it. Why won't he stop?

"I'm exposing myself, I know that, I'm leaving myself vulnerable, talking this way. But I think you're worth it. Because you and I — we're very much alike, you see. Very much alike."

Father Tetrault has risen from the Morris chair. He allows

himself a cigarette now. The smoke streams from his nostrils like incense.

"Try it," he says, motioning to the chair. "Sit down for a few minutes. I'll give you a quarter if you've ever sat in a more comfortable chair in your life. And . . . now that you're there . . . if there's anything more you want to tell me, just remember you're talking to a friend."

The boy stands at the door now, about to leave, but Father Tetrault's hand covers the knob. A bomb will detonate if he tries to get out without permission. And Father Tetrault has just remembered a detail which makes him laugh. "After that whole affair I was telling you about, I went away for a good long rest, of course, and I was as good as new again. No, better. Better than new. But there was one rather funny development. It seems the old rector was afraid to enter my room after I left because of the wiring. So he called up the Portland police and they called up the Portsmouth naval yard and, lo and behold, one fine sunny day four armored trucks pulled up on the circular driveway in front of the seminary and out popped a whole demolition squad of men in Buck Rogers suits and helmets and visors and Geiger counters. Naturally all they found was a mess of wires." He laughs and opens the door, and as the boy slips out, the hand ruffles his hair again and the priest, laughing more softly now, says, "Take good care of yourself, now . . . my little liar."

The hand in my hair is like an executioner's. I am hurtled out into the darkness.

I tuck the books under my jacket because a light rain is falling. I walk down Water Street in the raining darkness, my crossed arms holding in the swollen belly of books like a tumor.

Before reaching Miss Duplessie's house I cross to the other

side of the street for safety. A single light blazes on the top floor of her monstrous ark. I can see the old lady sitting in a rocker by the window, squinting at a newspaper through her half-moon glasses.

On the safe side of the street I step into the alleyway by the Monarch Furniture Company where they have discarded a pile of huge wooden crates. I climb into one, out of the rain, and set the four books down at the back. And watch the light in the window.

After a while the old lady gets up from the rocking chair and leaves the room. I step out of my crate and select two pieces of gravel from the alley.

Running now, the rest of the way home, hugging the books tight under my jacket.

No one is home. Paula is at the Opera House seeing Abbott and Costello. My father is probably at Jerome's. I throw the switch at the head of the cellar stairs and a pool of light spills over the area of the kitchen sink below.

The boy sits on the bottom step and stares beyond the iron stove into the half-light of the rest of the cellar. He is very tired. And suddenly overcome with sadness. This is the cellar. This is home. Forever. Unchanging as a photograph.

The photograph shows:

Front left corner: my mother's dresser, a hot water bottle on top, part of an old blackboard nailed onto the side. The plank door leading to the furnace and bathroom. To the right of the door a china holy water font. A timetable of the Grey Lines Transportation Company tacked over that. Against the left wall the Dutch cabinet, with books on the bottom shelf, my half-finished (never to be finished) ship model over that, and St. Joseph and several glass figurines on the top shelf. A

124

few feet in front of the cabinet, one of the iron posts that keep Grandma Vigue from caving in on us.

Far left, kitty-corner: the easychair. A brown slipcover with orange oak leaves. A plaid cover on the seat cushion over the torn brown one. A piece of nubby violet bedspread stitched on the back over the torn plaid. Doilies stitched on top of that and on the arms. Layer on disintegrating layer. Under the feet of the chair a small rug braided out of my father's old clothes. The rest of the floor is linoleum, cracking already in places from the uneven rocks in the cement. Over the chair a whatnot shelf with an empty glass planter shaped like a horse.

The back wall: fifteen feet of paneling from Grandpa Vigue's bar, whitewashed like everything else, making a three-foot-high dado, and resting on its ledge, the left front leg of the highboy. A thermometer and Gabriel hanging on the paneling. Over the paneling the stone and cement, with more pictures: Pope Pius XII and Grandma Vigue.

Against the back wall, moving right: Gabriel's maple table that once had all the letters of the alphabet painted on it in bright yellow. My mother's sewing stuff there now — an Easter basket with yarn, a black Bokar coffee can for buttons, a corduroy pincushion. Paula's blue jeans on the floor under the maple table. Moving right: the collapsing highboy. In the foreground the edge of the porcelain-topped table. The rest is darkness, hidden from view by the iron stove.

We live in a photograph. My father never talks about getting out anymore, even though there are more real estate ads in the paper than last winter. He suffers like Job with his boils. The cellar is an incurable disease.

The boy tries to superimpose on the photograph the happy one of his dream. He shuts his eyes and slowly, dimly at first, like reluctant stars coming out, the dogwoods blossom by ones and twos, till the whole forest of white has reappeared.

But in the clearing in front of the trees — nothing. He crushes his eyelids down on his eyeballs, but no figures appear, only the beautiful and frightening whiteness of flowers. There is nobody in the picture. Will there ever be again?

But out of the darkness to the right, outside the picture entirely, a voice whispers, "My God, must've fallen asleep." The cat-crying springs on my father's couch. A cigarette cough. Zzzrrrnnng: a zipper singing along metal teeth. Zzzrrrpp! "O damn!" in a small panicky voice, "it's stuck!" Rising from the bottom step the boy advances into the cellar on the other side of the stove, stretches for the light cord and yanks on the fluorescent light.

My father is sitting on the edge of the couch in his Sartor Resartus briefs and one sock. Jean, standing, startle-eyed under her tangled hair, is fighting the zipper on the hip of her skirt. She has no blouse on. She covers her tits with her hands and cries, "Tom, get him out of here!"

But my father is saying to me, "I guess we must have fallen asleep. We've both been working hard, you see, and I guess we just sort of dropped off after dinner . . ."

"O crap!" Jean says, scooping up the rest of her clothes and retreating to the gloom of the entryway to finish dressing.

My father climbs into his pants and gropes in his pockets for the Dill's Best.

"I imagine this must look a trifle strange, but actually it's not that at all . . . Jean?"

She is pushing open the bulkhead doors and bolting into the darkness.

"Jeannie, you wait in the car, OK? I'll be out in a minute."

She doesn't answer.

"My mother," the boy says.

"No no no, it's not that at all. Listen, sometimes boys your age think they see things and the things aren't that way at all. You know what I mean?"

The boy does not know. "My mother!" he says.

"Your mama'll be home tomorrow. And the last thing in the world she needs is to have you upsetting her about something you're not altogether clear about. Now I think Mama should be our first consideration, don't you?"

The blood is going to flow. That familiar draining feeling just before it comes; inevitability; a sluice gate has opened somewhere; too late to halt it now.

"So you don't want to go getting funny notions that you've seen something because . . ." He is coming toward the boy, silly-smiling, groping with a peacemaking hand for his shoulder. The black pelt of hair on his naked chest is horrible.

"Don't, Papa. Don't touch me."

"Now look here, it's a fine kettle of fish when a father can't even try to explain something to his own son."

"Don't! I'll be sick. I will!"

The father stops short, bobbing against an invisible glass wall like a helpless balloon, transfixed by the boy's imploring hands. As if he too sees it — what the boy sees before everything goes dark. How the bright blood trickles from a fresh wound in the center of each palm.

Eight

Before the final blackness, this — the terror of the voices. The voices of my father, the angel, the doctor with hairy nostrils. Then the voices no longer separate or separable, nor even voices, but all the sounds of the world converging on my ears, the fan wailing in the hospital window, cars colliding outside, beetles grating their teeth in the grass. The capital city of Poland in Europe explodes in flames.

But no longer separate or separable. The boy crushes his ears with his hot hands but the sounds do not stop. He hears his hands, he hears howling around him the din of a monstrous ocean. He drowns, gladly, in the final blackness.

But it is not final.

"What do you hear now?" the hairy-nostriled doctor asks.

"Your voice."

"Anything else?"

"Somebody is playing a radio at the other end of the ward."

"That's right. Does it bother you?"

"No."

"Good boy."

It is difficult to talk because I am full of tubes. There is a tube in my nose which the doctor says leads down to my stomach. A tube in my arm for plasma. Another tube to drain out of my pecker.

"The ear," says the doctor, "is a marvelously subtle instrument. First of all there's the eardrum. The eardrum is a very thin membrane — you know, like a tissue paper, say — and that's the first thing to pick up the sounds. While I'm talking to you, right now, that sensitive little membrane is vibrating and it's sending messages to the inner ear, where there's a complex and mysterious apparatus that turns those messages into electrical impulses that travel up the nerve pathways to the brain. Do you see?"

"Yes."

"Well now, whether you realize it or not, your ear — everybody's ear — is sensitive to the tiniest little rhythmic disturbances in the air. Constantly it's hearing far more than you actually think you're hearing. Thousands of sounds are bombarding us at every moment. Well now, you might well ask, why is it then that every moment we aren't confused and overwhelmed by a continuous roar of unrelated sounds? And that's a good question. You'd certainly expect that, wouldn't you? But the answer is that the ear, for some reason unknown to medical science, *masks* sounds — one sound makes other sounds inaudible. That's nature's way of protecting human beings from — well, from what apparently happened to you. All the sounds coming at once with no selection, no defense you might say. For some reason, you see, the masking process broke down . . . but the important thing is that you're getting well again. That's the important thing."

He does not mention the blood. After he leaves I unfold my palms; they are without blemish. Then I go to sleep, but this time it is not black but a soft brown.

STATUE WEEPS?

Police last night were summoned to the Church of the Holy Angels on Water Street by the Rev. Eugene R. Tetrault, assistant pastor, to clear the church of what he described as "an unruly and hysterical mob scene." According to Father Tetrault this was the third night of such disturbances, but on previous nights he and the pastor, Monsignor Joseph F. X. Fallon, had been able to disperse the crowds without summoning police aid.

Center of the disturbance, it was said, was a plaster statue of an angel which allegedly sheds tears. Reporters arriving at the church about eight-thirty last night found a noisy crowd estimated at over two hundred persons, comprised of devout parishioners and curiosity seekers from as far as Skowhegan, blocking access to the so-called "miraculous" statue. Local police, unsuccessful in enforcing some semblance of orderly procedure, found it necessary to remove the image, over loud protests, from the church and take it to a secret hiding place.

Captain of Police Onasime Giroux reported that he found no evidence of anything "peculiar" in the physical appearance of the statue. But several witnesses, interviewed by reporters, contended that the statue had been weeping for three days and stopped only hours before police were summoned. One elderly lady, whose identity could not be learned, but who is said to have come down from Farmington Falls each of the three days to witness the "miracle," claims to have been cured of an undisclosed ailment.

Father Tetrault was not available for further comment. It was learned from reliable sources that Monsignor Fallon had left town earlier in the afternoon to confer with his bishop.

Ansel brings me the paper so I can keep up with Joe Palooka. Ansel is my new friend; though he is only an orderly, they let him take all the tubes out of me yesterday. He likes to sit at the bottom of my bed and tell me stories about his life — his job as a short order cook, a bouncer in a nightclub, a merchant mariner (who killed a man in Singapore but it was self-defense), a gandy dancer on the railroad. But especially about the morgue.

"Always it's me, Ansel. I think they must know when I'm on duty alone. They wait for me, you know, hanging on the edge of their rubber rafts, just keeping their heads bobbing above the water. Then sometime after midnight one of them'll say to himself, 'Ansel's on the night shift tonight. I think I'll wheeze off now.'

"So I get this call to come up to Second General and bring the keys. I gotta show you those keys sometime, these two keys on a steel ring with a fat brass medallion saying MORGUE. Like you were going to open up a cathedral or something. And up on Second General there's this old stiff waiting for me, and I plug up his hole and tie a little string around his watercock . . ."

"Why do you do that?"

Ansel laughs. "Blatt! Pssst! They'll try to go all over you quick as that. A little present they save up for you for taking such good care of them. So anyway, I wrap him up in paper like an Egyptian mummy and throw a sheet over to make it look professional and start wheeling him all over this goddam hospital. And that's the craziest thing of all.

"You want to know why? I'll tell you. Because whoever built this place had me in mind, he said to himself, 'We don't want to make it too easy for Ansel, we want him to spend a little time getting acquainted with the stiffs,' chauffering them clear across to Second South, then down the elevator to First Obstetrics, then clear across to the other side of the hospital, then down another elevator to the *sub* sub basement, then down that corridor to the morgue. And every few feet I gotta stop and turn on the lights ahead of me and turn off the lights behind me, because God bless the good sisters, they have all these little signs with 'Turn Off The Lights,' only that last 's' isn't an 's', it's a dollar sign. Get it? So here I am, and I don't scare easy, but here I am wheeling him down these long corridors with only this little pool of light where we are, and ahead of me it's dark as sin and the dark is creeping up on my heels behind me."

The boy's eyes are wide to keep the room as light as possible.

"OK, so here we are, down in the sub sub, and there's nothing here at all except this dark corridor leading to the autopsy labs and the morgue, and all along the corridor they have shelves of things in bottles of formaldehyde. All sorts of trophies in those bottles — brains and livers, appendixes, unborn babies with two heads, stuff like that. Inside the morgue we've got four wooden icebox doors, and I say a little prayer that the bottom ones are empty, so I can just slide him off onto the tray. But they're always full, so I have to lift this guy up — he weighs about five thousand and eight pounds — and put him in the top freezer. Then I tie a label on his big toe and another one on the door and keep a third one for the desk. And that's when it happens."

"What happens?"

"Every time. I told you I don't scare easy. But every single time, when it's all over, just when I'm turning out the light, that's when it happens. Every single goddam hair on my head and the back of my neck stiffens up like a hard-on."

A large nun flaps into the ward like a fat sea gull trying to fly, but too heavy for the little white wings starched onto each side of her flowering face. She chases Ansel on his way, checks something off on her clipboard, rolls the boy over briskly on the bed and inserts the cold glass rod. And every single hair on his head and the back of his neck stiffens in terror.

*

The boy is only an instrument, he knows that. People do not stop doing what they are doing just because of him. There is Professor Quiz of Radio Fame, shown at the Veterans Administration Hospital at Togus yesterday, entertaining veterans of four wars with card tricks as Governor Horace Hildreth looks on. And there are Mr. and Mrs. Bernard Rabideau of Norridgewock, who were guests of honor Saturday afternoon at a fortieth wedding anniversary observance. Mrs. Rabideau's suit is buttoned to her neck and she wears a gardenia. Mr. Rabideau has a plaid, short-sleeve shirt, with a combination eyeglass case and fountain pen holder in the front pocket, and a carnation pinned onto the wide lapel of his shirt. He is admiring a money tree presented by the guests. For them nothing has changed.

For Joe Palooka the fight has finally begun, but he is not in condition. Phantom Dill draws the first blood — "a right to the face brought the claret gushing from Palooka's nose." Joe staggers back from the barrage of blows, and suddenly spots a familiar face in the crowd. It is the man with the beard! When he gets back to his corner Knobby Walsh is talking to him, but Joe does not listen. His glassy eyes are searching the crowd, trying to find that face again: "Who is he? . . . that voice . . ."

There is something I must know.

"MIRACLES" MOUNT IN LACRIMATION CASE

More instances of alleged miracles have been reported in the wake of Sunday's incident concerning a so-called "weeping angel" statue in the Church of the Holy Angels. The statue has been returned to its niche in the church, and although no further accounts of lacrimation have been reported, crowds continued to circulate in the church throughout Monday and Tuesday. Captain of Police Onasime Giroux reported that he has assigned a special traffic patrolman to the Water St. area to alleviate "a real bottleneck situation down there."

Sister Mary Alfonsina, of the St. Francis de Sales Sanatorium for Respiratory Diseases in Hallowell, told this paper yesterday that one of their patients, Emily Bolduc, 18, of Lewiston, had experienced a "marvelous favor" through the intercession of the angel. Miss Bolduc has been suffering from a speech defect for over a year, the sister said.

Had Tonsillectomy

A sufferer from pulmonary consumption, the Bolduc girl has been given shelter for the last five years at the Hallowell sanatorium. Last year, owing to a degenerative repercussion of her infirmity, she had to undergo tonsillectomy, and from then on was no longer able to speak, Sister Mary Alfonsina related.

On Tuesday Sister Mary Alfonsina said she and the girl came to Deauville, arriving at the church early in the afternoon. Struggling to make her way through the crowd, the girl reached a place directly in front of the image, and her appeal to the angel was so fervid and confident that the miracle took place, the sister said. "All at once the young child moved her lips to speak, and at first she could produce only a hoarse and inarticulate sound which aroused the pity of those around her. Then she invoked the merciful angel with a loud voice, her first clear words being 'I love you! I love you!' "

Dr. Hyman Rothstein, Director of the Sanatorium (and a non-Catholic, it was learned) confirmed Sister Mary Alfonsina's statement that the Lewiston girl had not responded to speech therapy treatments for over a year. "I just don't know," he replied to queries about the possibility of a miraculous cure. "I'm a doctor, not a clergyman. But faith can accomplish strange things. You don't just rule things out."

Deauville Man

The second incident involves a Deauville man, Perley Arsenault, 47, of 19 Gold St., an employee of the freight yards of the Central Maine Railroad. Co-workers claim Mr. Arsenault was cured yesterday of a crippling form of neuritis. Reporters were unable to reach Mr. Arsenault by telephone or at

134

his address. A friend of the family indicates that he may be visiting his sister-in-law in Augusta to avoid the press of well-meaning callers.

If the Antarctic ice cap melted at a uniform rate, it would produce about 6.5 million cubic miles of water, enough to feed the Mississippi River for more than 50,000 years.

A woman was brought into Emergency last night for rabies shots, because while she was sleeping with her mouth open a bat mistook her warm mouthhole for a cave and flew in.

Ansel leaves the room still shaking with laughter.

The fat nun rolls me over.

They enter the ward timidly. My father holds back at the foot of the bed, pretending to find some reading material on my chart. Finally he comes up toward the head where the others wait — my mother (I offer up my sickness to make her well) and Paula (whose eyes are still remembering the garage). He says sadly, almost inaudibly, fearing to damage my eardrums with human speech, "We each of us brought you a present. Here's mine." Awkward, like a child, he shoves it onto me, a wooden model kit of the *De Witt Clinton*. "Not that you'll be able to work on it here, but I thought maybe looking at the plans . . ." He smiles sadly, shaking his head at something inside his head.

None of them is going to say anything about It.

O Father, I forgive you! See, I am already taking the pieces out of the box, I am reading the directions on the glue and unrolling the plans, I forgive you. I am your son. Don't be afraid of me.

All I ask is love.

135

by Omer Rossignol

Some years ago, when I was a cub reporter for the *Lewiston Sun*, an old-timer on the city desk asked me, "Suppose an item came in on the teletype that Joe So-and-So, former resident of Lewiston, had been killed in a hotel fire in the Roxbury section of Boston. How would you go about doing a story on that item?" I thought for a moment. "I guess I'd find out if he had any family or relatives in town, then go and interview them. Right?" "Wrong!" he thundered. "You'd go to the almanac and look up Roxbury and find out if it's really in Boston, that's what you'd do. A reporter takes nothing on faith."

I've never forgotten that advice. I had need of it yesterday when I had the distinction of being the first "outsider" to interview Perley Arsenault, 47, of 19 Gold St., the beneficiary of an alleged "miracle" earlier this week. Mr. Arsenault, who has been in seclusion since word leaked out, was reluctant but cordial to this reporter.

Alert Eyes

Mr. Arsenault is a large man, with a shock of gray hair, a face heavily lined by sickness and hard work, but with sparkling, alert eyes. I listened intently to his story over coffee amid the somewhat faded surroundings of his sitting room in the five-room frame house he shares with his two unmarried sons, Albert, 25, and Roland, 22.

A Catholic, but by his own admission "maybe not as good as I should be," Mr. Arsenault is employed at the Freight Yards of the Central Maine Railroad. Born in Poland, Maine, the son of Alice and the late Louis Arsenault, the widower has been suffering for the last five years from a form of neuritis which completely stiffened his right leg, which he had to drag along while walking with the help of a cane. His left leg was also pretty weak. He had tried every possible treatment, going as far as Boston to consult specialists, but with no result.

Finally, after hearing of a "miraculous" statue in the Church

136

of the Holy Angels, Mr. Arsenault decided to go and ask a favor from the angel. "I didn't put much stock in this talk of miracles," Mr. Arsenault confided, "but the boys kept talking it up so I decided, why not give it a try?" Nothing ventured, nothing gained has been his philosophy throughout his long bout with illness, it was learned.

"Lift Your Leg"

Monday evening, accompanied by his two sons, Mr. Arsenault visited the controversial statue. He lighted a vigil lamp and kissed the toes of one foot of the angel. Did he pray for a miracle then? Mr. Arsenault isn't telling — at least to this reporter.

Tuesday morning, as usual, he went to his work. "I sure wasn't thinking of any miracles!" he adds sardonically. About one o'clock in the afternoon, taking time off for a lunch break, he unconsciously made a movement which for years he had not been able to accomplish. Though his work is done from a sitting position, he arose from his desk without first getting hold of his cane, and walked away. He did not even notice the lack of his old friend the cane. Only when he sat down again did he realize what had happened. A co-worker realized it too and kept urging him, "Stand up! Lift your right leg! Lift your left leg! Bend your knees!" Arsenault followed orders "as if," he says now, "in a dream." And now the other man (in the excitement Arsenault has forgotten which of his friends this was — he thinks it might have been "Bunky" Worden) could not restrain himself any longer and started shouting, "A miracle!" The whole yard became tumultuous. All the men left off work to crowd around him, wanting to see him walk without his cane, wanting to touch him, while the cry echoed around, "A miracle! A miracle!"

Remains Skeptical

Perley Arsenault is a "cool cookie" indeed to remain as calm as he does amid the enthusiasm his case has awakened. He admitted to this reporter that he doesn't need a cane anymore and

137

demonstrated how he can stand on his feet and walk about, not exactly sprightly, but freely enough. But he remains skeptical about a miraculous "cure." "All I know is I never felt better in my life," he opines.

Perhaps he doesn't think himself worthy of such a special favor as his friends claim for him. Perhaps there is a medical explanation for what has taken place. Yours truly is only a reporter and can only tell what he has seen and heard. But for the sons, neighbors, and co-workers of Perley Arsenault, it is clearly a miracle.

"We're going to come and see you every day till you get better," Mrs. Goodman says. "It won't always be me, of course. I'm eighty-eight years old and I don't take too well to over much traveling. But don't you worry, somebody will be here. Every day."

"That's right," Mr. Fortier says.

"We're all so grateful," Mrs. Goodman says. "And honored. To think that you would come to us first."

"We're grateful to the angel for all he's done," Mr. Fortier says, blessing the boy with clear, untainted eyes.

"*Here's* the angel!" Mrs. Goodman cries, and puts her head down on the pillow next to the boy, and kisses him with her tooth-smelling mouth. And kisses him again, this time for Evelyn. "Evelyn's very shy. She wanted to come and tell you herself how sorry she is that she didn't believe you at first. But she's such a shy girl. She got an upset stomach about it all. So that kiss is from Evelyn."

CHEMICAL ANALYSIS OF TEARS CITED

Evariste Lavallier, owner and founder of the Lavallier Rexall Drug Stores in Deauville and Skowhegan, asserted today that he had made a chemical test of the tears of the so-called "miracle statue" in the Church of the Holy Angels. Such a test, he claims, was made during the absence of Very Rev. Joseph F. X. Fallon, the pastor, but with his knowledge. "It was just a few hours before the tears stopped flowing," Lavallier added.

Own Words

In his own words he recounted the events of June 2 leading up to the chemical analysis of the reputed tears.

"About five in the afternoon, when I visited the statue, liquid was still flowing from the eyes. In a few seconds I collected more than a cubic centimeter of the liquid in a syringe, even though a number of people had already soaked handkerchiefs in it to keep as relics. I then dried the image with a wad of Rexall cotton and after a few minutes I noticed that a fresh tear had formed in the angel's right eye, then another in the left eye.

"My first thought was that maybe a refraction of light was causing the impression, because the statue's face is painted with a glossy enamel. I took various positions around it and observed it from various angles, but the same thing was happening. Afterwards I tried to figure out, just what is this statue made of?

"It seems to be made of a thin plaster, probably hollow. Its back was perfectly dry. I don't see how the tears could be caused by anything like a vapor condensation, especially when you consider that there was a lot of liquid given off before I even got to the statue. I myself decided to taste the liquid and it was just like I was tasting one of my own tears.

"Later I checked this out scientifically at the pharmacy and my impression was exactly right. These are human tears. Don't ask me how they got there but that's the scientific fact."

No Hurry

Questioned about Lavallier's report, Monsignor Fallon advised caution. "The Church does not speak except after mature investigation because she is wise and prudent and is in no hurry," he said. "I would therefore urge all to remain calm in the face of this extraordinary manifestation, without any fanaticism or exaggeration."

According to an informed clerical source, the Council of

Trent (a famous council in the history of the Roman Catholic Church, 1545–1563) has this to say about the worship of statues: "Images of the Lord, of the Blessed Virgin, and of Saints are to hold in veneration, not because there is in them some divinity or power for the sake of which they deserve to be the object of our cult, nor because something may be asked from them, nor because some trust may be placed in them as it was done of old by the pagans who put their hopes in idols, but because the honor given them refers to their prototypes."

The same source agreed that this would also apply to statues of angels.

Father Tetrault came to visit this morning, moving down the ward on stiff Tinkertoy legs. For an instant the boy did not recognize him — like somebody you had known very well before the war who went overseas and changed. He made no mention of what was in the newspapers, but talked instead of the rumor that the Pittsburgh Pirates were going to go on strike because everybody else was doing it. He gave the boy a card from the members of the confirmation class at Holy Angels, for if the boy had not become sick he would be making his confirmation along with Paula and the others.

The card was a spiritual bouquet, in which the twenty-three members of the confirmation class promised to offer up a total of forty-six masses, forty-six rosaries and forty-four worthy receptions of holy communion for his recovery. In the picture on the card a priest was celebrating mass in front of the crucified body of Christ, from whose wounds streams of the most precious blood gushed into the elevated chalice. Seeing that, the boy looked up from the picture to the priest, but the priest gave no sign of recognition. The picture was just a coincidence.

After Father Tetrault left, the boy suddenly realized why he looked different. He had not shaved.

*

Day after day the fight goes on. Joe is battered and groggy. On a darkened roof, overlooking the darkened stadium, a gunman draws a bead on the arc-lighted ring. Once he has the champion in his sights, the black cross centered on Joe's bruised body, and his finger tightens on the trigger, but the referee steps between. And once again, and he pulls the trigger, but the gun jams. And the terrible fight goes on and the gunman waits his chance.

But the boy is going to be well. Tomorrow — or the next day at the latest — they are letting him go home again. It has been a lonely struggle.

For not once has the angel appeared to comfort him in his suffering.

PAY PHONE DOESN'T,
BUT CALLER DOES

Thomas F. Dolan's frenzied attempt to recover a nickel from a pay telephone Wednesday cost him $25 in Criminal and Traffic Court a few hours later.

Dolan, 49, of 54 Water St., pleaded guilty to a charge of destruction of private property resulting from his demolition of the phone in a Deauville drinking establishment.

Asst. City Atty. Richard Joubert said Dolan tore the phone from the wall and smashed the receiver in pieces. Dolan said he was angry because the phone didn't return his nickel after an uncompleted call.

He didn't get the nickel.

Nine

The union has gone out on strike against the paper company. For the first few days the boy's father lived for the strike. "The lines are drawn," he announced. "The lines are drawn and it's about time we found out who's standing on which side of the fence." He divided his time between the picket line that inched around the outside of the Anchor Post fence and the strategy huddles inside Jerome's bar. On the first day of the strike somebody set fire to the big chip pile; it was obviously a scab who was paid to discredit the union. At supper that night the boy's father recreated John L. Lewis' defiance of FDR. At the end of the porcelain table the President appeared, ashen-faced, his paralytic body trembling under the velvet-lined cape, and at the head of the table John L. Lewis, eyes smoldering under massive eyebrows sketched by a mad artist with hunks of coal. And the boy thrilled to the beautiful words of wrath: "It ill behooves one who has supped at labor's table and who has been sheltered in labor's house, to curse with fine impartiality both labor and its adversaries when they become locked in deadly embrace."

But then the drama went out of the strike when it became clear that there would be no early settlement. The boy's father sat over second and third cups of coffee before going out to join the picket line, and returned an hour or so later for another cup of coffee. By the end of the week he had found things to do around the house, like painting with an old can of red enamel the iron posts under Grandma's feet, and teaching the boy how to drive the Dodge.

"Tom, he's just a child. And he's still not completely recovered."

"He's thirteen years old now. I wish somebody had taught me a skill when I was his age. Jesus Christ, there ought to be *something* that a father can show a thirteen-year-old."

So the boy and his father sat out in the driveway shifting gears, the boy on the edge of the seat, barely able to reach the clutch with his toes, and when he had mastered that they practiced going back and forth in a ten-foot strip of the driveway. It was a hot afternoon, and he kept stalling the engine and finally flooded it. But his father would not let him leave. "A man doesn't simply walk away from his mistakes. He sticks with them." They stuck with it, waiting for the car to unflood, the fierce sun striking down on the tin roof and thickening the gas fumes inside. When they came in for supper they still hadn't got it started again, and the boy was nauseous and in tears, and his father's face was dark with quiet anger.

But today we are all driving down to Camden to see the ocean. I have never seen the ocean. Yesterday morning, while my mother was making her thanksgiving after mass, Father Tetrault came out of the sacristy and sat down in the pew beside her. He asked her how I was. They ought to take me down to Camden to see the ocean, he said. It would be a natural tonic. There is a strip of empty beach just below the harbor where the view is spectacular, he said.

My mother was up at five-thirty, making sandwiches and filling the thermos with iced tea and hunting up everybody's bathing suit, before she went off to mass. When she got back she had a quick breakfast and we left. Though it was nine-thirty, the mists were still rising off the Kennebec. "It's going to be a scorcher," my father said, obviously pleased.

"I've seen the ocean four — no, five times before," Paula says.

"What's it like?"

"What do you mean, what's it like? It's not like anything, you stoop. It's just the ocean."

Just past Albion it begins to rain, black billows of cloud appearing out of nowhere in the perfect blue sky. "That's a good sign," my father says, as the hard rain pings on the hood. "That's going to blow over in no time. That's an inland storm. You won't find any of that down on the coast."

And he is right. The storm lifts as suddenly as it came, and the cleansed air roars into the car, smelling of warm wet roads, of fields of drenched daisies, and once, of enormous lilacs pouring out of the foundation of a collapsed barn. They never tear anything down in the Maine countryside. They let the buildings collapse like old trees. When houses start to go they simply add on more rooms, and move the furniture into the new rooms while the old ones cave in, and then maybe fifty years later somebody adds some more rooms onto them and they move all the furniture again.

"Do you hear that?" my father asks me as we begin to climb a hill.

144

"What, Papa?"

"Listen. What do you hear?"

I do not know. The engine, of course. The wind whistling through the butterfly window. The yellow splat of bugs against the windshield? Maybe even the ocean, miles away? What do I hear?

"The engine, I mean. How's it sound to you?"

"Pretty noisy."

"Right. OK . . . *now* how's it sound?"

"That's much better."

"OK. So you see what I did? Obviously this car can't take these hills in third. And the engine warns you. It starts to lug, so that's how you know you have to shift down to second. Always listen to what your engine's telling you. It doesn't matter what the speedometer says, it's the engine that knows what's going on in a car."

On the other side of the hill he pulls over to the edge of the road by a red sign saying WHY DID THE CHICKEN and cuts the engine. "Your turn," he says, sliding out from behind the wheel.

"O Tom! Please, not now."

"I'm going to be right here beside him. There's nobody on the road and we've got a straightaway for a good mile here. Just take it nice and easy."

The boy takes his father's seat, waves of fear pulsing between his legs.

"Nice and easy," his father says.

The boy reaches for the choke knob and the windshield wipers are swishing furiously. Paula, in the back seat, giggles. The boy's cheeks flush with shame. "There were still some drops of water," he says. "I wanted to get all that water off there."

And now the car is moving with a will of its own. It is incredible that the car should be moving. Up until this moment he never really believed in that possibility, he expected and even counted on the fact that the car would refuse to go. The needle trembles at fifteen miles an hour, but the engine is screaming and the outside world is already beginning to blur past them.

"Second!" his father cries. "Slide her into second!"

His left foot depresses the clutch, but his right foot is still pumping the accelerator, and the motor makes a crazy detached sound as though it has left the car altogether. Then he takes his right hand off the wheel and grips the knob on the end of the stick and shoves it forward. The Dodge is in second.

But it is no longer on the road. They are lurching through high grass, and nobody says a word about it, except that his mother is making a thin moan in the back seat, and a black cow in a nearby pasture looks over her stone wall at the car with placid wonder. The car bounces back onto the road just in time for them to read the last of the red signs. BURMA SHAVE.

The boy's father lets out a low whistle and says, "Holy Immaculate Mother of God! That takes the bananas, that does . . . OK, just turn right at this intersection up here and pull her over to the side."

The car goes through the intersection and continues straight ahead.

"I can't!" the boy cries. "I can't do it!"

"OK. OK, now, don't panic. Just take your foot off the pedal and let her die."

The car slows down. Once again the boy is surprised: it was his foot that was making the car move. It coasts to a stop, shudders, gives a final angry jerk and dies in gear. His armpits are soaked with sweat.

His father is back in the driver's seat. The boy, in shame and exhaustion, is in the back seat with Paula. "He just isn't ready yet, Tom," his mother says. "He's not old enough to handle it yet."

"It's about time he learned how to handle something besides his own little pecker."

We drive on to the ocean in silence under a perfect blue sky.

We are still several miles from Camden when suddenly, on the downside of a hill, the air is cool and we smell the ocean. I know that is the ocean smell even though I have never been near it. My father glances over his shoulder, nods at me and says, "Sorry I lost my temper back there. You're a good lad, you'll get the hang of it. All it takes is a little practice."

By the time we get to Camden he is laughing at the memory. "Can you imagine what old Bessie the cow thought, seeing us barrel-assing through the daisies?"

> Break, break, break,
> On thy cold gray stones, O Sea!
> And I would that my tongue could utter
> The thoughts that arise in me.

"Nobody's been able to improve on that in all the years they've been writing poems," my father says. "I memorized that poem in school when I was your age. Break, break, break . . ." He is sitting on a large rock in the sun, his pants rolled up to the knees, his shirt off. He peels an orange contentedly. My mother is about ten feet away, lying on a blanket on the pine needles in the shade, dozing now that the picnic lunch is over. Except for that gentle movement of my father — the thumbnail under the orange skin, the slow turning of the orange like the rhythm of the sea — they are two people in a photograph. In the half light under the pines the worry lines have left my mother's face; she seems almost to smile, as if she knows something we don't know. And my father in the white sun watches the sea and turns his orange, and remembers in his happy eyes the sad words of the poem. My father and my mother.

> O, well for the fisherman's boy,
> That he shouts with his sister at play . . .

"Where's Paula?" my mother says, suddenly opening her eyes.

"She's down in back of that big rock, putting on her bathing suit."

"Well, tell her it's just for wading or she'd be crazy enough to try swimming in those waves."

"Yes, Mama."

Someday I will be a poet and write tragic poems about the sea. But what is the ocean really like? What are you supposed to feel the first time? I have seen the ocean and now I can die. No, but what if in the fall the eighth grade nun asks them to write a descriptive essay. The stones are not gray at all; they flash with sunlight through the white froth, and the blue of the ocean is almost black. The scarred pines grow out of the boulders and the boulders grow out of the sea. No two waves are alike, never in all the history of time. There are voices in the waves, sand-tombed men raving under the sea, stories and prophecies, the Flying Dutchman, gaslight sails, St. Elmo's fire, the bird that sits on spars. But it is hard to have real thoughts about the sea.

Paula's head appears from behind a large black rock down on the beach, then the rest of her, as she scrambles up it on all fours, then stretches upright, shakes out her hair, looks back toward them and turns to the sea. Her bathing suit is too tight. The bottom piece pulls up in the crack, strips of white cheek showing between the suit and the tan lines on her thighs.

The boy already has his on; he got into it in the back seat of the Dodge while the others were finishing lunch.

> Break, break, break,
> At the foot of thy crags, O Sea!
> But the tender grace of a day that is dead
> Will never come back to me.

"Hey," Paula cries, "come on down. I want to show you something."

The boys picks up his sweat shirt and makes his way gingerly down to the beach, his bare feet picking their way over the round stones. He climbs the big black rock and looks for her, but she has disappeared.

"Where are you?"

"Around the bend. Come and look at this."

She is standing in a tidal pool, the water just below her tan lines, and a ledge of rock between her and the sea. Her clothes are in a pile on the beach behind her, a stone weighting them down, her underwear out in plain sight. The boy would not do that: whenever he changes into his bathing suit he rolls his underpants up neatly and puts them in his pants pocket.

"Come look at all the fish."

The water is so cold it burns, and he would withdraw at once but hundreds of iridescent minnows are darting through and around his legs as if they were two stone pillars.

"How clear the water is here," the boy says.

"Yeah. But that's nothing. Down in Stratford, Connecticut, where I'm going to go as soon as my father gets enough money, the water is so clear you can see to the bottom twenty feet down. And you can bet there's a lot more than just minnows down that deep."

"I don't believe you."

"It's true. It's because it's not like the ocean, it's called Long Island Sound. There aren't any waves. You could just

149

float on your back for an hour if you wanted to and read the newspapers."

Suddenly a large breaker curls over the ledge of rock and rushes into the tidal pool, knocking them both off their feet. When it retreats the boy is sitting in the icy water up to his neck, his sweat shirt floating ten feet away like the bloated carcass of a fish, and something slimy has coiled around his neck. He reaches for his throat in terror and pulls off a long black strand of seaweed. Then he staggers up, wades toward his floating sweat shirt, and heads for the beach, trembling with the cold and the menace.

"Your lips are blue," Paula says, sitting down beside him on a patch of sand. "And your teeth are chattering like castanets."

"I can't help it. I wish my sweat shirt hadn't got wet."

"It's better to dry off in the air. You get warmer faster." She picks up some of the sharp sand and rubs it between her fingertips. "Down in Stratford, Connecticut, the sand isn't like this at all. It's miles and miles of soft sand as white as sugar. You could lie in it nude and it'd be like being in bed."

A large sea gull circles over the tidal pool and plunges.

"First thing I'm going to do in Stratford, Connecticut, is get Dirk to take me up in one of those helicopters. They can take off straight up — like this. And stop in midair. And land any place — like on that rock if you wanted to."

What is all this stupid talk? Who is Dirk?

"Dirk's a test pilot. He's a real dreamboat. His kisses make me tingle all over. When I'm sixteen I'm going to live with him."

There is no Dirk. Paula reads those comic books called *Just Married* and *Teen Love*.

"Suppose he doesn't want to marry you."

"I don't care. I'll be a concubine, that's what. There's no point in marrying a test pilot anyhow, because a lot of them get killed. I don't want to be married to somebody and then have them get killed. Besides, when you get married people just expect you to sit home laying eggs."

"You made that up. Humans don't lay eggs."

"Don't be so sure."

The boy is not sure. What if that's another one of those horrible secrets that happen to women in the bathroom or in bed?

"Do they?"

"That's for me to know and for you to find out."

If they did it would be monstrous, like the hen that belonged to a farmer in Burnham that laid an egg measuring three and an eighth inches long and six and three-quarters inches around. After bringing it forth the chicken staggered two feet from the nest and died, and the farmer donated the egg to the University of Maine in Orono.

"You know what I wish sometimes?" Paula says. "I wish you weren't my cousin. You could be my brother maybe. Or nothing. I wish you were something or nothing. You're not much good to talk to. Particularly now that you're a saint."

"I'm not a saint," the boy says, but his blood suddenly races with her words, denying his denial.

"*I* know that, but maybe there's some people who don't." Her eyes narrow shrewdly under the thick eyebrows. "Hey, how come you never saved any of the tears from the statue?"

"I just didn't, that's all."

"Because if you'd of saved those tears, what we could of done is put them in little bottles and sell them. We could put our pictures on the label and call it 'Miracle Tears' and sell them to people."

"I don't want to talk about it."

When he left the hospital, what he expected, waited for and even feared was the talk. But nobody had anything to say about it. Not even the newspapers, since there were no new miracles to report. And the boy was surprised to find that he was relieved. He did not especially like those people he read about in the papers, Perley Arsenault in the freight yard and the girl from the Hallowell sanatorium and the druggist who tasted the tears. He wasn't even sure that he believed everything that they said about his angel.

"How do you know you're going down to Stratford, Connecticut?"

"Just as soon as the divorce comes through and my father has enough money he'll want me to come down and live with him."

"Maybe they'll make you live with your mother."

"No, they can't. She's a deserter. My father will get custody."

"How come he never writes to you?"

Paula picks up a stone and drops it carefully onto the sand, like a sea gull dropping a mussel shell to crack it open.

"How come he never writes?"

She turns her face to him and her eyes are burning.

"How should I know? Maybe he's busy or something."

"I don't think he's coming back."

"He is too! My father loves me. Not like your old father, fooling around with you know who before she went to Vermont."

"That's not true," the boy whispers.

"Of course it's true. It's as plain as the stupid nose on your stupid little face."

"That's not true, I said!" The boy springs to his feet and advances on Paula, doubling his fist up to defend his father, but just as he is about to punch her in the stomach he sees tears in her eyes, so he pushes her shoulder with his open hand and sends her sprawling in the sand.

"God damn you!" Paula cries, scoops up a handful of sand and comes at him. He throws up his hands to protect his eyes, but she doesn't go for the eyes. She seizes the front of his bathing suit with one hand, pulls it out from his body, and dumps the sand down in. The boy lashes out and his fingers find her hair and close on it and he yanks her to her knees. Then she has him pinned on his back on the sand and is straddling his chest so that he cannot breathe under the painful weight, and she slaps his face with both hands, one after the other, deliberately, again and again. He catches one wrist and twists it, and then Paula is on her back.

But something ends it. Paula is lying on the sand with one leg straight out and one bent, but suddenly the ankle of the bent leg is fastened to the knee of the other by her bathing suit bottom. And the boy realizes that that was his doing, his hands remember catching hold of it, and it came down with frightening ease. He backs away in confusion, staring at the incredible white flesh there and the clump of hair exposed to the bright sun. Paula's eyes are wide with astonishment and her face is dirty with crying.

"You filthy little hotpants bastard!" she cries.

The boy turns and runs across the stinging sand, and does not stop until he has rounded the point about a hundred yards away.

No.

Nothing.

Nothing happened. So that's that.

The sky is a perfect blue. The black pines drinking right out of the ocean. The boy does not lie.

I am a divine instrument.

OK, so that's that. That's that. That's all there is to it. That's that. Though sometimes.

No. That's that. Stop. Hard round stones, lungs. Break, break, break.

Consent.

No because sometimes when they think they see things and the things aren't that way at all. The mind is a liar.

Because.

But what if?

Stop!

Two fiddler crabs in the mud, one halfway out of his hole, the other in the open, vulnerable, to lure his adversary out, they sidestep dance, each his proud claw raised, lumbering, prehistoric, back to the dark hole, then half out, all out into the sunlight, the dance again, a dodge, a jab, a sideways scurry, a retreat into the hole, then the claw out, all out, advance, retreat.

Why?

For instance what if.

Stop!

Like water down the wrong pipe, lungs burning with water, lub dup lub dup lub dup, that's how your heart sounds, look at the crabs.

That's OK. That's that. OK now. Break, break, break, nobody's been able to improve on that in all the years.

Her.

Because unless but what if and that's not any different from before when it wasn't so that's that.

Why?

No.

The gulls. Soaring ever closer to an invisible sun in the unbelievable blue sky, above the atmosphere, the stratosphere, the ionosphere, till suddenly their wings melt, and in an instant, a blazing white instant out of all eternity, plummet into the black waves.

That's ridiculous.

The boy laughs out loud.

He is not like the others.

How long though?

A blink of God's eyelid? Brightest of all the archangelic hosts, Lucifer, resplendent from all eternity in the courts of heaven, an instant swift as thought.

No. I am a divine instrument.

Scaling a large rock. The encrusted barnacles score his bellyflesh and the boy whimpers, but there is no blood. At the top of the rock there is only black and white. The harsh exposure of sunlight on black human words. Kilroy Was Here. 43 Forever. Judy Libby Sucks. Hubba Hubba E. M. C. Polycarp's A Pill.

The boy climbs the bank behind the rock and is in a pine grove. The footing is treacherous. Sharp twigs lie in wait under the soft bed of needles. A strand of spiderweb lashes his face and he swats it away in panic. Then he stops and looks about him in the green shade. Sun sifting through the needles, the surf breaking below him, but other than that nothing.

He takes off his bathing suit, inverts it, shakes out the sand. Then he brushes the wet sand away from himself, being careful. Very careful not to. Because what my father said in the car, this is not true. The boy does not.

He puts his suit on again.

So that's that.

But what really happened?

Nothing happened. It was like this.

And he loops his thumbs on the band of his bathing suit and yanks it down again to show himself how it was that nothing happened. When he did that to her. See? All there is to it. That's all. No, because she started it. Hotpants.

He pulls them back up and runs from the grove, slipping on the needles once, scrambles over the large rock and across the hard round beach stones, and into the icy water up to his ankles.

Better now.

Calmer now, my head numbed by the icy water around my

155

ankles. I can think clearly now. Let's just think this all over.

My shoulders are beginning to sting from sunburn.

But.

And what if.

And it will come again, slowly, like the sweat that forms, drop by drop, on the rusted water pipes. God is not mocked, whose eye travels around the globe, even to the dark side, like radar, that's radar spelled.

No. Look at the ocean. What is the ocean like?

It's not like anything, you stoop, it's just the ocean. It says nothing. There are no voices. History has lied. There is only myself alone.

And the tender grace of a day that is dead.

Unfair!

I will not confess it. There is no sin. There is nobody to confess to. I am alone.

The boy crouches on the sand now, hugging his knees up against his scraped belly, and the sobs wracked from his body are black gouts of blood.

At first he is aware only of the dog. He is sitting on the sand, crying to the ocean that is only the ocean and does not answer. Then he feels a presence, and turns to find a large black police dog sniffing him. He recoils.

"Get!" he cries. The dog flinches but does not retreat. The boy scoops a handful of sand and flings it at the dog's feet. "Get out of here!"

The dog backs off a few feet and shows a mouthful of yellow teeth. He barks once, moves back a few more feet, feigns indifference, lifts a leg to pee on a nonexistent rock, pees drily, and looks at the boy again. Then the dog sees the man and scampers off to join him.

The man is bearing down across the sand. He wears a yellow bathing suit and carries strings of something black in one hand and a white shirt in the other. In the glare of the sun a trick of vision turns him into Father Tetrault, and the icy waters rush to the boy's temples, for God has seen and has sent the priest to hear his sin, to make him kneel in the sand and confess the impurity of thought and action.

The man waves the shirt.

And is, in fact, Father Tetrault, now no more than fifty yards away and still bearing down on him, his sneakered feet measuring the seconds, ticking off the distance between now and never. Because the boy, smearing away the tears, knows what he must do: even to sleep one night in mortal sin is to risk eternity. He knows that the minute those feet stop he will say to the priest, in broad daylight, in the fullness of sorrow and contrition, "Bless me, Father, for I have sinned." And still the feet come on, like Johnny I'm on the first step, Johnny I'm on the second step . . .

Or must the priest be wearing a stole to hear valid confessions?

Then again the dog is sniffing at his side, and Father Tetrault has come to a stop, and the boy, looking up at that familiar (but once more unshaven) face, has nothing to say.

"I don't know who he belongs to, but he insists on following me around," Father Tetrault says. "Well. I'm glad to see your folks took my advice. How are you coming along these days?"

"Fine, thank you."

"Good boy." He drops his shirt and the black strings that turn out to be dried seaweed. "And I see you've been swimming, too. Now I call that brave!"

"I got hit by a wave."

"Oh? . . . That water *is* cold, isn't it? It never really warms up. I suppose because we don't get the advantage of the Gulf Stream."

Father Tetrault has been in swimming himself. Beads of

water trickle down his face from his matted hair. His words remind him that he is cold and he begins a little dance, alternately spreading his arms wide and slapping them into his body again like the wings of a giant moth. And as he bobs from one foot to the other his sex jiggles around in the wet wool suit.

It is impossible! How can the boy ever have dreamed of confessing to the man in the yellow bathing suit? Even supposing there was anything to confess.

"How about yourself? You look cold."

"No."

"Oh, but you are. Here, put on my shirt. Go ahead."

Obediently the boy puts on the oversize white shirt. It has no collar. The priest sits down on the sand and the dog settles beside him, his wet tongue hanging loose from his jaws.

"Here's something I bet you've never done," Father Tetrault says. He picks up the dried seaweed and runs it between his thumb and index finger, squeezing the air bubbles and making a series of small explosions.

"Just like ladyfingers." And he giggles — not a laugh, a giggle. Then his face clouds over.

"Well," he says. "I'm glad to see you here."

But he has already said that.

"Actually, I've been hoping for a chance to have a talk with you." But there is no real hope in the dry and toneless way he says it. The boy suspects a plot. Have the priest and his mother conspired to get him here? Why?

"First of all, I have a confession to make to you. You see, when you first started confiding in me about — about what you were seeing and experiencing — well, I didn't really believe you."

"But you do now?"

"Yes. I do now."

"Did you see them too? Did you see the tears?"

The priest is slow in replying, and his answer is not an answer. "The tears are not the issue," he says. "No, that's not what I mean. I'm not talking about physical manifestations. I'm talking about what's taking place in your soul."

How does he know what is taking place in my soul? I cannot look at him, or his long-distance eyes will look through my eyes and into my soul. Or the dog, lying beside him, will see that my eyes are afraid and leap for my jugular vein.

"I pray for you," he says. "Daily. Every time I offer up the holy sacrifice of the mass I pray for your soul. Because God is putting you to a great test. You must be very dear to Him, otherwise he wouldn't place such burdens on you. Only a small child." Something catches in his throat and he clears it.

"I must speak to you about this angel of yours — this sorrowing angel, I think you called him."

"That was before I knew his real names."

"The Angel of the Bottomless Pit."

"Yes."

"And — how was it you said it?"

"Samuel. He's the angel Samuel."

The priest shakes his head.

"That is not his real name."

"What do you mean, Father?"

"That's what it sounded like to you. I can understand that. It's not your fault, and you mustn't think you're to blame. I want you to understand that, that you're in no way to blame for any of this."

"What do you mean?"

"I have been studying. And praying. The prophet Enoch in the Apocrypha, the ancient rabbis of the Jews, they knew your angel and spoke of him. But his name is not Samuel. It is Sammael. And his name is Legion."

Why is he whispering? His voice is horrible; it is dredged up from the bottom of the sea.

"I don't understand."

"His name is Sammael and his name is Legion. He is indeed a great angel, but he is also one of the foulest angels who fell from heaven. Some say he was the father of Cain, or the dark angel who wrestled with Jacob. Perhaps even the Prince of Darkness himself, who goes by many names."

The sun is darkened, and something in the boy's brain tears like an enormous curtain rent from top to bottom. "No! My angel is beautiful and good!"

"Yes. Yes, I can believe that. That's how he has to make it appear. That's why Eve ate the apple, not because she thought it was evil, but because it seemed good and beautiful. Do you see?"

The boy begins to tremble under the priestly shirt. Father Tetrault starts to put an arm around him.

"Don't touch me!"

"Please. I'm not trying to frighten you unnecessarily. You mean a great deal to me."

"I . . . have sunburn," the boy says.

"Yes. And to God, also. Never forget that. It's only those souls very close to God who are worth the devil's time. I know how upsetting all this is. But it would be on my conscience if I didn't tell you what I know. At all costs we must be prepared to resist this spirit. He is a truly terrible spirit, this Sammael, an angel of death."

The boy cups his ears with his palms, pressing his fingertips into his temples. He is going to drown. He hears the black waves breaking over his head. But gently the priest pulls the boy's hands from his head and holds them in his own hands. When he speaks again his voice is calm.

"We know something, you and I, that many people don't. Many people today who claim they believe in God don't really believe in the devil. And nothing could make him happier. Because he's the father of lies, you see, and his greatest lie is to pretend he doesn't exist. But as long as you stay close to God you needn't be afraid. Together we can battle this spirit. Above all you must continue to frequent the sacraments."

"I am in the state of grace," the boy whispers.

"Of course you are. And if you should ever have the misfortune of falling into sin, never lose hope, because that is precisely what the devil wants. He tempts us into sin, and then is the first to accuse us of it, to try to get us to abandon hope. The only thing worse than sin is to doubt forgiveness."

At this moment another figure comes around the point and is intercepted by the black dog. It is Monsignor Fallon, in drooping bathing trunks that reach almost to his knees, a pack of Lucky Strikes tucked in the waistband. A large gold watch band flashes on his wrist. His slack belly is overgrown with silver hair. He, too, carries a shirt, but it is weighted down with something, the arms and corners tied into a knot.

"Hello there," he says. "I've been doing some collecting. Would you like to see what I found?"

He sets the shirt down in the sand and unfastens the knot, and inside, hundreds of wet pebbles glitter like precious jewels.

When the boy gets back to the picnic grove the orange sun is slanting through the pines. Up above the needles are shooshing, but down below even the ocean breeze is at rest. Paula is sitting on the running board of the Dodge reading a comic book. Both his father and his mother are lying on the blanket now — he on his back, his eyes shut, his arm under her, and she on her side, her face buried in his shoulder. Again it is a photograph. If the twigs stay silent under his feet, if the boy says nothing, they will remain like that forever. And he remembers how on winter mornings in the farmhouse on

China Lake he and Gabriel would gather their clothes into a ball and hurry down to the central grate to dress. And one morning they found Mama and Papa hugging each other, for no reason at all, and seeming so happy that he and Gabriel wanted to get in on the happiness. And pretty soon they were all knotted up together over the hot air grate, all four of them, he and Gabriel still in their underwear and still clutching their clothes bundles with one arm, and all of them together in the remarkable hug.

Ten

It is only a matter of time now. Either the sniper's bullet will tear into his brain or Phantom Dill will send him crashing to the canvas. Black stars are circling Joe's battered head. And now Phantom Dill moves in on the champion, his face contorted in savage triumph: "I'll cut ya ta pieces before I finish ya!!"

But that voice! Those words! Memory balloons bubble over Joe's head. He and Jerry Leemy, stripped to the waist, hang from their wrists while a Nazi bullwhip rips into their flesh. And watching with cool pleasure, in his tall black boots, a monocle screwed into his eye, is a high Nazi officer, who says to his underling, "Cut him to pieces before you finish him!" It is the same man, the man whose face I have been trying to place all these months. At last I know his name: "That voice . . . it's BIMMELLMAN."

At last I recognize my enemy!

*No one in the entire stadium realizes that Joe, half-con-
sciously, thinks he is fighting the Nazi Bimmellman . . . As
he struggles to get out of the corner and finish the kill . . .
his crazed mind, tortured by blows, wants to tear into Dill
who has taken the place of the Torturer . . . Bimmellman.
Simultaneously with the bell he tears away from his handlers
. . . He doesn't know he's in a ring . . . He's back on
Drooten's Island . . .*

"I'll kill 'im, Jerry . . . Killer Nazi . . . Got a beard
. . . Get him . . ."

Instantly the tide of the fight turns. Joe unleashes a blind
barrage of lefts and rights. *Through the sight the killer has a
bead on Joe's heart . . . As Dill, out cold, falls past him . . .
the gunman fires . . .*

Phantom Dill lies motionless and a pool of blood widens on
the canvas from a wound in his side.

One day last fall my father and I were in Freddie's Spe-
cialty Store and I handed Freddie a dime for a Baby Ruth.
He rang up five cents on the register and was reaching into
the till for my change when a huge man in a dirty lumber
jacket appeared in the doorway. He glowered at Freddie,
then at me and my father, then at the shelves, as if he expected something dangerous was hiding behind the Wheaties.
Then he strode up to the cash register and Freddie scooped
up five pennies, pressed them into my palm and slammed
the drawer shut. But the man didn't go for the register. He
came up very close to Freddie and whispered in his ear. Freddie shook his head. The man began to talk very loud French
Canadian, but still Freddie shook his head, so he stalked out of
the shop, slamming the door behind him.

"What was that all about, Freddie?"

"He wanted a half a cup of olive oil. He just come out of the woods. Been lumbering up river. He figured now he's in the city he'd go down to the Chez Paree and get himself some poontang."

"But the olive oil?"

"For his hair."

And Freddie and my father laughed.

That was how the boy got the 1871 Indian head penny, because if it hadn't been for the lumberjack Freddie would have noticed that he was giving him a rare coin in change. The penny was coated with a dark green skin. When the boy got home he scrubbed it with a toothbrush and it gleamed like a new issue.

But later he read in the Sunday coin column that the green skin was patina and he had ruined his coin by cleaning it. It is a breach of numismatic ethics, the writer said, even to handle somebody else's coin except by the edges. He tried to make his coin look old again, rubbed it with shoe polish, soaked it in wet sulfur, once even buried it behind the garage for a week. But it only ended up looking dirty and he had to scrub it again.

Patina. You can never get it back. The boy, sitting on his couch in the furnace room, pulls the coin out of its paper envelope, hoping unreasonably that somehow, this time maybe . . . The penny gleams unnaturally. He winces and puts it away.

Things that you can never get back. And the more you try the worse everything gets, like Mama with the oil painting. What's done is done, my father says. The other day he picked the yellowing geranium off the ledge and said, "What the hell, this thing isn't going any place. I don't know why we have it taking up space," and he tossed it into the trash. That night the boy awoke from a troubled sleep and thought of the plant lying in the darkness at the bottom of the trash barrel, broken, ruined, but not completely dead yet. Lying unconscious in the dark trash barrel. His father should have killed it before he threw it away. What's done is done, the boy told himself, over and over, trying to fall back to sleep again.

He thinks of these things now as he sits on his couch in the furnace room, of things that will never be the same, the rare penny and the ruined geranium, of Gabriel and the house on China Lake and the story in the paper this morning about the gentle people of Bikini Atoll. Their mournful eyes look back for the last time on the little homes in the coconut palms. And then the bomb comes in a B–29, and the bomb is named Gilda and has Rita Hayworth on its flank. An enormous pillar of water climbs the sky. The battleship *Arkansas* takes off like a twig and is never seen again. Loss. Change.

And in the bathroom behind the plank door his father asks, "What is iniquity?" There is a pause and he says again, "I asked 'What is iniquity?' and I found that it is not a substance. It is perversity of will, twisted away from the supreme substance, yourself, O God, and towards lower things, and casting away its own bowels, and swelling beyond itself . . . By God, that's appropriate now. Its own bowels."

It is Wednesday night and the boy and his father are alone in the cellar. Paula is upstairs on the sun porch, probably rereading her comic books, and the boy's mother has gone off to St. Francis Xavier devotions. And behind the plank door his father is reading the *Confessions* of St. Augustine on the toilet. Whenever he comes to a passage he likes he reads it out loud. He has been reading everything he can get his hands on lately, because the union is still on strike. He leaves notes to himself around the cellar on small slips of paper — "Every disordered mind is its own punishment" — "How then shall I find you, if I do not remember you?" Yesterday he had an argument with the boy's mother about St. Augustine.

"This business about the pear tree. I think he's all wet here. You remember how he climbs into somebody's orchard and steals the pears? Well, then he tells us that he was evil without purpose, that there was no cause for his evil but evil itself. What do you make of that?"

"What do you mean, Tom?"

"What do you make of it? You're the one who went to college. How can you have no cause for evil but evil itself?"

"I don't know. I guess it's all very . . . theological."

"Balderdash! It's a pear tree, plain and simple, that's what it is."

He tossed the book down on the table and went out to Jerome's. After he left the boy thought for a long time about evil without purpose. He wishes his father would not read St. Augustine. This, too, is a change and it makes him uneasy.

"Who will bring to my mind the sins of my infancy?" his father says now. "For in your sight no man is clean of sin, not even the infant who has lived but a day on earth. Who will bring this to my mind?"

The toilet flushes and the plank door swings open.

"Well, hello there, Little Beaver. I didn't know you were out here eavesdropping on your papa."

He hasn't called me Little Beaver since before the move.

"How's the coins? Find anything valuable lately?"

"No."

"Let's see if I've got anything here." He sticks his thumb and forefinger into his watch pocket and pulls out a little stack of change. "How about another zinc penny? Have you got enough of those yet?"

"I'll take it, Papa. They're calling them all back, so they're going to be rare some day."

"Catch!" The penny takes off from his thumbnail, spins end over end, arcs just under the beams, plummets through the boy's fingertips and smashes to the concrete floor.

"Sorry. Bad throw . . . Hey, what are you so glum about tonight?"

The boy picks the penny from the floor and says nothing. His father sits down beside him on the couch.

"Well," he says. "It's good to have you home for a change, Little Beaver. I would've thought you'd be gallivanting off to the novena with Mama."

"I didn't feel like going tonight."

"Uh huh. Well, I suppose once you've got nine of them under your belt it pretty much takes the bloom off the rose. How's your old friend Father Tetrault these days?"

"He's not my friend."

"Oh? What's the trouble?"

My father's eyes are mild. I do no know how to explain this fact: I cannot remember the last time his eyes were like this, like warm meadows. I want to tell him something. I want to tell him to stop reading St. Augustine, and to take us back to China again, and call me Little Beaver.

"Papa?" the boy says. "Papa, I think maybe I should go to Blessed Sacrament Church instead of Holy Angels."

"Why's that?"

"Well, I mean that's where I go to school, and it would probably be better if I went to church at the same place I go to school."

"Hmn. And what's Father Tetrault going to say about losing his prize altar boy?"

"Papa . . . he touched me."

A wind blows through the meadows. Clouds gather. The light burns cold before the eclipse.

"He touched you."

"Yes."

"Father Tetrault?"

"Yes."

"Well, you seem to have survived it all. I mean you're not made of Wedgwood China, are you?"

"I don't mean that. He touched me . . . where you shouldn't."

The Dill's Best in the familiar yellow package with a face in the oval. He sprinkles the tobacco carefully into the half-cylinder of paper like a farmer seeding a furrow.

"OK, now let's get this straight. Where did he touch you?"

"Down . . . you know."

"No, I don't know. Down where?"

"Down . . . down there. He touched it."

He licks the cigarette paper and several strands of tobacco stick to his lower lip. He spits onto the concrete and says, "Are you telling me now that this priest touched you on your — *penis?*"

The word is ugly, like anesthetics, hysterectomy, uterus.

"Yes."

He has left the room. He is out in the kitchen area slamming drawers, talking to himself. He was looking for matches, for he returns carrying the tin matchbox holder that hangs over the iron stove. There is an explosion of sulfur in the cellar air.

"When?"

"Papa?"

"When? When did this happen?"

"Last Wednesday night. After benediction."

"OK. And maybe this was just an accident? For instance, did he just brush against you, or what?"

"No. It was after benediction and Walter Caron and Philip Proulx, who were the other altar boys, had already left. And I was helping Father Tetrault fold up the vestments and put them away, and he reached down and — and touched me. And I got frightened because I didn't know what he was doing, but he just laughed and said that wasn't anything to worry about."

My father whistles a jet of smoke. "Good Christ! That explains a hell of a lot of things, I guess."

169

"What, Papa?"

"You're sure of this? You're absolutely sure of what you're telling me? Because this is pretty serious business."

"Yes."

"Good Christ! Last Wednesday . . . What was last Wednesday's date?" He opens his wallet and runs his finger down a pocket calendar. "Last Wednesday night . . . God! I knew there was something funny about that bird the minute I laid eyes on him."

He sits at the porcelain table under the fluorescent light, a bottle of black ink and blank stationery at his left hand, scribbling on a pad of scratch paper. He is composing a letter to the bishop. It is like no letter he has ever written before: he will not stand up when he finishes and read it to everybody like the underwear letters with a smile of happy anger on his face. Every so often he draws a large X across the pad, crumples the paper, and tosses it on the floor. Then he opens the bottle of Poland Spring Gin and pours another warm glassful. The glass is the bathroom tumbler, crusted with calcium deposits from the hard water.

"I could have told you," he says to the boy, who is sitting on his father's couch. "Just the way he smokes his cigarette. A fag with his fag. That's a bad joke. What's the name of those other two boys who were with you?"

"Walter Caron and Philip Proulx."

"But they left?"

"Yes."

"How the hell do you spell Proulx anyway?"

My mother comes back from church. "It's raining out, Tom, but just a gentle summer rain . . . What are you doing?"

"I'm writing a letter to the bishop."

She does not follow it up. She assumes that he is being sarcastic, fixes herself a cup of tea, drinks it standing up by the kitchen counter, kisses him good night on the cheek and goes upstairs to bed.

"What are you still doing up?" he says to me. "It's long past your bedtime."

Maybe he won't finish the letter tonight, and tomorrow we can talk it over again. I lie awake and listen to the sounds on the other side of the door — the crumpling of papers, the tumbler filling again, the chair grating against the floor. Once the furnace room fills with light and he passes through on his way to the bathroom. After he returns there is a long silence and I cannot tell what is happening. Then the chair makes a very final sound, and he is walking around the room and moving things.

I slip out of bed and peak through the crack at the edge of the door. My father is putting on his raincoat.

Hurriedly, in the darkness, I get dressed. I am still groping for my sneakers when I hear the cellar bulkhead groaning open to the night.

He is about a block ahead of me, moving unsteadily but with great determination through the night rain. He bobs into clarity under a streetlight, the rubber raincoat hanging stiff from him but the body moving queerly underneath. My father is a penguin. At the next streetlight he stops, looks up, looks down at his coat, pulls the envelope from his pocket and drops it into the mailbox.

What's done is done. I back into the doorway of the laundry because he is bearing down on me and I pray that he will not see me. But halfway here he stops and lights a cigarette. Then he returns to the mailbox.

He is pulling wooden matches from his pocket and trying

to light them on his shoe, on the wet side of the mailbox, on the pavement. Then he stoops down and strikes a match on the concrete post just under the box. It flares up and he raises it, cupped under his other hand, pries the lips of the mailbox open with his elbow and aims the match at its mouth. It sputters out in the rain. He repeats the whole process again. And again. He is littering the pavement with burnt-out match carcasses. Finally a couple comes down Water Street, wrapped in each other's arms, and my father abandons the mailbox.

He passes the doorway of the laundry muttering, in a wet voice, "O Christ! O Jesus Christ!"

"I think you know who I am, young man?"

"Yes, Father. You're the bishop."

"Yes, Your *Excellency*," Monsignor Fallon says. "The bishop is His Excellency."

"Yes," the bishop says. "I am the bishop."

The bishop removes his biretta, which is topped by a lilac-colored pompom, and reveals yet another hat, like Bartholomew Cubbins, a lilac-colored satin skullcap. He hands the biretta to Monsignor Fallon who hangs it up, all alone, on one of the bony fingers of the hat rack by the door. Then everyone sits down — the monsignor and the boy on the sinking velveteen cushions of the sofa, the bishop in the leather club chair by the window, and the other man on a straight chair in the shadows. Father Tetrault is not with them. The afternoon sun blazes on the gems of the mammoth pectoral cross. The bishop folds his hands on the lilac sash which he wears higher than his belly, like a woman with child. The even row of small buttons down the front of his cassock is interrupted just below his folded hands by a button that has no buttonhole; the cassock is carefully misbuttoned the rest of the way down.

"And this is the young fellow you were telling me about, Monsignor?"

"Yes, Your Excellency. He was the first."

"I see. You look like the sort of chap who would tell the truth. Are you?"

"Yes, Your Excellency."

"You'll have to speak up," he says, tilting his head on one side. "I don't hear very well."

"Yes, Your Excellency."

At this the bishop chuckles, and the wattles under his chin tremble; they are raw from too much shaving.

"I understand that there have been no . . . disturbances lately concerning the statue?"

"That's correct, Excellency. Things have pretty much quieted down . . ." The bishop raises his hand to stop Monsignor Fallon and turns to the boy instead. "You haven't seen anything lately, have you?"

"No, Your Excellency."

"I see. That's just as well. I think, however, that Mr. Rafferty here has something to say which might be of interest to all of us?"

Mr. Rafferty is the man in the shadows. He has shiny hair and a pencil mustache, and is deeply tanned. He has been staring at the boy for several minutes with a disturbing intensity. He reaches beside him, now, for a brown paper parcel and begins tearing at the wrappings. "If you will allow me, Your Excellency." The paper falls to the rug, and in his hands Mr. Rafferty holds a small but perfect replica of the statue of the angel.

"Mr. Rafferty is an artist. A sculptor," the bishop explains. "In fact the very sculptor who made the statue in your church."

"Well!" says the monsignor.

"Not so much a sculptor, actually," Mr. Rafferty confesses. He does not look like a sculptor — more like a real estate

173

salesman or an elderly boys' gym teacher. "Actually, I'm a modeler of plaster figures, though I think I can lay claim to being one of the best in my field. I've turned out thousands of these figures over the last thirty years in my factory in Somerville, Massachusetts — Plaster Arts Products, we're called. The one in your church was done — oh, about twenty-five years ago, anyway, because that's when I stopped making the larger items in that line. There's been more sales potential in these smaller ones, I find."

"How did you find out about our statue?" Monsignor Fallon asks.

"I come up to Winthrop every summer to stay with some friends, get a little fishing in. Aurele La Flamme of Winthrop. Maybe you know him?"

"I'm afraid not," the monsignor says.

"Well, this year when I arrived I found the *Dispatch* running pieces about a weeping statue up here in Deauville, and you can imagine my surprise when they showed a photograph of the statue and it turned out to be my very own!"

"And I think nothing like this ever happened to any of your other products?" the bishop says.

"Never. I have, as I indicated, factory-produced thousands of statues in my career. They're scattered throughout New England and New York State. But the phenomenon which occurred in the statue under question has never occurred in any of the religious or profane images produced in my factory."

He picks up his chair and hobbles it out of the shadows now, to a point midway between the sofa and the bishop's chair. With his knowing right hand he hefts the statue in front of their eyes.

"The raw material in this statue is pure gypsum. Gypsum is dissolved in water and then poured into molds made of glue or gelatin . . ."

"I beg your pardon," the bishop says, tilting his head again. "Glue or . . ."

"Gelatin."

"I always thought gelatin was something you put a fruit cocktail in, didn't you, young fellow?" He smiles at the boy.

"Yes, Your Excellency."

"Following that," Mr. Rafferty says, "as soon as it has coagulated, the image is taken from the molds and placed to dry in the open air and the sunlight. When a piece is thoroughly dried, it is checked for possible imperfections, then turned over to my painting department. The painting is done by means of spraying machines, using varnishes with a nitrocellulose base. The plaster piece forming this angel, like the one in the church, was taken from the molds all in one block, without any further addition."

"I'm afraid that's a bit too technical for me," His Excellency says. "Tell us, Mr. Rafferty, is it conceivable that a bubble — that somehow a moisture bubble, say — could have been trapped inside the statue and caused the . . . leakage?"

"No. Such a thing is impossible. Plaster images are not fired in a kiln and cannot hide internal bubbles or cracks. They are all in one piece and rather thin. The weeping angel — the one in the church — is only about an inch thick throughout. The varnish is absolutely waterproof and no dampness could rise to the surface from underneath. Even if there were any dampness present — and after all these years — but even if there were, it would drain out the back of the image — right here" (his finger drums on the angel between the wing blades) "and at most could leave a small stain in its trace. It is inconceivable, it is absolutely inconceivable that there can be any natural explanation for the volume of tears that people saw flowing from the eyes for several days."

He stops. The bishop is tapping the tip of his nose thoughtfully with his forefinger. Are there actually tears in Monsignor Fallon's own eyes? And Mr. Rafferty says, in an altered voice, for the first time unsure of itself, "I wish I had the faith that I lack."

"How's that?" the bishop says.

Mr. Rafferty does not repeat himself, but the bishop must have heard anyway, because he says, "We all need to strengthen our faith in these evil times. To emulate, perhaps, the faith of little children. Suffer the little children. We are a supersophisticated age. But we still have much to learn from innocence. I think" (smiling at the boy now) "you were due to make your confirmation last month?"

"Yes."

"But I don't recall seeing you. He was ill, was he not, Monsignor?"

"Yes, Your Excellency."

"I'm sorry to hear that. Tell me, young man, what *is* confirmation?"

"Confirmation is a sacrament through which we receive the Holy Ghost to make us strong and perfect Christians and soldiers of Jesus Christ."

"Yes. And which are the effects of confirmation?"

"The effects of confirmation are an increase of sanctifying grace, the strengthening of our faith, and the gifts of the Holy Ghost."

"Good. Very good. What do you mean by the gifts of the Holy Ghost?"

"The gifts of the Holy Ghost are Wisdom, Understanding, Counsel, Fortitude, Knowledge, Piety, and Fear of the Lord."

"Good again! Excellent! Let's try one more. Which are the twelve fruits of the Holy Ghost? Be careful, now. This is a tricky one."

"The twelve fruits of the Holy Ghost are Charity, Joy, Peace, Patience, Benignity, Goodness, Long-Suffering, Mildness, Faith, Modesty, Continency, and Chastity."

"Home run!" the bishop exclaims. "Monsignor, this young man does not disappoint me."

"He's a very devout boy, Your Excellency."

"I can see that. Now then. Suppose, young man, suppose I told you that I was about to offer you the one thing you wanted most in the world right now. What would that be?"

"I don't know."

"Well, think now. Would it, for instance, be a truckload full of ice cream?"

"No."

"Did I hear correctly? Did you hear that, Monsignor Fallon? A boy who wouldn't want a truckload full of ice cream?"

"I don't usually eat ice cream."

"Oh. I see. Well, what would it be then?"

"There is nothing I want."

The bishop laughs. Is he pleased with the answer or amused by it? He loops his thumbs into the gold braid holding the pectoral cross.

"Excellent . . . As you may know, your church, the Church of the Holy Angels, celebrates its centennial anniversary two weeks from Sunday. That means one hundred years. Your bishop will be here for the rededication of the church. And at that time I would like to give you the most precious gift that it is in the power of a bishop to confer on a deserving boy. What I am going to do is, I think, without precedent in the history of this parish. Monsignor Fallon, on that Sunday afternoon in the sacristy, as a very special privilege, I shall confirm this boy."

Monsignor Fallon bobs on the sofa as if everything was rehearsed, as if he was in on the surprise all along. A set of bright, approving teeth materialize under Mr. Rafferty's pencil mustache. Paula lies on the sand with her bathing suit bottom tangled around her knee and ankle. And everything

— the room, the biretta absurdly alone on the hat-rack peg, the three men smiling approval — turns into gray cardboard. In my despair I feel nothing.

"I am afraid, Your Excellency, that he's too overcome to thank you properly. This is most generous of you."

The bishop rises from the club chair and the leather cushion sighs. He comes over to the sofa and extends his right hand. His fingers are soft and pink like a baby's, though hair sprouts from the knuckles, and the fingernails are cut or bitten back to the quick. On his ring finger an enormous ruby, fatter than the finger itself. As he draws near, the odor of bishop: of incense and male underwear and extinguished candles. The boy kisses the ring.

"God bless you, child."

"I think, now, that you may leave," the monsignor says. "May he not, Your Excellency?"

"Of course. Now I'm sure you understand, young man, that there are things that it's best for your bishop not to pass judgment on until we're sure of all our facts? Let me exhort you to humility. Do not become puffed up. Listen especially to what your pastor counsels you. Until you hear from him, it would be most wise to refrain from saying anything about — things. *Nihil nimis*, wouldn't you say, Monsignor? The important consideration at the moment is to prepare yourself for the reception of the sacrament of confirmation. In the meantime, discretion. Discretion . . . it's the better part . . . by the way, there is one other matter."

This? What he has been waiting to say all along?

"I believe that I've had a piece of correspondence from your father. A somewhat — emotional correspondence, I must say. I don't think there's any need to go into the particulars at the moment."

The boy desperately wants to blink. Silver specks are floating in front of his eyes like lazy summer flies and he wants to blink them away, but does not dare.

"Your father, as I put it together, was somewhat concerned about Father Tetrault's health. Well, that's all been taken care of. I'm sure he'll be pleased to know that Father Tetrault is getting a well-earned rest at our retreat house. I had a long chat with him just the other day and, at his own request, I'm assigning him to a — quieter parish. A good man, Father Tetrault. Very active with the younger element. So. Well. God bless you, child. You may go now."

The parlor door shuts behind him. At the end of the corridor Della opens the kitchen door, impales him with her eyes, wipes her hands on her apron and disappears. The smell of boiled cabbages floods the corridor. The parlor door reopens and Mr. Rafferty comes out.

"Wait . . . just a minute here." He is carrying the statue. "I'd like you to take this home with you as a present from me."

The boy thanks him, but Mr. Rafferty is staring at him intensely again, as though he expects more than thanks. His hand goes into his pocket and he pulls out a dime and a quarter. He studies them for a moment, puts the quarter back and awkwardly presses the dime on the boy.

"Would you do me a favor? On your confirmation day, would you — would you say a prayer for me? Just a little ten-cent prayer for an old sinner?"

The boy leaves the rectory carrying his trophy, its lacquered wings glistening in the afternoon sun.

On the side away from the rectory there is a narrow alley between the church and an abandoned bicycle warehouse, where drunks pee on the way home from Jerome's. Here, alone for the first time with the statue, I take a real look at it.

It is not my angel. The eyes say nothing. They are not the

passionate dark eyes of my angel but a milky light blue. These eyes will never weep. There are thousands of them — scattered all over New England and New York State.

Where is my angel now? To whom does he belong?

And Father Tetrault is gone.

But the bishop is confirming me in an act without precedent in the history of the parish. What are they all doing with me? Is it to make up for what Father Tetrault did? Are they trying to get at the angel through me? What is the price of it all?

In the late afternoon sunblaze I bear my tragic trophy down Water Street.

Eleven

In the wooden belfry the iron bell gongs steadily on this sunny Sunday morning. Under the sound of the bell, the swelling of the organ and the ladies' choir singing "Panis Angelicus." Every seat in the church is taken, and the crowds spill down the front steps and about a hundred feet along Water Street. Monsignor Fallon has had an electrician string up a loud-speaker in the catalpa tree for those who could not get seats inside. Intermittently a voice explodes in the catalpa leaves, testing one-two-three. It is the centennial anniversary of the laying of the cornerstone of the Church of the Holy Angels.

The procession organizes in the parking lot behind the church, where waves of summer heat undulate from the asphalt. First come the little girls of the first communion class, in white dresses and veils, long white stockings, and patent leather shoes. They carry baskets full of flowers; once inside the church they will shred the flowers into petals, and the petals into particles of petals, all along the route of the procession. One of them is whimpering because a nun has just slapped her hand.

"Bless the Lord, all ye his angels," says Monsignor Fallon, and a nun at the head of the procession tinkles her bell, and the flower girls begin to move. "Bless the Lord, O my soul: and let all that is within me praise His holy name. Glory be to the Father and to the Son and to the Holy Ghost."

"As it was in the beginning, is now, and ever shall be, world without end, Amen," say the visiting priests, some of them grinding out cigarette butts under their heels. One hikes his cassock up around his hips, like a lady about to sit down on the toilet, pulls a wad of hankie out of his pants pocket and blows his nose. Monsignor Fallon pats the crimson pompom on his biretta to make sure it is still there.

Now the second unit of the procession starts to move, the boys of the first communion class, in navy blue short pants and knee socks, white shirts, and white satin ties. Then the older girls, including Paula, who wear, instead of veils, coronals of yellow flowers. Then the oldest girls, in dresses like gauze, sashed with blue for the Virgin, and blue felt badges embroidered in gold letters, TWIF. Each of them carries a single shivering lily.

"O God," says Monsignor Fallon, turning to the bishop and nodding that the time has come, "Who in Thy unspeakable Providence has deigned to send Thy Holy Angels to watch over us, grant Thy suppliant people to be always defended by their protection, and to rejoice in their companionship forevermore. Through Our Lord Jesus Christ who liveth and reigneth world without end."

"Amen."

At the head of this final section of the procession — the altar boys, priests and monsignori, His Excellency the bishop

— is the boy himself, who carries a bronze cross taller than he is. He has been chosen to lead them because he is the smallest of the altar boys. But for other reasons too. He keeps his eyes devoutly fixed on the hands that hold the cross, but can feel the pressure of all eyes upon him. This afternoon the bishop, wearing on his head a mitre of white silk embroidered in gold and silver thread, its stiffened halves rising in front and behind like two splendid horns, will seal him with the sacrament of confirmation.

There is still time. Time to think everything out again and absolve himself once and for all of the fears. Would God really let a boy whose whole life was remarkable for its piety not only be tricked into mortal sin but into the great sacrilege of receiving a sacrament of the living unworthily? The fears are unreasonable. They are temptations from the devil and must be laid to rest.

"August Queen of Heaven," Monsignor Fallon prays, "sovereign Mistress of the Angels, who didst receive from the beginning the mission and power to crush the serpent's head, we beseech thee to send thy holy angels, that under thy command and by thy power they may pursue the evil spirits, encounter them on every side, resist their bold attacks, and drive them hence into the abyss of woe."

The procession passes through the front doors of the church, carried on a wave of women's voices. It will circle the inside of the church once along the side aisles, then the altar boys and the priests and the bishop will make their way up the center aisle and onto the altar for the solemn high mass. They step carefully: the floor is treacherous with shredded daisies and chrysanthemums and, occasionally, an entire rose petal like a drop of precious blood. The boy keeps his eyes on his hands. He does not look into the crowd, though he knows that somewhere in their midst his mother watches. And his father, too. "I promise you," the angel said, "the joy of his conversion." Today, for the first time in years, his father has come to church. But the boy does not look around — not until the procession comes to a momentary halt and he finds himself by the eighth Station of the Cross. Jesus, bowed under the weight of his cross, is surrounded by women, some kneeling, one with her hands outspread in anguished prayer, one touching the hem of his garment. Jesus meets the Sorrowful Women. O Jesus, Thou didst teach the women of Jerusalem to weep for their sins rather than for Thee.

And here, as if for a sign, as if God stationed her here, a woman reaches out from the pew on the aisle and touches my surplice. She opens her mouth to speak but no words come. But her glitter-green eyes are soft with tears. "Forgive me," the eyes say, before she turns her face away in distress. It is Miss Duplessie.

Jesus Falls for the Third Time.

Jesus is Stripped of His Garments.

At the head of the procession the smaller children have already filed into pews reserved for them. Then the bigger girls. Now there remain only the oldest girls, and us. The girls halt in the center aisle, each turns and faces her partner, and at the tinkling of a bell they raise their lilies.

We pass between them. Under the trembling lily cups, under the bare arms of girls, white and tanned and freckled, under the arching arms of girls who are growing tits, we pass to the altar.

But I am without sin.

When the sun hides behind a cloud — as it must be doing now — the stained glass window over the altar is simply a large black disk.

— From all evil,
    O Lord, deliver us.
From all sin,
    O Lord, deliver us.
From Thy wrath,
    O Lord, deliver us.
From threatening dangers,
    O Lord, deliver us.
From the scourge of earthquake,
    O Lord, deliver us.
From plague, famine, and war,
    O Lord, deliver us.
From sudden and unprovided death,
    O Lord, deliver us.
From the snares of the devil,
    O Lord, deliver us.
From anger, and hatred, and ill-will,
    O Lord, deliver us.
From the spirit of fornication,
    O Lord, deliver us.
From lightning and tempest,
    O Lord, deliver us.
From everlasting death,
    O Lord, deliver us.

But when, suddenly, the sun breaks through, it is a rose on fire whose petals are not petals but a multitude of angel wings, and there is still time.

The epistle for today, from the Book of Exodus, chapter twenty-three, verses twenty to twenty-two: "Thus saith the Lord God: Behold, I will send My angel, who shall go before thee, and keep thee in thy journey, and bring thee unto the place that I have prepared. Take notice of him, and hear his voice, and do not think him one to be contemned, for he will not forgive when thou hast sinned, and My name is in him. But if thou wilt hear his voice, and do all that I speak, I will be an enemy to thy enemies, and will afflict them who afflict thee: and My angel shall go before thee."

"Thanks be to God," says Monsignor Fallon, and ascends the pulpit.

"In the name of the Father and of the Son and of the Holy Ghost, Amen.

"My dear people. For thirty-seven years it has been my inestimable privilege to labor in our Lord's vineyard, and twenty-nine of them I have spent right here in the Church of the Holy Angels. I need not, I think, tell you how rewarding that labor has been and what joys I have experienced here. Many of you I have joined together in holy wedlock; I have poured the revivifying waters of baptism over the heads of many of these children here today and placed the eucharistic wafer on their tongues for the first time; I have sealed the eyes of many of your loved ones in the sleep of the just. You know, then, that I do not choose my words lightly when I tell you that today, as we rededicate this church that God has singled out for so many special graces, is my happiest day as a priest.

"It may, however, startle some of you to hear me say that the Church of the Holy Angels is a wealthy parish. What, I hear you ask, can the old fellow possibly mean? Surely he knows, as well as anyone, how slowly the building fund inches along, how sadly in need of reshingling is the exterior of our little church, how worn these old pews are which have seen one hundred years of the faithful come and go? Yes, my dear people, all these things are only too regretfully apparent. Yet

I say to you that this is a wealthy parish, though its riches are recorded in no earthly ledger. What are those riches, what is the most precious treasure of Holy Angels? It is, to put it quite simply, its innocence.

"Its innocence. You may recall how, in the gospel of St. Matthew, the disciples came to Jesus and asked Him who was the greater in the kingdom of heaven. And Jesus called a little child to him and set him in their midst and said, 'Amen, I say to you, unless you be converted, and become as little children, you shall not enter into the kingdom of heaven. Whosoever, therefore, shall humble himself as this little child, he is the greater in the kingdom of heaven. And he that shall receive one such little child in My name, receiveth Me. But he that shall scandalize one of these little ones that believe in Me, it were better for him that a millstone should be hanged about his neck, and that he should be drowned in the depth of the sea. See that you despise not one of these little ones: for I say to you, their angels in heaven always see the face of My Father who is in heaven.' "

Monsignor Fallon pauses and looks searchingly down the side aisle. He evens up the sheaf of papers on the lectern. He coughs. Then, with mild impatience, he snaps his thumb against his forefinger, but noiselessly. Finally a nun appears from behind a pillar and hurries to the back of the church. Some parishioners turn their heads to watch her. The organ begins to play, softly.

And now, slowly up the side aisle from the rear comes Mary Margaret Pelletier, pushed by a boy from the first communion class. Like the other little girls she wears a white dress and veil and carries a basket. But Mary Margaret, who caught infantile paralysis last summer swimming in a polluted pond, is in a wheelchair, and her basket is full of untouched flowers. When they reach the statue of the angel she leans over in her wheelchair and places the basket of intact flowers at the angel's bare right foot. Monsignor Fallon bows his head in a moment of silent prayer. Her attendant turns her chair around and they start back down the aisle.

From his priedieu on the gospel side of the altar the boy watches them until the wheelchair comes to rest at the end of the aisle, and he sees the expressions on the faces of the people as Mary Margaret passes, full of pity and expectation: it would not surprise anybody if she suddenly got up from the wheelchair and started walking.

"The eyes of children, my dear people, the untainted and innocent eyes of children often see things when the jaded and world-weary eyes of their elders fail them. For theirs are the eyes of simple faith. Again and again history has taught us that lesson, the lesson of Fatima and the lesson of Lourdes. It should come as no surprise, then, that when our Lord singles out our own church for his special graces, for strange and wonderful manifestations of one of the heavenly host, it is a child who is chosen as the instrument of those graces. Not one of the learned or the great, not a distinguished lawyer or doctor or even your own pastor, but a little child of humble parents. It would serve no useful purpose for me to name this pious family to you, to cast upon them the unfamiliar glare of publicity or notoriety. For them our Lord has ordained the sheltered and hidden life, in emulation of the life of his own family at Nazareth, three hearts beating in unison with the love of God, hard-working parents who have raised their child, from his tenderest years, in the strictest piety and devotion.

"Out of the mouths of infants and sucklings Thou hast perfected praise, says the holy gospel. By now you are all familiar with the events of early June which took place in this very church. What you may not know is that long before then the angel had apparently manifested his power to a child in our midst, and, I do not hesitate to say, it may well be that it is

188

because of the innocent and persistent faith and prayer of that little soul that the angel has thought us worthy of the extraordinary favors that have been so widely reported. Many of you, I know, have been waiting for me to speak out on this subject. To those who have urged me to do so I have repeatedly maintained that it is not our province to pass judgment upon these facts. Do not wonder, therefore, that both your bishop and I assume the same reserved and dignified position as does Holy Mother Church, who does not speak except after mature investigation. Final judgment on such matters is always reserved for the Holy See in Rome, to whom, you may rest assured, everything has been scrupulously reported and whose verdict we must await with patience and humility and prayer.

"It is none the less proper, however, to ask two questions. What must we think of these facts which have shaken, and do shake, not only good faithful souls, but also those who usually show no interest in things spiritual? And, secondly, what does the angel desire to teach us?

"In the first place, as to the widely observed lacrimation of the statue, it has undoubtedly occurred to many to question why this particular manifestation, why in such a place and in such surroundings? Would it not have been more appropriate if the angelic tears had flowed from some classic statue in a cathedral, in a great city of the world, in the presence of a devout multitude? What can we think of the divine strategy, if we may use this term, which selected a city of no great size as cities go today, a city where the people are no more pious than anywhere else, nor more wicked, for that matter? And which selected this humble church of average, hard-working folk?

"We like, as a matter of mere curiosity or as a matter of intellectual yearning, to explore the fitness of things and delve into the inner congruity of things and facts. However, much

189

as such inquiry is natural, it is altogether unnecessary and vain. When we, roaming on a California mountain, come up against a gigantic redwood tree which started to grow centuries before the coming of our Lord, we may wonder what particular combination of soil, climate and general surroundings has produced such a marvelous structure; yet our ignorance cannot be enlightened; no scientific research will tell us the secret of a redwood tree. It is there! Nature, under the will of God, has produced it. Be content with that, ye mortals.

"Let me repeat, my dear people: extraordinary facts have been witnessed in this church, but we must leave it to wiser heads to declare whether they are miraculous. The Church is ready to admit a miracle upon certain and incontrovertible proofs but is equally ready to exclude it, if the proofs are insufficient. Our holy faith has no need of new miracles to defend itself and to triumph. Nevertheless, in recent days I have seen many things that are, to my own way of thinking, of a miraculous nature. In recent days many hearts, hardened by years of sin, have been touched with repentance; many have come back to the Church, many have received the sacraments they had neglected for a long while. Tepid souls have become fervent, as witness the record-breaking attendance we are now getting at St. Francis Xavier devotions. There has been a dramatic increase in public and private recitation of the rosary. No thinking man can ignore such proofs of divine favor.

"As to the second question: what does the angel wish to teach us by his tears? As the poet has said, 'All things call for tears, and thoughts of death touch the mind of men.' Holy Church reminds us that this earth is, indeed, a vale of tears. It is not out of place to think that the angel weeps over the mystical body of Jesus, his Church, and over all humanity so wounded and tortured. He weeps in sorrow for so many of those who have been redeemed by the Divine Blood and yet live in oblivion of their redemption. They are not only oblivious of Christ, but often inimical, yes, diabolically inimical, to Christ, to his Gospel and to his Church, fit subjects for punishment by Divine Justice. The angel weeps upon our sins which fill to overflowing a world that is becoming daily more atheistic and materialistic. Our twentieth century witnesses the triumph of matter and sensuality, while the flame of the spirit is obscured . . ."

Monsignor Fallon stops momentarily because somebody has started talking in church. He looks around him in annoyance and resumes:

"But there is hope in tears, too, my dear people. It is said that the angels gather up the tears of innocent children to offer them to the throne of God and to implore mercy for sinners. So too . . ."

Monsignor Fallon stops again. He can no longer ignore the disturbance because the voices are as loud as his own, though the words are unintelligible.

"I would like to request that whoever . . ." he says.

But the voices grow louder and several people are on their feet in the pews, turning their heads. The nun on the side aisle is suddenly racked with sobs. From his vantage point on the altar the boy sees what is happening and a point of ice pierces his brain. It is as if one of the spiders in his collection, supposedly dead, were to start heaving the pin out of its midsection and rise from the balsa mounting board. Slowly, horribly, Mary Margaret Pelletier is rising from her wheelchair and setting one rubberoid leg in front of the other.

Then the boy's eyes see nothing and he slides from the priedieu in a faint.

When he looks back on the afternoon that the bishop, in a simple ceremony in the sacristy before his mother and father and Paula and Monsignor Fallon, confirmed him, he will remember two things. The first is how, after all the time, there was no time. Up to the beginning of the ceremony he still was not sure. And then, just as the bishop, smiling like an uncle, bent over him to sign his forehead with the sacred oils, he knew, with cruel and complete certainty, that he was in the state of mortal sin. He hoped to faint again, as he had that morning, but though he heard the ritual slap on his cheek like a distant impact on another person's flesh and though he lost track of everything else — what the bishop looked like in his vestments and where his family stood — he did not faint.

The second is how his father shook the bishop's hand. After the ceremony the bishop came over to his mother and father and presented his right hand. The boy's father, his face flushed from a collar whose stiff wings stuck out horizontally and his tie turned over so the label showed — "Wembley. Wear with green or brown suit" — seized the bishop's hand and pumped it up and down like a car jack. But when he let it go the bishop's hand failed to drop, remained resting on the air as though the air were something solid, able to support even the weight of the mammoth ruby ring.

"Kiss it!" the boy's mother said, in a loud whisper.

Paula snickered.

"You may kiss His Excellency's ring," Monsignor Fallon explained with patient annoyance.

Suddenly his father turned into Charlie Chaplin, his body collapsing in a grotesque genuflection. Humiliated, he kissed the ring.

And the boy hated everybody for what they did to his father.

But now it is over. We are walking home down Water Street and no one can speak. I am carrying the box camera in whose darkness lie images — of me and the bishop on the side

192

lawn, and me and the bishop and Monsignor Fallon by the catalpa tree near the rectory, and my mother and me and the bishop on the rectory steps, and even one of Paula and the bishop. When the film is developed the images will become what really happened.

Paula lags behind because she has found a tennis ball in the gutter and she bounces it hard against the sidewalk as she walks.

Pung. Pung.

Pung pung pung. Pung!

"Please don't do that, Paula," my mother says.

Pung.

"Why?"

Pung pung pung.

"Because I asked you not to."

Paula waits a minute before she starts bouncing the ball again, lazy little slaps this time, and my mother doesn't seem to notice. Her face is not of this world. It is like moonlight on a rain-beaten rock. She is thinking: now I can die.

I fall behind my mother and my father, so that now there are three groups—my parents, then me with the box camera, then Paula with her tennis ball. My father has a curious walk. Because he is not a big man, he walks with something like a swagger, but he doesn't really believe in the swagger anymore, so his weight comes down on the backs of his run-down heels. He will have to take those shoes down to Ralph's one of these days and have the heels reversed.

He stops now, turns and looks at me, and finding nothing to say, gives an odd little laugh. It is impossible to describe the laugh because it is not attached to any object, just a little spasm of nervous noise. In that moment, however, my mother has gone on to take the lead of the procession. Now there are four of us.

Everybody is alone.

A tiny silver plane sails out of the sun and across the blue summer sky. I measure it between my thumb and forefinger, no bigger than that, yet maybe there are as many as a hundred people inside the tiny plane.

For Joe Palooka the long night is finally over, the night that began, months ago, in the ring with Phantom Dill, and ended with the archfiend Bimmellman crashing through the palm trees on a tropical island and Joe relentlessly in pursuit. In his briefcase Bimmellman carried the secret of the atom bomb. "I am the Fuehrer's heir . . . and I shall control the world. These American Schwein, I shall snuff them out like Hiroshima . . . Ha-ha . . . ha . . ."

The airplane is curving slowly into the path of a solitary mountain of cloud. I strain the muscles of my eyes; I will make it miss the cloud.

Then two figures locked in a death embrace, the champion, exhausted by the terrible ordeal in the ring, and the berserk Nazi, whose hand inches toward a fallen Luger on the ground. Then the enormous Bang, and a breath expelled in darkness, HUHHH! and it is all over.

Bimmellman is no more. The long night is over.

But more will yet be required. I am talking to a doctor in the hospital where Phantom Dill lies wounded from the assassin's bullet.

"Gee . . . I wish I could help him."

"Wait a minute . . . maybe you can . . . he needs a transfusion . . . We just possibly might use you if you're the right blood type . . . We haven't his type of blood at the moment in our blood bank."

"Certainly, sir . . . I hope I am . . . I was Type 4 on my dog tags . . . a universal donor . . . They said I could give to anybody . . . and often did."

I cannot make the airplane turn. I try to stare it away from its course on the cloud, but softly and silently it collides with the white mountain and disappears.

The universal donor. But how much more can a human being give? What more can they require of him?

Pung pung pung pung.

Grandma has been waiting for them on the front porch. She is dressed to go out: the brown felt hat a bell with a dent in it, the purple dress of some slippery substance, white gloves up to the elbows, a cameo brooch with a lady in profile whose nose is chipped, and, draped around her neck like a sleepy python, a scarf of rose-colored feathers. She rises from the rocking chair and takes the boy by the hand.

"We are going to take a walk," she says.

The boy's father frowns. "I think the kid's done enough walking for one day. You must be bushed, right?"

"Yes."

"Pooh!" Grandma says. "This is only a little walk. It don't hurt anybody."

Paula flips the tennis ball into the air with her right hand and catches it in her left. "I'll come too," she says.

"No."

"Why not?"

"Never mind. That is our secret."

"O for Christ sake!" Paula says, flinging the ball into the porch screen; it leaves a pocket in the screening. "Why don't you grow up, Grandma?"

Walking again. Grandma does not release the boy's hand. That close to her on the humid afternoon he can smell, under all the clothes, the confusing odor of Grandma: vanilla perfume and her own body and the memory of whisky. He hopes that no one will see them, a thirteen-year-old boy walking down the street holding his grandma's hand, and when they come to an intersection he tries to slip away but she tightens her grip. And while they wait for the traffic to clear she turns to him and smiles — a smile without malice: "You are a good Vigue," she says. "You are more of a Vigue than you are of a Dolan."

"Where are we going, Grandma?" he asks, simply to cover his embarrassment, for the question is unnecessary.

"You'll see," she says.

At the Temple of God they go not into the little shrine with the vibrations but directly to the main house where only members are allowed. Grandma presses the bell and a hand pulls a curtain back from one of the front windows. "They're here," somebody announces as the front door opens.

The living room of the main house is just like any ordinary living room except that an enormous Stromberg Carlson — the largest radio the boy has ever seen — is centered against one wall, and the familiar picture of the professor, whose eyes follow you, sits on top of the radio with a vigil light in front of it. The boy wonders if they try to contact the professor on some secret short-wave frequency that other sets are not powerful enough to get. In the center of the room they have set up a card table with a chocolate layer cake on which somebody has squeezed, in pink frosting, the crude outline of an angel. They are all here: Mr. Fortier and Mrs. Goodman and Evelyn and the women, but without their white robes, and in their ordinary clothes they are foolish and pathetic. What has he to do with these people?

"Go ahead, Evelyn dear," Mrs. Goodman says.

Evelyn steps behind some drapes into another room and comes out with a gift-wrapped box with a card stuck under the ribbon.

"This is for you," she says, handing it to the boy. "It's a present from us."

From the beaks of bluebirds come musical signs, quarter and eighth notes dancing in air, and the card says:

> On this day of days
> We hope and pray
> That all good blesings
> Will come your way.
> Your Friends of the Temple of God.

"Evelyn made up the poem," Mrs. Goodman explains.

Evelyn is older than I am and she doesn't even know how to spell "blessings."

The boy snaps the ribbon on the present and pulls the box out of the paper. A cowboy shirt. Red flannel with gold buttons and fancy gold braid around the pockets. And a leather belt with colored-glass jewels set in it.

"We hope the shirt fits," Mr. Fortier says. "It's size small."

"That's the right size," Grandma says. "He's a small boy . . . Well, what do you say about that, hey?"

What does the boy say? He looks from one face to another, foolish smiling faces waiting to be rewarded, even Grandma, who is proud because he is more Vigue than Dolan, and he says:

"There is no angel."

"Excuse me?" says Mr. Fortier.

"There is no angel. There never was any angel. I made it all up."

"That's not a funny thing to say," Mr. Fortier says.

"Or any tears either. There were never any tears."

Mrs. Goodman is shaking her head sadly. "He doesn't mean that," she explains to herself. Evelyn's wet mouth is curling into a smile. And the boy begins to scream, "I made it all up! I made up everything! There isn't any angel and there were never any tears! You're all wrong!"

"Hush," Mrs. Goodman says. "You're upset about something. But you don't have to talk like that . . . It's time for us to have some cake and beer."

Now that he has said it nothing matters anymore. He feels only an immense weariness as though his body and soul have both died, and yet something remains behind, but something which does not care. It does not care what anybody thinks or believes anymore. When Grandma is hustling him from the room, Mrs. Goodman detains him and says, "You didn't really mean that, did you?" and he does not care anymore and says "No."

"Of course not," she says. "Sometimes it's hard to believe all the time. I know because I've lived a long time." She is poking his elbow with an envelope. "This is a little present just from me," she says. "Put it in your pocket now, and make sure you don't lose it."

On the trip home Grandma speaks only once. "That is not a nice way to talk to people who give you presents, Dolan," she says. She does not take his hand.

The boy lies on his couch in the furnace room staring at Grandpa Vigue's workbench that has been turned into an altar, not so much for his sake as for them, because it seemed to be what they expected of him. On the altar is a large crocheted doily, his collection of blessed medals, a clutter of holy pictures, candles, a tumbler of wilted zinnias whose water has turned yellow and acid-smelling, and of course the replica of the statue with the bleared eyes. Nothing is anything.

He rolls over on his back and stares at the rusted water pipes overhead and listens to the voices of his father and mother on the other side of the plank door. He does not have to listen to the words to know what they are talking about. They are probably talking about his mother going back into the hospital for another operation, because the first one didn't get everything out. She postponed going in so that she could see the boy confirmed.

He gets up to yank off the light and suddenly remembers Mrs. Goodman. The envelope is still in his pants pocket, though mashed at the corners. Inside is an expensive card with a satin sachet bag on it shaped like a heart. And Mrs. Goodman has written very carefully: "For favors received bodily and spiritual and also I am eighty-eight years old and will die pretty soon. Please pray for a old lady. Yours truly, Teresa Goodman."

There is money, too, a lot of it, and at first the boy thinks it is a joke and this is play money, but the money is real. One-hundred-dollar bills with the portrait of Benjamin Franklin. Twelve stiff one-hundred-dollar bills.

Twelve

We are moving back to the little farmhouse on China Lake. At first the boy's father thought they should return Mrs. Goodman's money. But as time went on he found it difficult to offer any good reason why. If it made an old lady happy before she died, should they refuse her wishes? There were other considerations, too. The strike was over, but it had cleaned out what little savings they had. Then there were the hospital expenses from the second operation. When the boy's father had paid that off, slightly less than a thousand dollars remained which he decided to put into savings for the boy's college education.

But one day he came home from the mill and said to the boy's mother, who was recuperating on the couch, "You'll never believe what I heard today. You remember Romeo Tourtellot?"

"Who's he?"

"Don't you remember? He's the ex-Marine who bought the house on China Lake. Well, can you beat this? He's got the place up for sale already."

"Whatever for?"

"I think it's his wife. Misses the city. And I guess she can't take all that going up and down stairs, because's he's bought her a ranch house over to Winslow."

"What's a ranch house, Papa?"

"One of those little cardboard boxes that's all on one level."

They were all, of course, thinking the same thing. The boy's father was already slamming iron pipes into the ground to stake his huge Burpee tomatoes. His mother was resting on the oak swing on the front porch, getting better every day just from breathing the wisteria. It was the boy who said it:

"Papa, let's move back to China Lake."

"Whoa, there! Whoa, now! Let's not jump into things just like that. There are a lot of things you've got to think about before you go buying a house. Like money, for instance."

"Don't we have enough money now?"

"Do I look like Daddy Warbucks to you?"

"I mean my money, Papa?"

"Well, but that's *your* money, you know. That's for the future."

"Is it enough, Papa?"

"Well, whether it is or whether it isn't . . ."

"Is it, Tom?"

"Actually, yes. I think it'd go for eight hundred down."

"Then let's go back to China Lake, Papa. Please. I want us to."

The boy's father began pacing around the linoleum. Once he sat down at the porcelain table and flattened his palms down on it, getting the room level. A moment later he was up again, walking back and forth with his hands deep in his pants pockets. Finally he said, "We don't want to rush into anything. It's a big step and we ought to make sure it's the best thing for everybody. We'll talk this all out tomorrow when we're fresh. We want to be sure whatever we decide is the reasonable thing."

But his eyes were shining with unreasonable tears. And half an hour later he was saying, "What's to drink around the house? Do we have any cake? Let's all have some cake and something to drink. Let's have a celebration."

And that was how the boy brought the family back to China Lake in August of 1946.

Certain things have changed. When the boy's mother saw that the Tourtellots had hacked down the wisteria, probably to let more sun into the house, she cried. But new shoots are coming up from the ground. The roof is gone from over the old abandoned well. Mr. Tourtellot used the lumber to build himself a chicken coop, and fenced it in with the chicken wire that used to keep the rabbits out of the tomatoes. You can no longer tell just where the old garden was; it has all gone to thistle. And of course it is too late to plant anything now, though the boy's father plans to spade up the garden in the fall to be ready for the first spring planting.

Other things have not changed but only seem to have after the cellar. Like waking up in a room of sunshine. And the din of early morning birds. Then going back to sleep in the sunshine again and not getting out of bed till noon or after. Usually it is the boy's father who wakes him when he comes home from the mill for lunch. "Do you realize you've been sleeping for fourteen hours straight? I don't understand how anybody can possibly sleep as long as you do." But no matter how much sleep the boy gets his body thirsts for more. It seems to breathe sleep the way his lungs breathe oxygen. After lunch Paula puts on her bathing suit and spends the afternoon swimming and lying in the sun on Paula's rock. The boy's mother knits or takes her naps. The boy takes a book out under one of the crab apples in back and often falls asleep again reading.

Sometimes he wakes up whimpering from a bad dream but cannot remember what the dream was. He wonders if it was about the cellar. But already the cellar and its inhabitants are becoming remote. He sees them dimly, figures without faces in a black and white photograph. Sometimes a hand comes to life and lights a match and that is the figure of his father lighting a roll-your-own. Sometimes the figure of his mother pours a cup of tea. Someone speaks, and the words stick in memory but have no reason for being remembered. "It's time for supper." "Is Grandma up yet?" "Who's got the *Dispatch*?" The rest fades. It is a time of no-feeling.

On Sundays they go to mass at St. Philomena's, the church they belonged to before the move to the cellar. The whole church is no bigger than the classroom in the China school. Its windows are not stained; they are simple window glass in wooden sashes, looking out on the cars in the parking lot and on the pines beyond. Most of the time the windows are wide open to let the breezes in, and a large fan on the altar swings its head back and forth like a radar scanner. There are only two statues, in white marble, one of St. Philomena and one of the Blessed Virgin. On Sundays the boy receives holy communion with the family. He does not go to confession, though.

"Did I say grace?" the boy's father asks, putting down his forkful of potatoes just as he is about to bite into it. Before anyone can remember that he did, he is saying grace for the second time: "Bless us O Lord and these the gifts of thy providence which we are about to receive from thy bounty through Christ our Lord, Amen." This is the biggest change.

The boy's father cannot understand how he has deserved all the gifts he has received. "God knows it's not your papa who's gotten this family where it is," he tells the boy. "It must be all those prayers your mama's been saying. And you too, Little Beaver. I can't tell you how much . . . how many ways . . . the happiness you've given us all."

On Sunday mornings now he is the first one out of his pew to get to the communion rail. Then he kneels in the pew with his eyes shut and makes his thanksgiving out loud — "May this Divine Food preserve and increase the union of my soul with Thee" — so that people turn and stare at him. Once even the priest, who was still distributing communion, stopped and looked out at the congregation to see what the commotion was.

In the evenings, the four of them kneeling around the double bed, the boy's father leads the family rosary, for the intention of the mother's speedy recovery. He pauses frequently. "The fifth joyful mystery," he will say, "the finding of the child Jesus in the Temple." Then he will wait while everyone forms the mental picture, the sudden joy of the bereaved parents finding their twelve-year-old son, the boy savior, lecturing the elders in the temple. While most people say the Hail Mary at one speed, all the words of "blessed is the fruit of thy womb Jesus" getting equal time, he says, "Blessed is the fruit of thy womb," and pauses for a silent comma, then adds "Jesus" and bows his head. It takes a long time to get through the rosary.

At supper he relives the past.

"Do you remember, Anna, that time I went down to Portland looking for work? Not long after we were married — nineteen thirty-one, I think. Yes, because we still had the Ford."

"Those were hard times, Tom."

"You're telling me? But I remember one time I was driving

down toward the ocean . . . I could see the ocean down the end of the road, gray and cold . . . it was the middle of November and about four-thirty in the afternoon. The sun had already gone down. So there I was, tired after a long day of hunting for work and angry about wasting all the gas and just wanting a drink, and I noticed a little girl on the sidewalk. Kid about seven, maybe. Well, what do you suppose she was doing? She had a card table set up with a pitcher and some glasses on it, and be damned if she wasn't selling lemonade."

Paula laughs.

"Can you beat that? A gray day in the middle of November and it's half dark already and this little kid's selling lemonade . . . But that's not the point of the story. The point is, did I even have the common decency to stop and give her a penny or two? I did not. That's how much I thought about common decency in those days."

"I guess you needed those pennies as much as she did, Tom."

"Oh I needed them all right. I'll tell you how much I needed them. I needed them so much that I treated myself to two double whiskies, that's what . . . That's the kind of lunkhead your father was in those days," he says to the boy.

But it is not in the boy's power, or anyone's, to forgive him for not giving pennies to the little girl in 1931. "You're letting your peas get cold, Tom," the boy's mother says, because somebody has to say something.

And the next night he is remembering again. "You never knew my brother Andy's girlfriend, did you? . . . No, of course not, that was before I even met you. He was going with a girl for a while, a redhead from the secretarial school."

"I don't think I ever saw Andy with a girl."

"No, that's just it. He was shy around women. But he came to me once to talk about this girl he was going with. That was pretty unusual in itself, because in our family nobody ever talked to anybody. And Andy started telling me about her — how pretty she was and sensitive and the rest of it — and then he said, 'But you know, Tom, one thing that worries me is that when she talks to people she refers to the two of us as *we*. As if we were already married or something.'

"Well I should have had the sense to know what he was really saying. Obviously he wanted me to tell him that was fine. 'They all do that, Andy.' He was probably tickled pink that some girl thought that she and he were we. But what did I tell him? Me, the world's authority on everything? 'I don't like the sound of that at all, Andy,' I said. 'When a woman starts talking like that it's time to watch out. That's just too damn possessive. She must think she owns you.' What the hell did I know about women? My God, I could hardly tell one end of them from the other in those days.

"So a few days later he comes up to me and says, 'I've been taking your advice, Tom.'

" 'What do you mean?' I ask.

" 'Well,' he says, 'about Gracie. You're right about all that *we* business, that's getting a little too tight. I told her last night that we better just call the whole thing quits.'

"Poor Andy . . . he probably needed a good woman. A good woman might have helped him pull his life together."

So for the rest of the meal the ghost of crazy Andy Dolan, the best stand-up comic in Dorchester, hovers silently over the table, and no one can forgive the boy's father for the past. "Thanks be to God," he says at the end of supper, pulls out a cigarette and sucks on it. But the cigarettes are not real anymore. Though they are wrapped in what looks like real cigarette paper, the insides are made of chocolate. The boy does not understand all the changes, but they seem connected with his mother's sickness. Sometimes he sees his father looking at his mother miserably as though he were responsible for giving her the tumor.

"For the first time in my life," his father says, "I am at peace." But if he is at peace why did he smash the thermometer last Saturday? Saturday was the hottest day of the heat wave and even the boy was out of bed early because it was unbearable upstairs. Hourly his father would open the screen door in back, check the thermometer, and return to report the reading with growing indignation. "It's up to eighty-seven already." "That damn thing says ninety-one and it's not even noon yet." "My God, have you seen the thermometer? It's up to ninety-two." In the middle of the afternoon he grabbed his hammer and went out and smashed the thermometer. The red mercury trickled out of the broken column and left a small stain on the stone slab by the door.

The other night a woman on Mayflower Hill Drive thought she saw somebody out in her back garden and called the cops. When they arrived they found a man sitting in her dahlias with no clothes on. It was Father Tetrault. Naked as a peeled banana.

"O Jesus," Paula says, "am I bored! If anybody could be any more bored they'd have to be dead." She yanks up a weed by the edge of Paula's rock and throws it at the unmoving air. "Aren't you just bored right out of your skull?"

Paula, in her bathing suit, is sitting at the base of the rock in full sun. The boy, fully dressed, is a few feet away and in total shadow. "No," he says.

"Well why not?" she says. "What's there to do around this place anyway? There aren't any kids around here or anything. How come wherever we are there are never any other people there? I mean just me and you and your mother and father."

This is so. No one ever came to see them in Deauville, of course, because of the cellar. But it is true now, too, and the boy realizes that it has always been so. "God bless our little family," the boy's father says, but sadly, as if they were the only survivors of the atom bomb.

"You know why you're not feeling bored?" Paula says, squinting wisely. "The reason is because it'd be too much trouble. That's your problem."

The real reason is that he does not know how to feel. Sometimes he still hears a voice, but it is not the angelic voice. This one comes from inside the boy himself, from the hollow center that is like the center of the earth, and repeats, tonelessly, "Nothing is anything." Somebody died in the cellar, a thirteen-year-old boy, and they placed the green felt eyeshade over his eyes and laid him on his father's couch, behind the bedspread stretched out like a drape on the piece of clothesline, and everybody went away.

The wild blueberry bushes tremble. Paula reaches to the ground slowly and chooses several stones. Suddenly she is on her feet, charging the bushes and pelting them with the stones. But whatever was there is gone.

"You shouldn't have done that," the boy says. "Maybe it was Tigger."

"You're daffy. Tigger's dead."

"That's not true. You don't know that Tigger's dead. Maybe she's around the area someplace, and now that we've returned she'll come home again."

"No, Tigger's dead. She probably ate some rat poison and died. Or a pack of dogs killed her. She was pretty old anyway. Maybe she just went away to die someplace. They do that, you know."

"You can't just say that. You don't know."

"OK, so what happened to her?"

"She just got scared away for a while. She saw us packing to move and she went away for a little while. Cats can tell when you're going to move. But she wouldn't run away for good. Probably she came back looking for us after we moved and couldn't find us."

Tigger was a large striped cat who had been in the family since before Gabriel died. She had a brick red nose and a lucky extra pad on all four feet. She slept on the boy's bed, burrowing down on top of the blanket into the warmth between his legs. She disappeared the week before Christmas.

It was a Saturday and the boy's father had gone into Deauville to buy his three Christmas presents. Since they were moving and had little money, each person in the family agreed to buy one present for the others. The boy's father came home in the five o'clock darkness, his face flushed with cold and anger, the smell of whisky on his breath and no packages in his hand.

"How'd you make out, Tom?"

"How'd I make out? I'll tell you how I made out. You see before you the only man in America who's ever been spat on by Santa Claus."

"What are you talking about?"

"God's own truth. I'm down on Lower Main trying to get in those damned revolving doors at Bouchard's Department Store, which seems to be what everybody in Deauville is trying to do at the same time, and it's colder than a witch's whatzis — you know how the wind whips off the Kennebec down there — and right outside the door there's a mangy Santa Claus with his kettle and cowbell. All of a sudden he turns his head and without looking at what he's doing he spits over his shoulder. And it lands right on my sleeve, this prize-winning lunger of frozen spit."

He climbed out of his overcoat and held it at arm's length, as if the frozen germs were going to thaw in the warmth of the kitchen and become active. "What's the cat been up to today?"

What made him ask that? Did he sense something? For the first time they realized that no one had seen the cat all day. And in that instant the boy knew, despite what he told himself later, that the cat was gone for good. As if there was a connection between the two events. As if no living creature would stay around a family whose father was spat on by Santa Claus. Even the cat had deserted them.

That night the snow fell, about two inches of fine powder, but Tigger did not return. If she had come back even briefly during the night they would have known, because she had her own door, a linoleum panel with inner-tube hinges set over a hole cut in the back porch door, and there were no paw prints by the door.

After lunch the boy's mother went out for a walk in the snow, and a few minutes later he followed. He could not see her so he tracked the footprints. They set out in a confident line for the first hundred feet or so, then they became erratic, a few steps in one direction, an abrupt turn of ninety degrees, a retracing of the old steps. In the crab apple orchard the prints went berserk; there was no telling which way the person was walking. The footsteps of my mother! But beyond the orchard they moved forward again with new purpose, straight through the winter-blackened woods and down to the lake. When he saw his mother she was looking out over the skim ice on the lake that gleamed in the pale December sun and sobbing the cat's name. He went back to the house without speaking to her.

After supper it was his father. "Think I'll step out for a smoke," he said. The boy went upstairs to his bedroom and watched from the darkened window. He saw the black figure of his father against the snow, pacing about in the stiffened weeds of the back garden. Then he saw only the orange glow of the cigarette, brightening and fading among the crab apple trees. Then he saw nothing, but heard the whistling, audible even through the closed window, his father whistling a jaunty Sousa march into the night. That was apparently his way of calling the cat.

But neither of them would confess what they had been up to. With the loss of the cat suddenly everyone became separate. The next day, the first of the Christmas vacation, the boy went out on his own while his father slept and his mother worked at packing. It was a cold, gun-gray morning. He followed the main road toward East Vassalboro, planning to ask people along the way. About a mile down the road a striped cat saw him coming and scooted for cover in somebody's barn. He went after it and met the cat lady, an old woman who lived alone with seventeen house cats and an indefinite number of barn cats. She invited him in, gave him cocoa and made him take off his shoes and socks and put them on the radiator. Afterwards they went out to the barn to look. "Sooner or later all the strays end up here," she said. But the striped cat was not Tigger.

"Take him anyway," she said. "He's a pretty fellow. Go ahead."

"No, thank you."

"Then how about little Emily here? I call her Emily because she's so dainty. She's a lovable little thing. You'll love her in no time."

The boy had walked almost all the way to East Vassalboro and was on the point of turning back when a gas station attendant told him of a dead cat by the roadside just a little further up. He found the body badly mangled, the head caked with dried blood. It was a solid gray cat; it wasn't Tigger. But then a strange thing happened. As he realized in the cat by the roadside the possibility of death, he was no longer certain that this was not his own cat. He even found himself wanting the dead cat to be Tigger, and the only way he could prevent it was by shouting hysterically, "No! This is not Tigger! Tigger is striped! This is not her!"

When the boy returned home his mother had removed the latticework from under the back porch and, in a lumber jacket and a pair of his father's overalls, was crawling around under there with a flashlight.

"What are you doing, Mama?"

"There seems to be a strong odor coming from back here. I thought that maybe something might have gotten under here . . . and died. But I guess not. It must be the cesspool acting up again."

Every night they put out fresh food and water in the kitchen, and nobody mentioned the cat. For each of them it was a separate grief and a private guilt, and each had to be the one to find her, to say to the others, "Look, I found the cat. Everything's going to be all right now."

A few days before Christmas the boy's mother said, "Tigger's been sneaking in at night. She's eating her food. Look at that dish."

It was true. Then, for the first time, they talked about the cat. How they would let her take her own time and decide when she wanted to come back to stay, but how she would probably be back for Christmas. The boy slept happily that night.

In the morning he awoke to a clatter in the kitchen and ran downstairs. His father, returning from the mill just as it was getting light, had surprised the animal feeding. The water and food dishes were overturned on the floor. In the sudden blaze of kitchen light the eyes were Tigger's, dark vertical slits. But the animal was a fox, its white-tipped tail fluffed with fear. It looked at the boy blocking the doorway to the living room and his father blocking the back door, then scooted through his father's legs onto the porch, crashed through the linoleum flap and vanished in the Maine morning.

His father was white with rage. The boy had never seen him so intensely angry, as if he were not talking about cats and foxes at all: "That's the bastard that's been taking the cat's food! If I ever catch that animal here again, I'll kill it! By God, I will! I'll kill it with my bare hands!"

Of course the cat was never found. She will never be found, not even now that they have come back, and they will never know. The boy blinks tears away; for the first time in weeks he is in danger of feeling.

"But one thing I got to say for that cat," Paula says, "that was some hunter."

"Yes."

"I sure wouldn't want to be anything that cat got hold of."

The past is claiming him. The boy is powerless to hold back the flood of memory. He remembers a terrible summer morning when only he was home, and Tigger popped through the linoleum flap onto the porch with a bird in her teeth. He knew he should rescue the bird but was not sure how; he went into the living room and waited for the cat to finish it off. Fifteen minutes later the bird was still screaming. But by now undoubtedly injured beyond saving, he told himself. But half an hour later it was still screaming. The boy went upstairs and shut himself in the bedroom, telling himself it was, finally, too late.

When he came down, Tigger was in the center of the kitchen floor, crying for her breakfast. He fed her, took a paper bag from the closet and the coal shovel from the cellar, and went out onto the porch to dispose of the carcass. Long gold and brown feathers and wispy curls of white all over the floor, and in a corner, head to the wall, the bird.

But it was not dead. Its beak was smashed and perhaps its legs broken, for it lay on its side. All the feathers were torn from a spot on the back about the size of a silver dollar. But the raw spot pulsed steadily with horrible life.

He went outside and read for a while by the well.

But when he returned the bird was still thumping with life. He prodded it into the bag with the shovel and carried it outside, frightened by the small fluttering inside the paper prison. When he emptied the bag in the long grass by one of the crab apples, the bird flapped its wings but did not move.

By evening it still was not dead, and he could not tell anybody.

And still, the next morning, it refused to die, though now its eyes were closed. Had it gone blind? He dug two garden worms and placed them in front of the broken beak, but to his horror one of the worms started crawling right over the bird's head. "O God, please make it die," he prayed. But the bird refused to die. What was it trying to do to him?

The boy could suffer no longer. He took his father's ax from the cellar and standing over the damaged bird raised it shoulder high. But at the last moment he winced, for in bringing it down he missed the bird altogether and sliced off the rubber toe of his sneaker.

That evening the bird died of its own power. It had flipped over finally onto its back, its whole body gracefully arching backwards, diving into death. He poked its breast with a stick. Stiff. Finally dead. The boy wept tears of relief.

"Why are you crying?" Paula says.

For the boy is suddenly sobbing uncontrollably.

"Don't cry," Paula says. "It was just an old cat."

"No," he sobs. "Not that."

"What then? Tell me why you're crying."

He could not have told her even if he knew. He says, "My mother . . . my mother is going to die."

They are lying on the ground at the foot of the rock, Paula and the boy, his whole body shaking and his eyes blinded by tears, but now they are tears of laughter, and Paula continues the attack, tickling him without mercy.

"Oh stop!" he pleads.

"See!" Paula cries triumphantly. "See, you're not crying anymore, you're laughing."

"Nooooo," he says weakly.

"You are too. I'm making you laugh!"

She does not let up, her fingers playing his ribs like a piano. Then she too has a hysterical seizure of the giggles, though no one is tickling her, and finally she is too exhausted to continue the tickling and collapses on her back, looking up at the sky.

"Phwooo," she says, gives one last giggle like an afterthought, and falls silent.

They are both silent, lying on their backs at the foot of the rock, all their energy spent on learning how to breathe again.

"Are you still alive?" Paula asks, sitting on her haunches now and leaning over him.

"Yes. I just had to get my wind back."

"Hey," she says. "You want to smooch?"

He does not understand the word but knows, by the sound, by the way she says it, that it is something forbidden. Last spring Joseph Maroon and Bobby Durrell cornered him in the boys' room and would not let him out till he answered a question. "We got a question for you, Holy Dolan," Joseph Maroon said. "When you put your finger in your ear — like this — which has more fun, your finger or your ear?" How could you answer a question like that? But they made him, so he said, "My ear, I guess," and they both laughed, as though he had confessed to a dirty secret. "It's his ear! Did you hear that? Holy Dolan says it's his ear." He will not be trapped again, so he says to Paula, "If you do."

But it is no trap. "You have to close your eyes," she says. He closes his eyes and feels her lips on his.

And that is smooching. The press of Paula's tight lips with the hard teeth clenched behind them, painful, and he wonders when it is supposed to be over. But it does not stop; the longer they smooch the softer her lips become, and he lets his lips open like hers and feels her breathing into the inside of his mouth. And his soul leaves his body, sucked into the humid cavern of her mouth in the sinful smooching.

"Wow!" Paula says, pulling away. "Take it easy, huh?" She stands up, slips her hands into the elastic legbands on the back of her bathing suit and snaps them down smartly over her cheeks. "I'm going to go take another swim."

He lets her go, making no move to follow her, ashamed to have her see the stain on his pants from smooching.

At supper he cannot meet her eyes. When she asks him to pass the butter he almost drops it on her lap. He is glad that nobody expects him to say anything; his father is confessing his past sins again.

He lies in his bed, pressing two moistened fingers against his lips. Smooching. In his dream they are on the beach at Camden, and either they are fighting or she is tickling him, it is not clear. She picks up a handful of sand and stuffs it down the front of his bathing suit and her fingers touch him and it happens again. "I'm sorry," she says. "Did it hurt? I won't tell anyone." And when he awakens it is true, it happened again, and the hand is still there.

Thirteen

I am in love with her. She comes to me in my bed at night, sometimes in her slip, sometimes only in her panties, and her tits in the moonlight are two white flower buds. Sometimes she just stands by the bed, combing her hair with her fingers, swaying gently, her lips curled in a lewd smile. I plead with her to take her panties down, and sometimes she does, slowly rolling them down her hips, then stopping till I plead again, and they drop soundlessly to the floor. Or sometimes, still wearing them, she slides under the sheets with me, whispering dirty words into my ear, and I stroke her roundness under the petal-soft panties till I cannot wait any longer, and yanking them off I sin with her somewhere down there.

By day she is new and strange. She reads the funnies and ignores me at breakfast. Or else she finds little things to argue about — "Why do you always get toast crumbs all over the butter?" and "How come you always pick all the strawberries out of the jam?" — because she does not understand the tender shame that passed between us in the night.

She is no longer interested in smooching — only twice since the first time, and then just because there wasn't anything better to do. She forces the boy to humiliate himself, to wait endlessly for the right moment, to beg, in a voice thick with fear and anticipation, "Paula, do you want to smooch?"

"Jesus Christ, is that all you think about?"

"You used to want to," he says, hurt.

"Fish used to fly, too . . . Oh go away, stop pestering me. You're just a kid."

"I'm older than you are. I'm six months older."

"There's a big difference between chronological age and biological age," she says, out of a book. "Girls mature faster than boys."

The things she says now are sometimes different from the old crazy talk.

"People ought to care about other people," she says. "That's your problem. You don't care about anybody but yourself."

"That's not true."

"Who then?"

He cannot tell her. "Neither do you," he says.

Each time after she leaves he goes over what she said, again and again, like difficult sayings that will have a new meaning when you repeat them. When she talks about Uncle Fred and Stratford, Connecticut, now, he cannot contradict her, because though he does not believe it will happen, he fears that it will. And even though his love is doomed, and even though his father says she will turn out bad, he loves her.

School has started again, and Paula and the boy have returned to the one-room China school, but are not really there. Miss Lipchick, the all-grades teacher, took a while on the first

218

day remembering them, but when she did she remembered also that they were good readers, and satisfied on that point she promptly forgot about them again. They are the entire eighth grade class. At the beginning of the day Miss Lipchick gives them generous handfuls of paper to use somehow and turns her attention to the little ones. The boy spends the day writing letters to Paula which she must never see: long confessional letters about the secret intimacies between them. At the end of the day he tears them into bits and flushes them down the toilet. The next day he is at work on a new letter, or maybe it is the same one told differently.

After school on warm days Paula still goes swimming though the water is very cold. About a hundred feet down the lake from the sandy point where she swims, there is a clay bluff overgrown with blueberry bushes. Unseen on these heights, the boy watches her. Sometimes when she comes out of the water and shakes her wet hair out of her eyes and stretches her shining body in the too-small bathing suit, or crouches to pick the sand out from between her toes, he thinks: now! now she is going to take it off and lie in the nude! But she never does anymore. But still he watches until, picking up her towel and walking away from him, she heads back to the path through the woods. Before she disappears into the trees he tears her bathing suit off savagely. And the moment she is gone he strips off his own clothes and seizes a handful of blueberries, and swollen and stained with the purple juice he sins into the tight furrow between her bare cheeks.

It is Saturday, and his father has driven Paula and his mother into Deauville to buy Paula some new clothes for school. The boy takes the Sears, Roebuck catalogue up to his bedroom and opens it to the underwear ads for Debs and Sub-Debs. Lying naked on his bed he studies the pictures of girls in their underwear and the descriptions of them, in contour-fit cotton and luxurious lace, saucy, demure, cloud-soft, whisper-soft, ruffled and ravishing, page after page. On a piece of thin white paper he traces the picture of the nicest one, leaving off her underwear. Then, with trembling precision, he draws in her secret parts. He brings the finished picture into Paula's bedroom and puts it at the bottom of a drawer in her bureau, under a pile of panties.

He is standing on Paula's bed, then, in full view of her bureau mirror, wearing a pair of her panties, his flesh enraged by that softness. Dizzy, he falls onto the bed crying her name and sins again. Then he buries the stained panties in the garden full of thistles.

The next day, remembering all that insanity in shame and despair, he sneaks into Paula's bedroom to recover his picture. But the picture has disappeared, and neither Paula nor his mother says anything. Then where has it gone? And after-wards the boy thinks in terror of Paula's panties, of his father spading them up in the garden, but it is several days before he can get to the garden again without being seen, and by then he can no longer find the spot. Someday everything that is buried will be brought to light. But like the man in the side-show he cannot stop.

Last summer the Kiwanis brought a small traveling circus to the Deauville fairgrounds. One of the sideshow acts wasn't an act at all, simply a man in a loincloth lying on the dirt floor of a booth. He looked like a young man but had no hair on his head or body; his flesh was yellow and his cheeks sunken. He did not look at the crowd; his eyelids were closed, and he might have been sleeping, except for his right hand, which kept bringing a cigarette up to his lips. Hundreds of cigarette butts littered the ground. This, the barker said, was the Ciga-rette Fiend, who started smoking when he was a child and now could no longer control himself.

When it is not Paula it is anybody. Even in the *Dispatch*.

On the Women's Page he finds a picture of two teenage girls standing beside a large trash barrel, and the caption reads

Perform Good Deeds
Mary Olney, left, and Suzanne Foster do their good deed for the day at Foster's Beach on Lake Winnecook. The girls have been down at the beach many times this summer cleaning up after unwelcome visitors have left the area in a mess. The beach is owned by Zillah Foster, Suzanne's grandmother, and it is a pleasant bathing and picnic area in Burnham. (Photo by Rossignol)

In the photo by Rossignol Suzanne wears a stretchy T-shirt and gym shorts, one hand curves on her hip, and she pouts shyly at him. A few minutes later he is in the bathroom with Suzanne Foster torn out of the newspaper.

What death will end it all? For always after the sin the boy remembers death, he breathes death in his own acrid aftersmell. The stench of hell: a famous saint once said that if the earth were opened up to allow the air from hell to come to the surface for just one hour, everything on earth would die, so great would be the stench of rotting souls. But the boy has seen, too, the special hell reserved for him, and there are never any other souls; he is damned to an eternity alone in the abyss.

At night he still prays for the salvation that he cannot believe in. But when he comes to the end of the Act of Contrition — "I firmly resolve with the help of thy grace to confess my sins, to do penance, and to amend my life" — he knows it cannot be. He prays, then, that God will spare him just one more night, and God does spare him, so he sins again. Unable to confess, he has tried at least to amend his life. He has tried wrapping rosary beads around his hand at night, like the visiting Jesuit told the boys during the three-day retreat last spring, and has defiled the rosary. Repeatedly he has wounded the Virgin. Every sin of impurity, the Jesuit father said, wounds Our Lady, and he passed out little calendars like the banks give out. To make progress in weeding out vicious habits, he explained, you kept a record; every time you fell you put a pinprick in the date. Then, when you turned the calendar over, you saw what you had really done: it was a picture of the Blessed Mother standing on a crescent of moon. On the boy's once-undefiled calendar pinholes riddle the blue sky, moving ever closer to the Virgin's head, and on September seventeenth he puts out her left eye.

In his despair he cannot get enough of damnation. On Sunday mornings he damns himself over again, taking the sacred host on a tongue that neither burns nor withers away. And sometimes during the day, when he is less afraid of death than at night, he hates God for the injustice of it all: that he, who stood so high in God's favor, who had wanted only to be holy and good and to bring happiness to the family, should be made to suffer damnation like a common sinner.

It is, perhaps, evening. Everything is black or gray or white. The big willow at the front corner of the China yard has bleached white limbs and hairy black foliage. At the corner of the yard, too, as he comes up the road toward home, the three large stones set atop one another as a property marker a century ago are bone-white. But on that pillar now squats a black angel, his scaly wings at rest, waiting.

"I have been waiting for you," he says.

"You can't stop me!" the boy cries. "This is only a dream and you can't stop me!"

He passes into the yard unmolested.

But that knowledge does not keep him from waking up screaming in the night.

My father: I have made my father what he is and I have become what he was. On this hot Sunday afternoon in September, he sits at the dining room table over a second coffee and reads St. Augustine. My mother is washing the dishes from the noon meal. I am at the table, too, reading the Sunday papers. A trapped wasp is nose-diving crazily into the windowpane.

Paula, who has changed into shorts and a halter, is in the living room, in sight of both of us at the dining room table. Lying on the braided rug made out of my father's old clothes, she cleans her fingernails with a large boy scout knife that she stole somewhere.

"When I remember memory," my father says, "memory itself is present to itself through itself. But when I remember forgetfulness, both memory and forgetfulness are present: memory by which I remember and forgetfulness which I remember." When he wants to understand something, my father reads it aloud to himself. This time he reads it aloud twice and frowns unhappily.

Paula, barefoot, lying on her belly on the braided rug and scraping under her nails. She has a mosquito bite on the inside of her left thigh. She puts the knife down for a moment and scratches noisily.

I read about the war, the new one — how we may have to go to war with the Russians before they can learn how to make an atomic bomb.

My father finds another passage. "The unlearned," he says, "rise up and take heaven by storm, and we, with all our erudition but empty of heart, see how we wallow in flesh and blood!"

That is why President Truman has fired Secretary Wallace.

Paula spreads her legs on the braided rug. Her right leg doubles over, the heel journeying up the inside of the left leg. The heel stops at the upper left thigh, just at the opening of her shorts, and abstractedly begins to massage the mosquito bite, while her hands continue working with the knife.

All of a sudden my father says savagely, "You're getting

too big to be going around with your tits on show and those dinky britches riding up in your crack. Go upstairs and get into something decent."

Paula looks up at him in dismay, making sure she is the person he's talking to. The boy feels at once ashamed and angry, and to his own surprise says, "Leave her alone. She's not bothering you."

"What?"

"She's not bothering you."

Paula does not go upstairs. Brandishing the open knife she charges the back screen door in tears, slamming it behind her.

The boy's father steadies his coffee cup in the ring of the saucer with great care. "Now then," he says, "what's eating you?"

"Oh go to hell!" the boy's voice cries, and he too heads for the screen door.

He finds Paula in the crab apple orchard, slamming the knife into a tree about five feet away, sobbing.

"He hates me," she says.

"No, he doesn't."

"He does! He hates me because of my mother. Well, I can't help that. I didn't ask to be born."

The knife thunks into the tree. She twists it out of the trunk, taking away a slice of bark about the size of a hand.

"Please stop, Paula."

"I'll do anything I feel like," she says. "It's not my fault that we have gypsy blood in the family. My mother is part gypsy, you know. So that means I'm part gypsy too."

The boy has never heard this before: he is afraid to challenge her directly, so he says, "How can you be a gypsy and have blond hair?"

Paula snuffles scornfully. "I didn't say *all* gypsy, I said *part*, stupid . . . My mother had a cousin who was the gypsy queen of Perth Amboy, New Jersey. She was the guide for all the gypsies about love and marriage. She died when I was seven and we went to her funeral."

Remembering the funeral, she stops throwing her knife.

"All the gypsies in New Jersey were there, all in rags and tatters and not even washed, because it's against an ancient law to use soap when the gypsy queen dies. But she wasn't in rags — she was lying in her coffin in a gold and red satin gown with a necklace of gold coins and a jeweled star on her breast. People dropped coins into the casket. And on the outside of it there was the face of a clock with the hands put in by crayon at ten of nine, because that's when she died. She was the most beautiful lady I ever saw.

"And then, when they buried her, they poured some wine on top of her — that was the queen's share — and drank up the rest of it. Even me, and I got drunk because I was only seven."

Paula becomes strangely quiet, remembering the beautiful dead lady who was the gypsy queen. Suddenly she starts flinging the knife into the crab apple again, harder than ever. When she yanks it out it leaves tender green wounds.

"Paula, don't! That's bad for the tree."

"I don't care!" she cries. "All you people ever think about is good and bad. That's the whole problem with your screwy family, you think everybody's got to be either good or bad."

The knife thunks into the crab apple again and shivers wickedly. The boy reaches for it first, but just as his hand is about to seize the handle, Paula's darts in and pulls the knife from the tree, and his hand closes on the blade.

"O Jesus," Paula says, "that was a stupid thing to do."

The boy's left hand is doubled into a fist.

"Let me see it . . . How can I look at it if you keep your fist shut?"

She takes his hand and unfolds the fingers; he holds a palm

225

full of blood. She licks the blood away. The cut is really very small.

"Maybe you won't have to get the doctor this time," she says. "But you know you're not supposed to get cuts."

The boy wads his hankie into his palm and makes a fist again. But he doesn't really feel the hankie there. He feels, instead, the memory of Paula's warm tongue on his palm. And he thinks not of the hurt, but of his love for the angry gypsy girl who has tasted his blood.

The boy did not have to go to the doctor this time. His father cleaned out the little cut with Mercurochrome, spread a thick layer of Vaseline over it and wrapped his hand in gauze. It continued to bleed, but very slowly, and every hour or so his father changed the dressing. By the time he went to bed it had stopped bleeding. Still, they let him stay home from school in the morning. The boy lifts the gauze carefully now to check again; there is no fresh blood.

He is alone. Paula is at school, his father at the mill and his mother taking one of her twice-daily naps. The sky is cloudless. The abnormally hot Indian summer weather continues. But even so, even sitting in the full sun now on Paula's rock, the boy feels the chill of the air on his naked flesh. He stares at the skin protected all summer long from the light. Now, exposed to the September sun, it is a white beyond whiteness, an almost blue. He stares at the diseased little sex between his legs. He is desolate. He thinks of his old friend Father Tetrault, sitting like that in the moonlight in somebody's dahlias, a crazy smile on his face. The boy shuts his eyelids tight to drive the memory away.

But a clatter in the sky makes him open them quickly and look up. A flock of swallows, a hundred at least, passes overhead in front of the sun, migrating to their winter home. He watches them for several minutes until they disappear over the low chokecherry trees. Only then does he realize, in slowly mounting fear, what he has seen. The swallows are all flying north.

Suddenly the sky turns bitterly cold and the boy begins to tremble violently. But the cold, he knows, is not physical. It is because what he has feared for weeks has finally come to pass. He has been discovered. He feels the pressure of eyes watching him. He looks helplessly at his clothes, fully ten feet away at the foot of the rock.

But it is too late. The dark eyes bear down on him, and there is no compassion in them, and the terrible sword glitters in the cold sunlight.

"I find you in sin," the angel says.

"No!"

"I find you in sin. Is there any living creature so unspeakably foul as you are, so hateful to heaven? I offered you my heart. I offered you a life of intimate union with me, and you have forsaken me for the filth and degradation of the flesh. You have denied me to the people. You have abandoned me. From whom shall you find forgiveness now?"

"Please," the boy says.

"Where is the priest who can forgive you your sins?"

"The priest . . . what I said about the priest," the boy pleads. "That was for your sake."

"Yes. But you were only an instrument. The priest was my enemy. You see how I humble my enemies, how I drive them before my face. I have the power to give and the power to take away. I have given you much; I shall take away all."

"What do you mean?"

"The little girl — your cousin — do you love her?"

"Yes."

"It is a forbidden love. She will leave you. I shall take her away."

"Where?"

"Time will reveal that. It will be soon."

From the boy's throat comes a single strangled cry.

"And your mother . . ."

"I don't want to hear!" the boy cries. But he cannot stop the words that spring, like toads, from the angel's mouth.

"I shall take your mother, too."

"No!"

"Your tears are foolish," the angel says. "Tears cannot save your mother. She is going to die."

"But my father . . ." the boy whimpers, "not my father . . ."

"No, not yet. But he will drink of a cup more bitter than death. Do you see what you have done to your father? That is only the beginning. I have kept my bargain. I promised you his conversion. But I do not promise his salvation. I shall darken and confuse his mind, and he will know despair of the spirit, as you have."

"Please!" the boy cries. "I'm sorry!"

"Do you ask me for forgiveness? You have denied me. You have abandoned and betrayed me. One does not trifle with angels. You are only an instrument and I do not need you anymore. But I shall be manifest again."

"No!"

"Tomorrow, in my church, the tears shall flow once more. And then I shall do such things as you have never dreamed possible."

"NO!" the boy screams, but the angel is gone. He is alone with his nakedness, sitting on Paula's rock in the September sun.

But now he knows what he must do.

Fourteen

The darkness of churches. Churches are darker than the surrounding darkness, darkness clings to them, they breathe particles of darkness as a plant breathes light.

It is after midnight. All the doors will, of course, be locked, but in the rear of the church one small basement window is always left open in a hopeless attempt to air out the lavatory. When the boy puts his head in there the fumes are palpable — the unmoving odors that have saturated the damp stones and mortar of the foundation and will remain there forever. He withdraws and looks around him apprehensively. He rolls his little Indian blanket into a tighter wad and, slipping feet first into the window, sits on the ledge, gathering nerve. His body fears the descent; his feet, hanging free inside the darkness of the lavatory, have no assurance of a floor to meet them. Maybe they will simply keep on falling or touch down on some unnamable horror. His will forces his body to act, and clutching the Indian blanket in his armpit he drops several feet to the floor inside.

The boy trembles in relief. He is suddenly aware of a burning need to pee. He aims the hard stinging stream into that corner of darkness he remembers as the toilet. It hits the unseen wooden seat, finds the bowl momentarily and rattles into the water, loses its way again and splatters on stone.

He leaves the lavatory and is in the lower church, where catechism classes are held and, at nine o'clock every Sunday, the children's mass. While Monsignor Fallon says mass for the grownups upstairs, Father Tetrault — but somebody else now — says mass for the children, who sit on folding camp chairs and kneel on the cement, with the nuns making sure they pay attention, and some child who has been fasting from midnight always throws up after communion. The boy gropes in darkness for an aisle and cannot find one. He stumbles through the underbrush of wooden camp chairs toward the downstairs sacristy whose stairs lead to the one above. At the foot of the altar he collides with a stand-up microphone that smashes to the floor.

After the absolute darkness of downstairs the upstairs church is almost light, though there are only three dim sources of the light. One is the perpetual red flame on the main altar like the eye of God Himself. It is extinguished only on Good Friday when the Blessed Sacrament is removed, the door of the gutted tabernacle yawning wide, and God descends into hell. The second is a small wall lamp by the vestibule. And the third is from the votive candles — a solid bank of candles, though most of them have burned down — in front of the statue of the angel.

The boy is trembling again. There are figures in every niche and corner of the church, made lewd by the unfamiliar light. An alabaster angel hunches over in a grotesque and obscene act, a naked thigh protrudes from behind a pillar, a random shadow smears a gash of malign laughter across the face of a cherub. They are like figures in a fun house.

The boy passes in front of the altar, genuflects, enters the front pew on the center aisle and carefully eases himself along the pew toward the side aisle. He is sitting directly in front of the statue now. The eyes are not visible; their sockets are deep pools of blackness. The boy's own eyes are wide-gaping and do not leave the statue; his whole body is wound up beyond winding, like the mainspring of a clock. He falls asleep.

A chime, probably from Blessed Sacrament a mile across town, signals the half hour, and he awakes, but he does not know what half hour it is. He is clutching the blanket to his face and the binding is wet from sucking. Nothing has changed. The statue is exactly as it was before.

The boy leaves his pew and moves up to the side altar. He climbs over the railing and stands to one side of the statue. The terrible sword remains pointing downward at the votive candles. Suddenly, his arms spread wide and the blanket in his hands, he flings it over the angel's head, at the same time giving a frightened outcry and leaping back against the wall. Under the drape nothing happens.

He is moving toward the side door with the draped statue in his arms. It is hollow, and not much heavier than a small child, but his arms ache, and his fingers are so tightly constricted that they have gone numb. With his hip he leans against the metal bar that unlatches the door from the inside, and the night airs rush in at his throat. His feet go loose under him but he does not fall. He reaches the parking lot in back of the church and places his burden on the back seat of his father's Dodge.

Then, for several minutes, doubled over in darkness, he throws up, but nothing comes out of his mouth.

*

That is only the beginning: he must make it all the way home again in his father's Dodge. He does not clearly remember the drive to Deauville. Like the eight-year-old in the newspaper, who, when his father had a heart attack flying a Piper Cub, brought the plane in for a landing with the control tower guiding him down. But the boy does not know who or what guided him into Deauville — a boy in the belly of a mechanical fish, plunging through the depths of the night.

The boy turns on the ignition and when the engine catches tries to throw it into first. It stalls. He tries again. Again. A light goes on in the upper story of the rectory. Lost! All lost! The boy begins to cry.

And still crying he finds himself steering a car that is suddenly in motion. It cuts across a little patch of lawn and swings out onto Water Street in a wide arc, just missing the curbstone on the left side. He is driving the car again, sitting rigidly upright to see over the dash. He travels the length of Water Street before he thinks to bring the car over to the right. Luckily there is no traffic.

The engine is wailing. He hears his father shouting at him. "Never mind what your speedometer says, it's your engine that knows what's going on inside a car. Listen to what your engine tells you! Throw her into second!" The gears snarl into second as he passes over the Kennebec River. This time he holds the car steady in the center of the road, frightened by the closeness of the iron girders on either side of the bridge, and beyond and below them the river.

On the other side of the bridge he encounters blackness and realizes that he has forgotten to turn on the lights. His headlights carve a tunnel into the dark, and it is this tunnel he drives into now, fearful that at any moment he will scrape the walls of the tunnel of night. The gauze on his left palm is soaking wet.

Two blazing eyes appear down the road. As the eyes ap-

232

proach they lower but still come on. The boy swings to avoid them, feels the right wheels bouncing along the shoulder and hears the limbs of unseen trees clawing at the metal of the car, which does not stop. "O my God I am heartily!" he shouts, as the eyes come straight at him and then, miraculously, pass him by.

The boy is perhaps a mile from home when he sees, at the end of the tunnel, a figure waiting in the road. The figure becomes a beast with horns. It does not move. The boy leans hard on the brakes and the car, in gear, lurches to a stop only a few feet from the beast.

It is a moose. Remembering all he has heard, that the single most important thing is not to frighten them, the boy turns off the lights and waits for the moose to go away.

But after several minutes of waiting silence he knows, with growing fear, that he can never know. Is the moose still there or not? Motionless in the becalmed car, he becomes aware not only of the presence of the animal, a few feet from the nose of the car, waiting for him in the darkness, but of that other presence as well, lying on the back seat under the blanket. For the first time he is fully aware of his position: he has turned his back on the angel's sword!

He screams.

An instant later there is a loud trumpeting, tinkling glass and crunching tin, the moose dancing on the hood. Then the sound of hard hoofs trotting off down the road and crashing into the brush.

The lights on the Dodge are out for good.

*

A late moonrise. Objects are clear now. The boy walks along the road, carrying the shrouded statue in arms that have long since ceased to ache. He hears, when he is nearly home, a chugging noise behind him, and turns to see a single light coming along the road, so far to the right that it must be riding the shoulder.

A tractor overtakes him, a man in a straw hat and overalls in the driver's seat, and on a plank seat behind him a girl about twelve, facing backward, holding onto the upright mowing bar that cuts the air like a monstrous scythe. The tractor coughs to a stop.

"That your auto back there, sonny?"

"It's my father's . . . a moose . . . jumped on it."

"Eyah. Heard of things like that, haven't we, Debra?"

Debra turns her head slowly and looks at the boy in the moonlight with eyes that do not seem to see him. She says nothing. If she had not turned he would think she was asleep.

"You need a lift maybe? Debra don't mind shoving over."

"No. I'm almost there."

"Suit yourself." The engine begins to cough again. Over its noise the farmer says, "I've no call to be inquiring where you're going this time of morning. Any more'n you have with me and Debra. Just one thing, though. Debra was kind of wondering what you got in that blanket. A body, maybe?" He chuckles without smiling. Debra's face remains immobile, sleep-staring.

"It's . . . it's something I didn't want to leave in the car."

"Eyah," the farmer says, and the tractor moves on, mowing the night down.

In a few moments it will be all over. The boy has removed the plank cover from the abandoned well. He stands the statue upright on the rim, still wrapped in the Indian blanket, then gives it a shove and watches it topple. As the statue topples he shuts his eyes, awaiting the final crash as it hits bottom, the sound echoing from the depths of the pit like the last word of the broken angel.

The sound does not come. The angel is wedged in the mouth of the well barely two feet down, caught by a wing and the tip of the extended foot, and the blanket has come loose from his face. He stares at the moon with sorrowing eyes, fiercely alert, tragic with knowledge.

The boy panics. He sits on the rim of the well and kicks at the astonished face of the angel. The figure does not budge. With both feet he stamps on it, whimpering. Suddenly the plaster wing crumples and the statue falls, and the boy, stamping on air, falls with it.

The crying is over. At first he cried long and loud, from hurt — the bleeding hand, a foot broken or sprained — and from terror, but that was still in the first division of time in the well. At that time his mind was not right. Groping in darkness among shards of plaster, among rocks that were wet — but there was no water — his hand found a structure of bones, the rib cage of an animal, and he cried and called it Tigger but it was not so. When he had used up the crying he became cold, and finding the blanket beneath him he managed to wrap himself in it. He crouched in frightened silence then and listened to the sounds of the well — the small sounds, the chatter of crickets, of unknown beetles, and the large constant sound that is the moaning of the homeless sea. When you put a shell to your ear you can hear the sea, but inside a well in the dark earth you are swallowed up by the sound of the sea itself. And when nobody came the boy felt darkness in his brain and slept.

When he awoke it must have been morning, for the apple

trees up above were loud with birds. But looking up he saw a sky full of stars. Then it is true! he thought. You can see the stars by day from the bottom of a well. Could his father believe that? Down in the cellar in Deauville, from the little window over the steel tub, they tried but saw no stars; even from above ground the stars were hardly visible because of the perpetual glow in the sky from the paper company.

In this second division of time the boy feels a rare peace. He watches the stars that have never been so brilliant. Stars are the souls of the just; the evil become the spaces between them. Out of the depths he has cried and will be heard. It is only a question of time. They will find the damaged car and then the planks removed from the well, and they will save him.

As he has saved them. He sleeps again.

He awakens in confusion. On his tongue an alien taste, a milky bronze taste. The stars are still out. But maybe he was wrong and morning has not yet come, is hours away. Or has come and gone. How many suns have risen and set? I have been in the well for three divisions of time, he thinks. But there is no way of measuring these divisions except, perhaps, by his own heartbeat, and no man can count his own heartbeats. A man might be in a pit for eternity, and up above, on the earth, the sun have not yet risen on his first day in darkness.

What is this new fear? The well is becoming much warmer. He wriggles free of the blanket; he would remove his clothes if there were room.

There is a new sound in the well. He listens for it. He hears the blood flowing from his palm. And the new sound: a small whirring that grows steadily in volume, like the noise of a thousand locusts swarming from the roots of an old oak tree. Then the wings: a smothering multitude of wings, the press of angel wings around him. And the voices.

"Who are you?" the voices say. "What is your name?"

"No!" the boy cries, and curls himself small against the suffocating wings, and cups his hands over his ears, but the voices do not stop, over and over the same voices.

"Who are you?" they demand. "Tell us your name!"

The boy's voice is barely a whisper. He cries to the darkness.

"Sammael!" he says.